High School Reunion

'I can't let you massage me now,' said Roma. 'Not like this. I need a shower.'

Jake took a step towards her. 'You're fine as you are.'

She looked at him as if he were crazy. 'No, I'm not. I'm sweaty and stinky. Just wait. I'll be back in a flash.'

He reached out to stop her, but she was a wily one. She grabbed a robe from the wall and was gone before he could catch her. He started to follow her, but made himself stop. She'd said she'd be right back.

But who knew how long a flash was in female time?

He raked a hand through his hair. He didn't know why she was so fussy. They were just going to get hot and sweaty all over again. And that didn't even take into consideration the lotions and massage oils. Oh yeah, oil was definitely going to come into play once he got her onto that table.

Busying himself, he strapped Paul's belt of assorted lubricants around his waist. He had to adjust the bottle of almond oil when it rode just a little too close to his crotch. He'd been dealing with half a hard-on ever since he'd left her yesterday. The cold showers he'd taken last night and again this morning hadn't done the trick.

Not even close.

**For more information about Kimberly Dean's books
please visit www.kimberlydean.com**

High School Reunion

Kimberly Dean

In real life, always practise safe sex.

This edition published in 2007 by
Cheek
Thames Wharf Studios
Rainville Road
London W6 9HA

Originally published 2005

Typeset by SetSystems Ltd, Saffron Walden, Essex

Printed and bound by Mackays of Chatham PLC

ISBN 978 0 352 34123 5

Chapter One

Get out of the car, Roma.

No.

It's easy. Just open the door and step out.

I don't wanna.

I'm losing my patience. Get your butt out of the car!

Bite me.

The argument inside Roma Hanson's brain had been going on for the last fifteen minutes. Although it reminded her vaguely of an argument she'd had with her mother when she was six years old, it showed no signs of waning.

Move it!

Make me!

She scanned the building in front of her. Nobody else seemed to be having a problem going inside. In the short time she'd been sitting watching, dozens of people of various shapes and sizes had entered the place. Several, in fact, had even had – get this – *smiles* on their faces. Young, old, fat, thin ... They'd all just walked up to the door and stepped inside, easy as pie.

Pie.

Mm, now that sounded good. Distracted, she glanced around at her surroundings. There was a bakery just two blocks down the street ...

Oh, no, you don't! That's what got you into this predicament in the first place!

Taking a deep breath, she tried again to work up her courage. Her gaze ran hesitantly over the sign declaring JAKE'S GYM. It sounded so ... so ...

1

Rocky-ish. Visions of sweaty men with tattoos filled her head. Maybe this wasn't the place for her.

Then again, sweaty men with tattoos? That didn't sound too bad.

She stared at the plate glass windows, trying to see inside, but the reflection of the sun hid the club's activity. She really didn't like unknown quantities. Maybe she should try Workout World or Spa City. Surely they would suit her just fine.

But they don't have trainers, her brain insisted. *Not real ones. You know a pimply faced college student trying to earn beer money won't keep you motivated.*

'Ah, crud,' she muttered in defeat. Self-discipline had never been her strong point. If she went to another gym, she'd last three days. Tops. She couldn't let that happen. She needed to see results, and she needed to see them quickly. Procrastinating had only made matters worse. It was crunch time.

Before she could change her mind, she opened the car door and hopped out. Her heels skidded on the slick surface of the parking lot, and she grabbed the car to regain her balance.

Winter. The evil troll still had its grip on the city. Even though it was March, there were no signs that spring was on its way. Shivering, Roma wrapped her heavy coat more tightly around herself.

It's too cold. You can come back tomorrow.

'No!' Her eyes rounded when she realised she'd spoken out loud. Quickly, she looked around to make sure that nobody had heard her. Fortunately, the parking lot was empty.

She faced the building and braced herself. She'd never get up her nerve again if she left now. Her devious brain would find some other excuse to keep her away. She'd made it out of the car; she was going in. After all, this problem wasn't going to fix itself. Her high school reunion was only three months away, and she had thirty pounds to lose. Thirty!

She slammed the door, turned and marched determinedly towards the building. What was the worst that could happen anyway? She'd never been inside a real gym before, but she doubted that people would turn and stare at her. It couldn't be that evident that she was a newbie.

Just act like you know what you're doing. Just walk into the place and ask somebody about the training programmes. Easy.

It should have been easy.

It *would* have been easy if it weren't for a hidden, mischievous patch of ice.

The whole thing happened so fast, Roma didn't know what hit her. One moment, she was walking along confidently. In the flash of a millisecond, everything spun out of control. The smooth soles of her pumps lost their traction and, suddenly, her legs began churning like Roadrunner's in those old Saturday morning cartoons.

She yelped as momentum threw her forwards.

Her hands swung up to brace herself, but her luck being what it was, they landed against the one unstable thing she could find. With her nose plastered against the JAKE stencil on the front door, she went hurling into the gym.

She stumbled, gained momentum, and charged across the room in front of the reception desk. Her body was nearly parallel to the floor, her face only three feet above it, as she tried to recover. Like a duck out of water, her arms flapped wildly. Her purse connected solidly with ... something.

One more step and gravity finally won the battle. Sprawling face forwards, she executed a perfect swan dive.

'Ummmph,' she groaned as she came to a slithering stop.

At first, stunned silence greeted her. Then a deep voice rang out from somewhere overhead. 'Lady! Are you all right?'

3

Lady? Oh yeah, she felt real ladylike right about now. She kept her head down. Maybe she could get on her hands and knees and crawl backwards out of the place. If she kept her face hidden, nobody would ever be able to recognise her. She'd burn her coat and ditch the purse before it could be identified.

'Are you OK?' the voice repeated.

'Peachy,' she mumbled. Suddenly, the urge to laugh seized her. *No, they won't stare or anything.* Giggles shook her body, and she tried to hold them back.

'Oh God, she's convulsing!'

A hand settled on the back of her head, and Roma knew that there would be no crawling. A big body crouched down next to her, and she felt it loom over her.

'Don't move,' the voice instructed. 'Help will be here soon. Somebody dial nine-one-one!'

Oh, wouldn't that just be perfect? Call the fire engines. Bring on the ambulances. Nothing like a little more unwanted attention.

'No, no. Don't do that. I'm fine,' she insisted as she pushed herself back onto her knees.

Now what? she wondered. Just how in the heck was she supposed to get herself out of this mess?

Act like nothing happened, the devious side of her suggested.

Don't even look at me, replied the angel on her other shoulder.

Staring intently at the floor tiling, she mumbled, 'Um, I'd like to talk to somebody about joining the gym.'

The man with the deep voice chuckled with surprise. 'Sure, Goldilocks, if you're sure you're all right.'

A helping hand appeared in front of her face, and she grabbed it. The man pulled her up to a standing position, but she still couldn't bear to look at him. Instead, she took great care in dusting off her skirt.

4

'I apologise about the ice out there. This is our fault. Are you sure you're not hurt?'

He began to help her brush off her coat. His hand swiped down her back, and Roma let out a whoop when his touch curved around her bottom. 'Hey! Watch it!'

Unintentional or not, he'd goosed her.

Spinning around, she lifted her gaze and found herself facing a full house. Suddenly, she realised that the room was absolutely silent. Nobody had moved since she had entered – well, *flopped* – onto the scene. Everywhere she looked, eyes were wide and mouths were agape.

A groan slipped from her lips. There was absolutely no graceful way out of this situation. Deciding to go with the flow, she lowered herself into what she hoped was a graceful curtsy.

Across the room, somebody coughed. The sound was quickly muffled, but it was enough to snap the tension. Laughter and applause broke out in waves. She smiled hesitantly and bowed again.

'Tito, bring me some ice and salt that sidewalk before somebody really gets hurt.'

Roma whirled around at the sound of the increasingly familiar voice. Would he just let it go already? She just wanted to leave in peace. 'Really, I'm fine,' she assured. 'You don't have to –'

Her air caught in her throat and wheezed through her lips. Holy samoly! Electricity zapped backwards from her eyeballs and short-circuited her brain. If she'd taken the time to look at him before, she might have done something stupid.

The man connected to the voice was a Greek god. She fought the urge to lick her lips as she gave him the once over. Sandy-blond hair. Dark-blue eyes. And those muscles ... Oh my, did he have muscles. She nearly asked him to pick up something heavy just so she could watch them strain.

5

'The ice isn't for you, it's for me,' he said. He held his cheek with one hand, but a broad smile split his face. His eyes twinkled as he looked at her. 'You clobbered me with your purse.'

Oh, no. That had been the thud she'd felt on the way down. Good Lord, she'd just brained this gorgeous stud. Her wallet, keys, hairbrush, calculator and a million other things lived in her purse. In all, the bag had to weigh about ten pounds. 'Ohmigosh! Are you all right? Is anything broken?'

She fluttered about, not knowing what to do. How did one apologise for hitting such a sumptuous hunk of manhood – and a seemingly nice guy, at that?

'I'm so sorry. I just lost control,' she stammered.

'No kidding.' The man started to laugh, but bent over with a groan.

That did it; Roma lost it entirely. Hopping from one foot to the other, she charged towards him. He flinched at her sudden move, and she skidded to a halt. Carefully, she reached out and touched his cheekbone. A tingling sensation shot up her arm, and she pulled back as if burnt. Frantically, hands waving wildly, she looked around the room.

'Somebody get this man some ice!' she bellowed. She spun back towards him. 'How's your vision? Can you see me?'

Bent over as he was, his eyes were level with her chest. He let out a long breath. 'Oh, yeah. I can see you.'

'Am I clear?'

'There's supposed to be two, right?' Grinning, he stood upright and held out his hand. 'I'm Jake Logan.'

Jake – as in Jake's Gym. Roma winced. She'd just done a belly flop in front of the owner. And she'd managed to belt him on the way down! 'I'm so sorry. My clumsiness gets the best of me at times. I'll pay for any damage I've done.'

She reached for her purse, and tried not to take

offence when he instinctively moved out of harm's way. Quickly, she searched through the contents of her bag – forever forward known as the 'blunt object'. She finally found a business card, and she pushed it into his hand.

'I've got insurance. I'll pay for any medical care you might need.'

'There's no harm done.'

'No harm?' Her eyebrows shot upwards. 'Are you blind? I just bashed you. You might have a concussion. You could *go* blind for all we know.'

Tito appeared with an ice bag, and she literally ripped it from the kid's hands. She reached for Jake, but hesitated when he braced himself.

Guilt racked her. Of course, he'd be leery of her touch. She'd nearly knocked him out.

Disappointed, she turned her hand over and offered him the pack.

She went still when he caught her hand.

Quickly, she looked up at him. The humour in his eyes was surprisingly intimate – as was his touch. His callused fingers felt blistering hot in contrast to the ice pack. Her breath caught when the heat ran up her arm and settled in her chest. She watched, mesmerised, as he lifted their joined hands and pressed the ice pack against his cheekbone.

She cleared her throat. 'Better?' she asked.

'Oh, yeah.'

His gaze dropped to her opened coat and centred again on her chest. She nearly gasped aloud when her nipples stiffened instinctively. The heat. It was pouring into the sensitive tips, making them nearly burn.

She let out a quick puff of air and pulled her hand back. Surreptitiously, she began creeping towards the door. 'Well, I'm sorry for the intrusion. You've got my card, feel free to contact me.'

'Whoa, Goldie. I'm contacting you now.' Before she

7

could escape, he reached out and grabbed the hood of her coat. 'I thought you wanted to talk about joining.'

Damn! The blow to the head hadn't affected his memory.

'This was a mistake,' she stammered.

A huge mistake. She'd come here to get in shape, not make a fool of herself in front of dozens of people. He was too much of a distraction, anyway. If she worked out here, she'd spend half her time panting after him and worrying that she was nipping out. Jogging bras didn't hide that kind of thing.

He laughed and swung an arm around her shoulders. 'Just keep that purse away from me, and we'll get along fine.'

Roma hung her head. 'I can't believe I did that.'

'It's no big deal.' He finally looked at her business card. 'Roma ... Oh, you've got to be kidding me. Roma *Grace* Hanson?'

Her face flared. 'Rub it in, why don't you?'

'Well, it's a pleasure to meet you, Roma Grace. Come on into my office. I'm dying to hear what brought a woman like you to my humble gym.'

'Must have been temporary insanity.'

His lips twitched. 'Some of my best friends are insane.'

He gave her a quick squeeze, and Roma felt her body press against warm hard flesh. Incredibly hard flesh – the kind she'd like to test with her fingernails. She nimbly extricated herself from his hold. There were people around and most were still watching her. 'This cold pack is meant for your cheek. Would you please put it there?'

'Don't worry about me. I've got a hard head.' He lowered himself into the chair behind the desk, but obediently settled the ice pack against the side of his face. 'OK, why don't we start from scratch? What can I do for you?'

Roma's eyebrows lifted. Do for her?

8

She could think of quite a few things. Fun, naughty, impulsive things.

Nothing, her sensible side insisted.

This wasn't going to work. Did the Fates need to shove another neon sign in front of her face? Thirty pounds, shmirty pounds. So she'd be a little chunky at her reunion. It wasn't that big of a deal. She'd been pudgy in high school; nobody would even notice. Except her, of course.

'You mentioned that you were interested in joining the gym,' he said patiently. 'Can I answer any questions?'

She shook her head quickly. 'You must have heard me incorrectly – what with the blow to the head and all. I said I was looking for ... uh ... a "john in the gym".'

She pushed herself to her feet. 'Can you direct me to the ladies' room?'

He let out a snort. 'Nice try, but no.'

'No?' she sputtered. 'But ... But what if I really had to go?'

'Then I'd show you to one.' He laughed. 'As it is, I have very good hearing, notwithstanding "the blow to the head and all". I distinctly heard you ask for information about *joining* the gym.'

Roma fidgeted where she stood, but that watchful gaze of his didn't even blink. She couldn't get away from that intense blue stare. She could see amusement swirling in the fathomless depths of his eyes, but there was something more. Something hotter and deeper. The enigmatic expression made her nervous. 'I need to lose thirty pounds in the next three months,' she blurted.

His laser look intensified, and his eyebrows lowered. 'I don't think so.'

Disappointment filled her. It couldn't be done. She should have known. She'd waited too long to get started. This man said it wasn't possible, though, and he obviously knew his business. Just look at him.

Sigh. Just look at him.

'You don't need to lose that much.'

She blinked. She couldn't have heard him right. 'But I'm soft.'

'Soft can be a good thing.'

His gaze ran down her body so slowly, she could practically feel it caressing her skin. A tingling sensation started between her legs, and she pressed her thighs together hard. How could he do that? She was wearing a winter coat and a professional-looking blouse and skirt. That piercing look of his made her feel like she was naked.

He sat back in his chair. 'You haven't got that much to lose. Maybe ten to fifteen pounds. When you add muscle back, though, it will only be about five.'

Her jaw dropped, and she looked at him as if he'd just grown a second head. Was he insane? She knew her body. 'I jiggle,' she argued.

'I noticed.'

God, had he noticed. He'd have to be blind, deaf and dumb not to notice. Jake still felt thrown off-centre by the way this blonde whirlwind had crash-landed in his gym, but he wasn't stupid. He knew a good thing when he saw one.

And she was more than a good thing. He'd had a hard-on ever since she'd reached out and touched his cheek.

With her hand, mind you. Not the purse. That damn thing had nearly cold-cocked him.

He let his gaze run over her leisurely. She was curvy, all right, and in all the good places. He wrapped his fingers around the cold pack to keep himself from reaching out and grabbing her. There was nothing that scared off a woman more than jumping past the get-to-know-you stage right into the heavy petting.

He shook his head to clear the urge from his brain.

'All it will take is some weight and cardiovascular training to get you toned. I won't sugar-coat it, though –'

'No sugar?' she said with a pout.

The stupid grin on his face wouldn't go away. 'It will be hard work, but you'll like the results.'

So would he.

She sat down with a plop, and he had to hide his disappointment. He couldn't see her so well when she hid behind his desk.

'You're serious,' she said, disbelief colouring her tone.

'As a heart attack – which, by the way, exercise can help prevent.' He leant forward and tried to peek over the edge of the desk at her legs. He'd gotten a good view of them when she'd skidded across the floor with her skirt nearly up to her waist. 'But what's your rush? What's happening in three months?'

The minute he asked the question, he regretted it. Ah, shit. Was she getting married? Needles prickled at the back of his neck. He'd already started to get fascinating ideas about her. A fiancé would complicate things. Still, that didn't rule out the possibilities. He'd never shied away from a challenge before.

His gaze shot down to her left hand. No ring. That was a good sign.

'It's my ten-year high school reunion,' she replied, her lips twisting in distaste.

A reunion. The needles relaxed their pinch. Things were looking better and better. 'Looking for a little revenge?' he asked.

She smiled impishly. 'I've heard that it's sweet.'

That smile kicked Jake right in the solar plexus. God, she'd grabbed him by the cock with her looks alone. Add personality and a sense of humour, and he didn't stand a chance. 'So priority number one is a "killer bod"?' he asked, clearing his throat halfway.

She shrugged. 'I'd settle for a "nice figure".'

He gaped at her. Was she out of her mind? Had she looked in a mirror recently? 'Been there, done that. I've got clients that would kill for a body like yours.'

She flushed right up to her cute little ears.

He shook his head in bemusement. 'So a reunion, huh? I assume you have a suitably impressive car to take you to the event?'

Another shrug. 'It'll do, or I'll rent one.'

He thought back to his own reunion the summer before. Idly, he rolled a pencil between his thumb and forefinger. 'What about the boyfriend and the career? I've heard that they both score big points on the reunion scene.'

A funny look crossed her face, and she nervously reached up to try to straighten her mussed hair. 'I'm an accountant. It's not that impressive, but it's a respectable occupation.'

Jake pounced on the half-answer. No fiancé and no boyfriend. Things were definitely looking up. As to her career, it intrigued him more than she could know. He might be able to use that.

'I just want to look nice,' she said.

She already looked nice. Better than nice. Still, he knew what she was getting at. She wanted to be a drop-dead, stop-'em-in-their-tracks, bombshell blonde. He shifted uncomfortably in his chair.

She didn't have far to go.

'I can help you with that,' he said.

She nibbled her lower lip, causing his thoughts to scatter completely.

'I'll probably need more help than most,' she admitted. 'My willpower is nearly nonexistent.'

'You need instant gratification.'

Her flushed face turned nearly fuchsia.

Jake was feeling a little hot under the collar himself.

Business, he needed to concentrate on business.

Get her in the door as a client first. Then he could coax her into doing other, more interesting things with him.

'You need a trainer,' he said bluntly. Over the years, he'd seen thousands of people like her. Correction. None of them had looked like her; they were just in the same situation. They all wanted to lose weight and get into shape, but although they started out with good intentions, they quickly dropped out when they discovered how difficult the process was.

She flicked aside another invisible speck of dust from her skirt. 'How expensive would that be?' she asked.

The casual tone didn't fool him. He knew she was still looking for an excuse to leave. Well, she wasn't going to get one from him. 'We'll discuss that later. Let me show you around the place first.'

He put down the ice, stood, and circled the desk. She looked hesitant, but she shrugged out of her winter coat. A funny look crossed her face, though, when she stepped towards him.

Jake went still. He knew what that surprised look meant. He'd seen it when she'd crashed through the front door.

His gaze was suddenly drawn downwards. He watched in fascination as one of her stockings slid down her leg. It pooled around her foot like an invitation, and every muscle in his body clenched.

'Damn!' she hissed.

He couldn't have said it better himself. He looked at her helplessly. He wasn't a saint.

'It snapped during the fall,' she said with embarrassment. 'Could you turn around?'

Not likely.

She twirled her finger. 'Just for a minute?'

Stiff-legged, he faced the door – only to find her reflection in the window. Jake nearly groaned aloud. She'd lifted her foot and planted her high heel on the chair. The pose was something right out of a seedy strip club, only she was dressing herself. Somehow, it was just as erotic.

The clinging nylon slid over the curve of her calf, and his hands clenched when she smoothed the sheer material over her knee. Only women could move so sensuously. They did it instinctively, not even realising how it could jumble up a guy on the inside.

Especially one who wasn't supposed to be watching.

He couldn't help it. He was entranced as she hitched her skirt up high on her thigh. Lust hit him hard when he saw the dangerous curves. Her skin was lily white and smooth as silk. She worked the stocking up to nearly her crotch before she attached the garter belt, and he focused so hard on the little pink triangle of her panties, his eyes went dry.

Bless that loose catch, he thought a little desperately.

She smoothed her skirt back over her hips, and it was all he could do not to turn around and whip it back up. God, he wanted to touch her.

'I'm ready,' she said.

So was he.

He cleared his throat. 'This way,' he said as he opened the door.

He couldn't look at her. If he did, she'd see the bulge at the front of his exercise pants. He lowered his clipboard to try to hide it from the rest of the club. This was one muscle group he didn't have control of.

But it sure as hell was getting its exercise today.

His teeth ground together as he led her to the aerobics room. He needed to start thinking with the head on top of his shoulders. She was ready to bolt, he could tell, but there was no way he could let that happen. He had to find a way to keep her around.

This was one beauty he wasn't going to let get away.

The wheels in Roma's brain began to whirl as she followed Jake out of his office. Could anything else happen to embarrass her in front of this man?

She ran her hand over her skirt and felt the garter belt underneath. She'd been torn between taking off her hose entirely or putting her faith in the loose catch. She hoped she hadn't made the wrong decision. With the way he was looking at her, the more clothes she had on the better.

She stopped abruptly when she nearly bumped into him outside a classroom window. Her hip brushed against his clipboard, and he let out a harsh cough.

'This is our aerobics room,' he said in a voice that sounded strained. 'We teach around thirty classes weekly, so you should be able to find a time that fits into your schedule.'

She'd gotten too close. She could feel his heat radiating towards her, and the scent of clean soap and tangy aftershave filled her senses. It pulled her even closer. Only the clang of a weight stack brought her back to reality.

She quickly turned her attention to the activity in the aerobics room. A step class was in full swing. Her eyes rounded with amazement. A bouncy brunette was directing a roomful of people through precise, drill-team-like movements. The different combinations of stepping onto and off of the boxes made her head spin.

Jake cleared his throat. 'Uh, maybe you should save the step classes for later.'

Like when she could walk in the door without doing a face plant? She scrunched her nose. 'Good point.'

'Come over here and take a look at our weight room.'

She followed as he guided her through the rest of the gym, making sure she kept a better distance between them. She was nervous about facing her audience again, but she was relieved to find that everybody was friendly. And she had to admit that she liked what she saw. The equipment seemed to be very high tech, although she had no clue what it all did. She just liked the way everything glistened.

He'd conveniently evaded her question about the club's rates, though. Joining would be expensive.

There's your excuse, her devilish side told her.

But what's more important? the other side asked. *An excuse or a tight butt for reunion night?*

No question. A tight butt.

'How does personal training work?' she asked when they returned to the office. He'd succeeded in piquing her interest.

He sat down and put his clipboard on the desk. She'd noticed that he'd kept it with him the entire tour, but he hadn't taken any notes.

'We tailor workouts for each individual,' he said. He folded his arms across his chest and rocked back in his chair. 'We'd start by putting you through some preliminary tests to determine your current level of fitness.'

Uh-oh. She didn't know if she liked the sound of that. 'What kind of tests?'

'You'd start with a strength test and a flexibility test. Then, you'd get on the treadmill so your heart rate could be monitored. Of course, we'd take some baseline measurements so we can track your improvement over the weeks.'

We? Just what did he mean by 'we'? And what exactly were these measurements?

'Let me assure you that we keep everything confidential. Your file will be locked here in my office.' He pointed at a filing cabinet in the corner of the room. 'Believe me, I've learned that disclosing a woman's weight or dress size is an offence punishable by death.'

'I should think so!' She'd rather get a bad perm than let somebody know her weight.

But enough with this 'we' stuff already. He didn't expect her to hire *him* as her trainer, did he? She'd never be able to concentrate if he was hovering around her all the time, watching her, pushing her. *Tempting her.* That 'we' was more of a congregational term, right? We – as in his staff. Preferably another commiserative female.

Roma shifted uncomfortably in her chair. 'That aerobics teacher looked competent. Is she a personal trainer?'

He settled his elbows on the desk, and she couldn't help but be preoccupied by the way the muscles bunched up in his arms.

'Missy teaches a few classes a week to help pay for school. She's getting her master's degree.' He looked as if he were fighting a smile. 'I had someone else in mind.'

He paused, and Roma's heart tripped over itself. *Please don't say what I think you're going to say*, she silently begged.

'I thought I'd train you myself.'

'Oh.' Her brain flew in a myriad directions. Working with him would be so personal. He'd touch her. His big muscled body would loom over her. He'd see her sweat. 'Can't somebody else do it? I mean ... Hmm. Well, you must be very busy. I'd hate to put you out. I'd be more than willing to work with one of your employees.'

He leant closer, and her breath hitched.

That mysterious smile still hovered on his lips. 'No can do. It's me or nobody.'

'Excuse me?' she choked.

'I'd like to discuss a trade.'

Her belly clenched. The glint in his eye was

unmistakable. Was he talking about what she thought he was talking about?

He swivelled in his chair and pointed at a stack of papers. He sighed heavily and admitted, 'I need help with that.'

Roma looked at him dumbfounded. *What?*

OK, so he hadn't been talking about what she'd thought he'd been talking about. The paper. She looked at it incomprehensibly.

'I need help with the club's books.'

Dismay gripped her. 'Don't tell me,' she whispered.

He looked around his office as if he had gotten so used to the mounds of paper, he didn't even see them any more. At least he had the decency to look sheepish.

Roma's body sagged. His office was an accountant's personal version of hell. Some of the stacks stood so high, they looked like the Leaning Tower of Pisa. Worse yet, she knew it was probably just the tip of the iceberg.

He ran a hand through his blond hair. 'I need an accountant. A good one.'

Like a zombie, she stood and walked over to look more closely at the mess. There were receipts, copies of cheques, and electricity bills just in the handful that she grabbed. She looked through more slips of paper and nearly moaned. There were debits mixed with credits. Receipts shuffled between invoices. Cheques that hadn't been cashed. And here was even a birthday card from someone named Liz. She turned on him. 'You need a miracle worker. You do realise that taxes are due in just over a month.'

He grimaced. 'I'd heard something about that.'

She rolled her eyes. Taking a calming breath, she gestured at the room. 'This is your filing system?'

He shrugged. 'I had a full-time bookkeeper, but she left me about a year ago. Her husband got a job in Chicago. I haven't found anybody willing to take on the job since she quit. The staff and I do our best, but numbers really aren't our thing.'

'Can I see your accounting system?' she asked with dread.

'You mean the books?'

Oh, God. He didn't have things computerised yet? 'Whatever you have.'

He opened the bottom drawer and passed a ledger to her. More loose sheets of paper fell to the floor when she opened it. Her frown deepened as she looked over the entries. 'Let me see your personal training rate sheet.'

He picked up the phone book and found the information sitting underneath it. He pushed the paper under her nose. Her eyes bulged.

'That's why nobody else could train you but me,' he explained. 'My trainers get a commission. I refuse to ask any of them to take a pay cut so the club can have an accountant.'

'Oh. I see.' It was the most intelligent response Roma could come up with. She chewed her lower lip. She hadn't thought that the rates could be high enough to make all this work worth it. Unfortunately, he'd just proven to her that the trade would indeed be a fair one.

She glanced over at the imposing stack of papers again. There was a lot that needed to be done there. Still, she had lost Mr Dubcek's account just two weeks ago. He'd sold his men's clothing store for a healthy profit, but the new company had an accountant on staff. She had the time to do the job that Jake was proposing, but did she have the patience?

Her gaze flitted back to the rate sheet. Even if she did find another qualified trainer in town, she doubted that their prices would vary much from what he was showing her. Vaguely, she wondered if she was about to make a big mistake. 'You promise you can make me skinny in three months?'

She'd thought he'd smile. He didn't. Instead, his hot gaze slid slowly over her body.

'The men will be sweating in their beers, and the women will be green with envy.'

Roma felt a sharp thrill run through her. It was politically incorrect and very shallow of her, but she wanted that *bad*. She wanted all her male classmates to see what they'd missed out on, and she'd just love to see Ellie Huffington gape at her sleek and fit form.

But was it worth all this work?

Oh, yeah. No doubt about it. Watching Ellie eat crow would definitely be worth all the pain and suffering. 'You've got yourself a deal, Mr Logan.'

A smile broke out on his face. 'Jake. Call me Jake.'

He leant forwards across the desk and firmly gripped her outstretched hand. Little shocks of electricity hissed up Roma's arm at the contact, and her nipples tightened painfully. Her gaze flew to his, but he was looking strangely at their interconnected hands. He could feel it too, she realised. Slowly, he let her go. His fingers glided across her skin, and the friction made a fire start deep in her belly.

'When do we start?' she asked, her voice unsteady.

'Tomorrow.' He sounded a little winded himself. 'Definitely tomorrow.'

Chapter Two

The next day, Roma pulled into the gym parking lot. Her right foot itched to gun the gas, but she forced herself to find a spot and park. She'd been changing her mind all day long about the deal she'd made. Even on the drive over, she'd turned around twice to go home. Something, though, had made her turn back.

That something was those darn fifteen pounds.

Jake's assurance that she only needed to lose such a teeny-weeny bit of weight had her hooked.

And he didn't help matters.

That chest. Those arms. Those dark-blue eyes.

She felt an electric shiver shoot down her spine. No red-blooded woman could walk away from that.

Before she could change her mind again, she grabbed her gym bag from the passenger seat and got out of the car. She hefted it up over her shoulder, but nearly unbalanced when she saw Mr Hunk waiting for her. Jake stood outside the gym, casually leaning against the plate glass window as if he expected her to chicken out. His gaze caught hers from halfway across the parking lot, and Roma felt her knees go weak.

Stop it, Spaghetti Legs. The last thing she needed was to do another pratfall in front of him. Her pride was already wounded enough.

She carefully picked her way across the snow-covered parking lot. When she reached the kerb to the sidewalk, he quickly offered her his hand. Probably for insurance reasons. The sidewalk looked as if it had been extra salted today.

'I wasn't sure you'd come,' he said as he efficiently

relieved her of her gym bag. No doubt it would pack an even bigger punch than her purse.

'Neither was I,' she admitted. She looked up at him, ready to make an excuse to fall back upon just in case today didn't go well, but the lie never reached her lips. 'Your face!'

Oh, his beautiful face.

A dark bruise slashed across his cheekbone and shadowed his left eye. The colours of the rainbow were all there, right along with the puffiness. He looked as if he'd gone ten rounds in the ring. She felt a pang in her stomach. All he'd gotten was a sucker punch from her.

'I'm so sorry.' Impulsively, she reached out and cupped his cheek. She bit her lip as she gently caressed his bruised skin. 'I'm such a klutz.'

He didn't flinch under her touch. If anything, he leant his head down closer to her. 'You're sexy enough to make up for it.'

The husky compliment didn't help. Roma felt miserable. She let her thumb run across the puffiness under his eye. 'Does it hurt?'

His blue eyes glittered, even the one behind the purple and yellow eyelid. A dangerous smile crossed his lips. 'Like a son of a bitch. Want to kiss it and make it feel better?'

The pang in her chest slid lower, and she quickly backed away. Oh, he was a devilish one. 'I'm afraid I'd do more harm than good.'

He smoothly slid an arm about her waist. 'I'm a glutton for punishment.'

Roma jumped when she suddenly found herself trapped. His presence enveloped her as he pulled her closer. He was just so big. Her thighs brushed against his, and she braced her hands against his rock-hard chest.

She looked up sharply at his face. His blond hair was mussed, and his smile was cocky. Too cocky.

Had she said devilish? The man was a rake.

'Come on,' he said coaxingly. 'One little kiss on the cheek.'

She looked anxiously around him into the gym. People were already stopping mid-workout to watch. Great. This was just great. Hadn't yesterday gotten her reputation off to a good enough start?

'You don't play fair,' she hissed.

'Fair's no fun. Come on. Gimme a kiss. It hurts really bad.'

Oh, she'd hurt him really bad. Her eyebrows lowered. 'One kiss and you'll let me go?'

He smiled crookedly. 'If you want me to.'

'Fine.' Two could play at this game. Slowly, she lifted herself up onto her tiptoes. He took the opportunity to pull her closer, and she fell forwards. Her breasts flattened against his chest and she felt a distinctive bulge press against the notch at the top of her legs.

'Oh!' she gasped.

'I'm feeling better already.'

His hand slid down to cup her butt, and Roma felt arousal swirl through her. It shocked her. This was supposed to be an innocent peck on the cheek. A dare met. Things were quickly spiralling out of control.

And there were sweaty voyeurs inside watching.

She lifted her chin and gave him a quick peck on the centre of the purple bruise.

'Ow!' he yelped, flinching sharply.

She should have backed away then, but her own devilish nature suddenly grabbed hold. Feeling reckless, she moved even closer. He looked at her anxiously, but went very still when she caught him by the nape of the neck. She pulled his head down and daintily ran her tongue across his bruised eyelid. A low groan rumbled from his chest. His hips swivelled in reaction, and his arms went weak. She used to opportunity the wriggle out of his clutch.

He caught her hand before she could escape into the gym.

Roma felt a thrill shoot through her. She was playing with fire here.

'You pack a punch, lady,' he said gruffly.

'You started it,' she retorted. It had been a dare, and she'd met it. She knew it, and so did he.

He looked at her with the devil dancing in his eyes. 'I'll remember that.'

And so he should.

The door to the gym suddenly opened, and Roma glanced over her shoulder. She winced when she saw two big boy weightlifters grinning at her. They sent hoots of approval to Jake as they walked past, and she felt as if she'd been caught with her hand in the cookie jar. She quickly snatched her traitorous hand back.

'Now look at what you've done,' she hissed as she whirled around. 'I'm never going to be able to live down my reputation here.'

Jake pushed himself away from the window and adjusted her bag on his shoulder. 'What the hell?' he said nonchalantly. 'Reputations are overrated.'

'Yeah, but they're what people remember you by.'

His good eye narrowed. 'You're not talking about the gym any more.'

A tinge of uneasiness caught Roma, and she busied herself with her scarf. 'Sure I am.'

'No, you're not.' He looked at her for a good, long moment. 'You're thinking about the reunion.'

Damn the man. He was good. She reached for the front door, wanting to avoid the issue entirely. He caught her arm and pulled her back a step.

'It's a big deal for you, isn't it?'

She shrugged.

'Why?'

She started to shrug again, but his grip tightened and the look on his face went serious. That black eye made him look almost menacing.

She sighed. He looked stubborn, and she knew how a stubborn man could get. He'd let her freeze

24

before he'd let her walk away without telling him. 'High school wasn't all that pleasant for me,' she admitted. 'There were certain people – one girl mainly – who picked on me.'

She felt the old anger bubble up inside her, and the truth spilled out. 'I want to kick her ass when I show up at that reunion.'

The eyebrow over his good eye lifted. 'Figuratively,' he said.

She glanced away almost guiltily. 'Whatever.'

Out of the corner of her eye, she saw his lips twitch.

'Why didn't you say so?' he said. 'I've got a programme specially geared towards ass-kicking.'

He gave a tug on her hand, and Roma's shoulders sagged in relief.

He understood.

She entered the gym as he held the door open for her, but her steps slowed when she felt everyone's eyes on her yet again. Behind the desk, Tito stood with a big smile splitting his face.

'Hi, Roma,' he said.

'Hi,' she mumbled.

Jake followed her inside as if he didn't have a care in the world. He nodded towards a middle-aged man working out near the free weights. 'Tito, stop gawking at my beautiful bookkeeper and go help Henry. His form on those bicep curls is crap.'

Tito just grinned. 'You can't blame him. He got distracted by this big blob that steamed up the front window.'

'Yeah, I got distracted by that, too,' Jake said with a wink. 'Come on, Goldie. The women's locker room is this way. Get changed and then we'll take your baseline stats.'

Roma hated the feeling that settled in her gut when she stepped into the women's locker room. God, she hated these places.

A redhead stood in front of a mirror patting a thin layer of perspiration off her brow with a towel. Roma stepped around her so she could look about the place and shook her head in disbelief. Locker rooms hadn't changed a bit in the past ten years.

That was too bad.

Lockers were overstuffed with clothes, boots and winter jackets. Gym bags were stored overhead and one brave soul had even left her suit hanging on a shower rod. At least the place didn't stink to high heaven. Deodorants, shampoos and body sprays had given the place a definite powder-fresh smell. Still, the air had a damp, clinging sense to it.

'New?' the redhead asked.

Roma jumped as the voice brought her out of the past. 'Uh, yeah. Are the lockers assigned or can I use whichever one I want?'

'Just grab an empty one. Did you remember a padlock?'

'Oh, yes.' A padlock was the one thing she knew she hadn't forgotten. She could show up here without her gym shorts or tennis shoes, but she'd never, ever forget a padlock again.

'Have a good workout,' the redhead said. She threw her towel over her shoulder. 'Just ask if you have any questions. People around here are pretty helpful.'

'Thanks,' Roma called as the woman left.

She set her gym bag down heavily on a bench. She needed to get past this. So Ellie Huffington had pulled a nasty prank on her after senior high gym class. Big deal. That had happened a long time ago, and the people here were adults. She couldn't let one bad experience keep her from doing something she wanted to do.

And she wanted to get in shape. She wanted to be healthy.

But most of all, she wanted to show up that witch at the reunion.

'So get on with it,' she told herself.

There were machines and barbells waiting for her – not to mention a big, hunky blond trainer.

The thought of Jake made her start pulling off her shoes. She didn't doubt that if she stayed in here too long, he'd be right in after her.

She hung her coat on the hook inside the locker and opened her bag. Changing from her work clothes to scruffies was going to take some creative manoeuvring. Ten years may have passed, but she'd never be caught buck naked in a locker room again. She stepped out of her dress pants and hurriedly pulled on her shorts. She turned towards the locker to hide from any peeping eyes as she took off her blouse and bra.

Unfortunately, the spandex of her new sports bra proved to be a hindrance in her quick-change effort. The damn thing clung to her like a boa constrictor as she pulled it over her head.

'Mmmph,' she grunted as she tugged and pulled.

The tag on the Lycra and spandex had boasted about how much support the wonder material provided. No doubt if she could get the stupid thing on, her breasts would feel like they were propped up on a suspension bridge. That was if she didn't choke on the thing first.

'Oh, here! Let me help you,' somebody said from behind.

Roma was embarrassed beyond words, but she was fit to be tied. Literally. The sports bra cut across her diagonally. One breast was fully covered, but the other was half-squashed and half falling out. Her nipple looked as if it was trying to escape capture. Meanwhile, the shoulder strap was cutting across her windpipe with dangerous accuracy.

'You're trying to put your head through an armhole,' the helpful woman said. 'And it's twisted back here.'

'Get it off me,' Roma wheezed.

'You've got to be a contortionist to get one of these things on.'

Together, the women worked until Roma was able to pull the bra down over her head and both her breasts. When she let go, sure enough, the wonder material clamped down on her like a bondage outfit – *not that she knew what one of those was or anything*. Her breasts were plumped up and locked down. No jiggle there at all.

'Oh, thank you,' she said in relief. 'I feel like such a dufus.'

'Don't worry about it,' the woman said as she moved to a nearby locker. 'I always take time to stretch the material when I buy a new bra. You're taking your life into your own hands if you don't.'

'I'll remember that. Thanks again. By the way, I'm Roma.'

She turned to look at her helpful Samaritan and nearly groaned out loud. It wasn't the redhead; it was the bouncy brunette aerobics instructor!

Up close, the girl looked even more perfect. Her dark hair showed off her alabaster skin, and her close-fitting workout clothes flaunted a knockout body. There wasn't an ounce of spare fat on the young thing.

'I'm Missy,' the girl said with a bright smile.

'Of course you are.'

'Excuse me?'

'Oh. Sorry,' Roma said, flustered that her devilish side had talked out loud. 'I just ... Jake pointed you out yesterday during my tour of the gym. I watched you teach class for a bit. You're amazingly co-ordinated.'

A light bulb popped on in the girl's head. 'Oh! You must be –'

'The swan-dive queen?'

Missy giggled. 'I was going to say the woman who bashed Jake.'

Roma ran a hand through her hair. 'My reputation precedes me.'

'Don't worry about it. From time to time, we've all wanted to bop him.'

'It was an accident.' Roma shoved her work clothes into the bag and whipped out a brush. 'I feel so bad about it. I mean, really. Not only do I come crashing into the place, I clobber the best-looking man I've ever seen.'

Missy grinned. 'He is a hottie.'

'He's a shyster is what he is.' Roma cringed when her hairbrush caught a knot in her hair. 'He tricked me into coming back.'

Missy opened her locker and took out a heavy backpack. It thudded as she sat it down on the bench. 'Sometimes you have to give a person an incentive to work out. Believe me, I know. I couldn't get my boyfriend off the couch with a forklift.'

Funny, Roma hadn't pictured the athletic woman with a lazy boyfriend. 'Well, that's where I should be right now,' she said. She let the rubber band snap around her ponytail. 'On my couch with a packet of bonbons. What am I doing here?'

Missy smiled sympathetically as she pulled a bottle of shampoo out of her bag. 'You're here to get in shape, aren't you? I heard that Jake was going to train you personally.'

'See! That's what I mean. The man is a master manipulator. Who do I think I am working out with, Mr Universe? Just look at him. The guy has arms like Popeye.' Roma poked her bicep. 'See? No spinach there. I hate spinach.'

'Relax. Jake's great. He works with people at all levels. He's got an eighty-year-old man who's a regular, yet he's also training a woman who's getting ready for the Midwest Fitness Show.'

Roma paused. That sounded as if it was supposed to be impressive. 'Is that a big deal?'

'The biggest.'

'Oh, boy.' Her stomach soured. She'd wanted somebody who was qualified, but Jake was a top-notch trainer. She was so out of her league.

'His client has got a good chance of winning.'

Great. Just great. Roma looked down at herself. She poked her belly. Definitely squishy. 'This isn't going to work.'

'Oh, come on,' Missy said. She came over and began fussing with Roma's crooked ponytail. 'I didn't mean to scare you. Besides, Jake told me about the deal. You know – training you in return for your bookkeeping skills. You can't leave me here with him. He locked me in his office once with those books. I was clawing at the door to get out.'

Roma glanced over her shoulder. 'Are you sure I'm not making a fool of myself?'

'It's a good trade for everyone. You should grab it with both hands. It's really hard to get on his schedule.'

'He's that good?'

Missy turned her by the shoulders and looked her dead in the eye. 'He's *that good.*'

Roma shifted her weight uneasily. She still didn't know how she felt about all this. She'd been wishy-washy last night just because of Jake and his supreme hunkiness. This new info, though, made her feel even more intimidated.

'Do you think he can make me skinny in three months?' She scrunched her nose. 'I've got a high school reunion coming up.'

Missy rolled her eyes. 'Skinny isn't "in" any more. In three months, he'll do something even better. He'll make you sleek and strong.'

Sleek was good. It sounded even better than skinny.

'OK,' Roma said, letting out a nervous breath. She was already here, and she'd won the battle of the bra. What could it hurt to try? 'I'll give it a shot.'

'Great!' Missy said as she flipped a towel over her shoulder. 'Don't worry, you'll like it here.'

'Yeah, yeah,' Roma said as she reached for her T-shirt. 'My mom said the same thing when she took me to the circus when I was eight. A camel spat at me.'

She pulled her T-shirt over her head and let it drop.

Missy looked aghast.

'What?' Roma asked, looking down quickly. She liked the big pink flamingo on the front.

'Are you planning to wear that?'

'What's wrong with it?' The T-shirt came down to nearly her knees, but she liked it that way. If it didn't cover her hippo hips, it wasn't big enough.

'Uh ... nothing,' the brunette said with a sneaky smile. She shook her head as she walked to the showers. 'Jake's going to love it.'

Jake looked up when Roma appeared in the doorway to his office. She'd spent so much time in the locker room, he'd begun to wonder if he'd have to go in and get her. He pushed himself up from his chair and was reaching for his clipboard when he got a load of her get-up. He stopped short. 'What the hell is that?'

'What's what?'

'That,' he said, pointing at her. 'That *tent*.'

She quickly looked down at herself. Her fingers fisted into the T-shirt. 'You told me to wear something loose and comfortable.'

He scowled. Loose and comfortable was one thing. A muumuu was another.

That damn thing was coming off.

He had measurements to take, and he needed to see her muscles groups as she worked. More importantly, he wanted to see that body. He'd waited patiently for an entire day. She wasn't going to gyp him out of that. 'Get in here,' he said as he stomped around his desk.

He determinedly closed the door behind her and shut all the shades. Job number one, he noted on his clipboard, was to improve her self-confidence. For God's sake, his barber needed a muumuu more than she did.

He began filling out the form as he nodded to the corner of the room. 'Step up onto the scale, and I'll take your weight.'

Her eyebrows rose to nearly her hairline. 'A scale? Uh-uh.'

He took a deep breath. He dealt with this kind of a reaction all the time, but it still tested his patience. 'Roma, I told you that we need baseline measurements so we can watch your improvement over the weeks.'

Her ponytail swished as she shook her head. 'Uh-uh.'

'Come on,' he said in his best soothing voice. 'It's not that big of a deal.'

'For you, maybe. For me, it's huge.' She looked at the scale in distaste. 'Just about as huge as the number that's going to pop up if I step on that dang thing.'

Jake propped a hip on his desk and settled in for the battle. She was cute when she was stubborn, but he could outlast her. 'I really don't care what the actual number is. I only get concerned about weight when a client is obese, and you, sexy thing, are not obese.'

Her cheeks turned as pink as the flamingo on her shirt, and she folded her arms defensively. 'If you don't care, then you don't need the number.'

Damn, she was quick. 'OK, you've got me there. It's the change in weight that we want to track, but I'm more concerned with your lean body mass and percentage of fat. The three are interconnected. I'll need to track them all if I'm going to be of any help to you.'

She didn't budge.

He sighed. She was beyond stubborn. Reasoning wasn't going to work with her. He had to go for the jugular. 'I thought you came here for a reason. Wasn't there something about a reunion?'

Her mouth flattened into a straight line, and she glared at him. 'That's not fair.'

He recalled her saying the same thing outside, and he shifted uncomfortably on the desk. He was still half-hard from their little grope session. That tongue of hers was nimble. 'Do you want to get in shape?' he asked gruffly.

Her lips formed a pout that was more enticing than she knew. 'Yes.'

'Well, get your sweet tootsie up on that scale.'

Conflicting emotions crossed her face, but she wasn't willing to crumple just yet. 'Turn your back. I'll do it myself.'

'Fine,' he conceded. He handed her the chart and turned his back. He heard her step onto the scale. She fiddled with the weights, and he heard a groan. There was the sound of pencil on paper and then she quickly covered her tracks by resetting the scale back to zero.

'Here,' she said belligerently. 'Satisfied?'

He let her surly attitude bounce right off of him as he took the clipboard. In no rush, he flipped the pencil around and erased her handwriting.

'What are you doing?'

She bounded over next to him and nervously peered over his shoulder as he wrote the correct weight in the box. He fought the smile that pulled at his lips.

'How did you know that?' she squealed.

He jerked his thumb towards the wall. 'Mirror.'

She whirled around, and he used the distraction to whip a tape measure out of his back pocket. He could only imagine how much she was going to fight him on this.

It had the potential to be damn fun.

33

Unfortunately, she heard him when he tried to sneak up on her. She twirled around, and he held his hands up innocently.

'What are you doing?' she snapped.

She saw the tape measure before he could explain, and her eyes rounded as if it were a poisonous snake. Her hands came up to ward him off, and she began to retreat. 'Get that thing away from me.'

This time, he couldn't hide his smile. 'It won't bite – but I might.'

'Oh, you're a funny guy. So, so funny. Back off.'

He took a step towards her. He knew how to fight dirty. 'Reunion.'

'You ... You ...'

'Reunion,' he repeated. He took two steps towards her.

'Stop it.'

'Ree-ewe-nyun!'

'Ah, crud.' She stopped in place, and her shoulders sagged. 'You are a mean, mean man.'

'I like to think of it as being focused.'

She chewed on her lower lip. 'Is this really necessary?'

'Absolutely.'

Her fingers opened and closed as tension wove through her.

'Oh, all right. Just make it snappy.' She planted her fists on her hips, and her eyes narrowed danger- ously. 'But if I hear you breathe a word of this outside of this room ...'

'I know. My ability to have children will be severely limited.'

'Just as long as we're clear.'

'As a bell. Remember that filing cabinet? This will all be locked up right over there.'

She looked at the cabinet as if trying to see how secure it was.

He took a cautious step towards her. 'I'll make it fast. Just lift your arms.'

He stared at her almost dumbfounded as her arms came up obediently from her sides.

Well, that was almost too easy.

Before she could react, he grabbed the tent with both hands. The flamingo crumpled as he whipped it up over her head and tossed it behind him.

'There,' he said. 'That's better.'

He let his gaze run down her body as she sputtered and, for a moment, forgot to breathe.

This was *much* better.

She wore a jog bra that put Victoria's Secrets frilly confections to shame. The thing was an absolute engineering wonder. It lifted, bunched, and propped things up in a way that made his mouth go dry. Her breasts jutted outwards from her chest like twin soldiers leading the charge.

And as he watched, her nipples poked out to salute.

'Hel-lo,' he said slowly.

He had more than one idea on how to salute back.

Roma crossed her arms over her chest. She'd been right about nipping out. Even the super structure of her sports bra couldn't contain her perky nipples. This was yet another reason why she'd worn that T-shirt.

She leant to look around him for her flamingo. Maybe if she faked him out ...

'You're not getting it back,' he said, squashing that idea. His gaze had yet to leave her chest. 'Come on, now. Arms up.'

'You gotta be kidding me.'

'The sooner you let me take these measurements, the sooner it will be over.'

She wasn't going to fall for that trick. Having him know her weight was bad enough.

He ran his finger over his bruised cheekbone, silently manipulating her. 'Do it for me?'

Damn the man! Roma felt herself waver. In this

light, the purple of his eyelid looked nearly neon blue.

'The longer we stand here, the longer I'm going to stare at your boobs.'

Her spine stiffened.

'Unless you *like* having me stare at your boobs.'

Her arms whipped out to the sides. 'You are a fiend.'

'I've been called worse.'

She bit her lip and looked blindly over his shoulder as he came close. This was just awful. A virtual Adonis was analysing her doughboy form. Darn it, she shouldn't have had that piece of cheesecake last night. It had just looked so good at the grocery store, and she'd been embarrassed about yesterday, nervous about today . . .

He slipped the tape measure under her arms and around her back. Her wandering thoughts snapped back to the here and now when his hands brushed her chest.

What the —

He was measuring her bust line! Her breath caught on a sharp inhale.

'Stop trying to impress me,' he muttered. 'Exhale normally.'

'Hey!' she snapped as the back of his fingers rubbed her left breast. 'Hey, now!'

'Stop fidgeting.' He pulled the tape measure so it was snug across her bust.

'I . . . I . . . Oh!'

His fingers traced the line of her bra where her breasts plumped out over the top, and heat spread out along her skin. As if they hadn't felt huge before, her breasts suddenly felt heavy and all tingly. They were swelling to his touch.

He paused, and her eyes flashed to his face. The sharp interest in his blue stare nearly brought her to her knees.

'I hear that when you lose weight, that's the first place it goes.'

'I don't think you'll ever have to worry about being flat-chested.'

'Oh.' He was still staring, and zaps of energy centred in her sensitive nipples. 'Well, that's good. I think.'

'Definitely good,' he muttered. He inhaled as if he were having trouble with his oxygen supply.

He seemed to summon his professionalism and lowered the tape measure to her waist. Roma stood still. She wanted to chew up that tape measure and spit it out, but at the same time, he was touching her.

It felt too good to stop him.

Without her T-shirt, she was naked from her ribcage to her shorts. His fingers caressed her waist, and she sucked in her tummy sharply.

Skin to skin. The intimacy was shocking.

He took his time as he wrapped the tape measure about her. 'See?' he murmured into her ear. 'This isn't so bad, is it?'

Bad, no. Dangerous, yes.

'Just hurry it up, OK?'

'You don't hurry this sort of thing. In fact, you do it twice to make sure you've got it right.'

Oh, he was a naughty one.

His hands slid down the sides of her hips and over her backside. He crouched down before her in what could have been a tantalising position, but Roma's knees buckled when his fingers stroked against what she affectionately referred to as her Thunder Thighs.

'Whoa!' she said as she gripped his shoulders for support. His hands caught her hips to help her regain her balance, and the embrace nearly put his face in her crotch. She quickly tried to step back, but he stopped her with a tiny flex of the muscles in those sexy arms.

'Just a few more measurements,' he said with a knowing smile on his lips.

'Do you have to measure me there?'

'Oh, yeah. Right there.'

His gaze locked on hers as he slowly slid the tape measure between her legs. His palm cupped her inner thigh, and her air began thundering in her lungs. Just a slight turn of the wrist and he'd be cupping her mound. She stood there quivering with his hand pressed high between her legs as he measured her thigh.

Twice.

'Maybe I should take one more just to be sure,' he said.

Lord help her.

When he finished, his hand slid slowly down her leg. His fingertips glided over the back of her thigh, her knee and the curve of her calf until finally circling her ankle. Roma couldn't help but stare as his big hand gently cupped her ankle bone. She'd never felt so feminine in her life.

He cleared his throat and stood. 'Almost done.'

She tried to get herself to relax, but twittery feelings were coursing through her veins and converging low in her belly. She looked up at him, considering how he'd react if she gave in to the impulse to jump him, but the idea vaporised when she saw him coming at her with what appeared to be pinchers in his hand. 'What's that?' she asked slowly.

'It's a fat caliper. It's the last set of data I'll need. I swear.'

Fat caliper? She didn't think so!

Her fluttery feelings took a quick back seat, and she stepped away from him. 'Don't you even dare!'

'Relax,' he said. 'It's not going to hurt. It helps me calculate your body fat percentage.'

She hadn't expected it to hurt. She'd expected it to be embarrassing. And she'd been right.

She spun around. He'd left her T-shirt unguarded!

He caught her about the waist so quickly from behind that her toes left the ground. Roma let out a strangled yelp. With him holding her as he was, her backside was pressed firmly against his front side. And a very big and excited front side it was.

'You're not making this easy,' he growled.

She hadn't pegged him as the easy sort.

Roma Grace! her good side chastised. *Shame on you!*

What? He's a hot guy.

She groaned. He was hot all right. Her butt felt like it was on fire.

His hold shifted, but he didn't let her go. 'Are you going to fight me like this on everything I tell you to do?'

She felt a nip from the pinchers at the back of her arm. 'Depends on what you tell me to do.'

He let out a low chuckle. 'Now you're giving me ideas.'

Ideas that didn't take a genius to figure out. The bulge was rubbing against her butt ever more insistently.

'Two more,' he grunted.

He pulled her back so she was flush against him from her head to the backs of her tennis shoes. Heat flooded her system as his other arm came around her down low. She caught a moan at the back of her throat when he pinched the front of her thigh with the devious device.

'You didn't need to make this so hard,' he said raspily into her ear.

But hard had never felt so good. His cock felt like it was made of steel.

His arms tightened around her, and Roma watched as the hand with the caliper rose to her waist. Her lungs expanded and contracted with every breath. One more. Just one more. She jolted when he suddenly tugged on her shorts. The elastic waistband stretched wide as he pulled one side down to nearly her hip.

She grabbed for the other side as she felt her shorts start to slide down over her butt. 'Jake!'

He'd pulled them down so far, her panties were showing. She sucked in her belly sharply. The pinchers felt like a makeshift sex toy as he slid them across her skin.

'Lavender today, huh?' he said as he looked down at what he'd uncovered. 'Nice, but I think I liked the pink better.'

Her mouth gaped open. How had he known the colour of the panties she'd worn yesterday?

This was too personal. Way too personal. She squirmed to try to get away.

She gasped when she felt the true strength in those arms clamp down. He held her still as he slid the waistband of her panties down to give him better access. Her face flamed when her blonde curls were revealed.

The caliper slid to a spot a few inches above her hip bone. Her lungs heaved as she watched it pinch her skin. It was only after he was done that she realised that he'd taken the measurement nowhere close to her panty line.

'You sleaze!' She kicked back at him with her heel, and he let her go. She darted away, yanking her clothes up as she went. 'You didn't need to nearly strip me for that.'

He threw her a wink. 'For that? No.'

She let out a sound that was nearly a growl and dived for her T-shirt.

He chuckled as he wrote down the measurement on his clipboard. 'If I'd known you were going to like it so much, I would have started with the pinchers.'

Roma pulled the T-shirt over her head and felt her face flush. 'Are we finished?'

'Oh, baby. We're just getting started.'

She stomped towards the door, but he moved fast.

He straight-armed it shut before she could open it. She could feel his body heat as he hovered close behind her.

'If I'm going to train you, we're going to do it right,' he said into her ear. 'You should know right now that I'm going to work you hard.'

'Just wait until I start drilling you on your financials,' she fired back.

She turned around and found herself trapped. He ran a finger along her chin.

'No more fighting me,' he warned. 'If I tell you to do something, you need to do it. That is, if you want to do some ass kicking at that reunion.'

He didn't scare her. 'Ever heard of the Internal Revenue Service? I can sic them on you.'

He pulled back.

'Fair enough, Goldie. Here's the deal. I'm in charge when we're in the gym. You can have your way when you're sitting behind that desk. All right?'

She sniffed and crossed her arms over her chest. 'All right,' she finally agreed.

The move brought his attention back to the pink flamingo, and he scowled. 'Good. Now take off that ugly T-shirt. I want to see you sweat.'

Chapter Three

'Excuse me?' Roma said in disbelief.

'Take it off.'

'You can't be serious.' She understood – sort of – why he'd needed access underneath her shirt for the measurements. Bunched-up clothes added to the numbers, and she wanted those puppies as tiny as they could possibly be. This, though, was totally different. 'I can't go out there in just my jogging bra and shorts.'

'Why not?'

'Why not?' she snapped. 'I can think of two pretty good reasons.'

'Ah, the headlight problem.'

Her jaw dropped. 'I was counting that as one.'

Flustered, she wiped a hand across her face. If only the red colour would be so easily removed. 'I'm not exactly in strip-down shape.'

'Bullshit.'

She was not about to be sweet-talked.

They stood in a silent stand-off until he finally cocked his head and looked at her speculatively. 'Would it help if I joined you?'

Before she could answer, he reached for the bottom of his sweatshirt. Without an ounce of shyness, he pulled it over his head and tossed it back on his desk. The T-shirt he was wearing underneath was a pale reminder of what it once might have been. The material was so threadbare she could see through it and the sleeves had been ripped off – or maybe torn off by his teeth.

Now there was a picture . . .

43

'No,' she sputtered, trying to get her thoughts back on track. 'That doesn't help at all.'

She was gaping, she knew. She couldn't help it. There were only so many things a girl could control at once, and drooling was currently at the top of her list. Darn him, he wasn't playing fair!

'Your turn.'

'No way.'

'Backing out of our agreement already?'

Her eyes narrowed. Oh, she was going to get him for this. Just wait until it was her turn to play boss.

'Fine.' Jerkily, she pulled the flamingo over her head. Honestly, it was like giving up a security blanket. She crumpled the material up in her hands and, before she could back down, held it out to him.

Wordlessly, he took it and draped it over the chair. He knew better than to smile. 'I can see your muscle tone better this way,' he explained.

'Yeah, yeah. Let's get it over with.' Trying to show bravado, she flipped her ponytail over her shoulder. With a deep breath, she turned on her heel and yanked open the door. Maybe it would be less painful to do it quickly – like pulling off a bandage.

She remembered too late that that always stung like hell, too. The minute she stepped out into the gym, she felt naked.

'This way,' he said with a guiding hand at her waist. 'We'll start on the treadmill to warm you up.'

Warm her up? Between his touch and her embarrassment, she was pretty toasty already, thank you very much. Self-consciously, she crossed her arms over her chest and followed him. She glanced around shyly as she stayed on his heels. The gym was busy and, fortunately, everyone seemed to be doing his or her own thing. Nobody was paying much attention to her.

But they were to Jake.

It didn't take long for Roma to realise that the women on the cardiovascular machines were more interested in his flesh than hers. They were eyeing his muscled arms like fresh meat.

Why, the skinny little nymphets! A wave of flirting followed his movement across the floor. As he passed by, one woman arched her neck and sensuously wiped the sweat off her throat. The next nearly threw her hips out of joint as she exercised on a cross trainer, but the last one was the worst. She raised her hands over her head in a supposed stretch and her tiny boobs lifted in silent invitation. Roma threw them all a glare. Could they get any more obvious? There was flirting, and then there was flaunting. Some of these hoydens were wearing even less than she had on – although none were nearly as well endowed.

'Ha!' She had them there. Taking on their silent challenge, she dropped her arms, squared her shoulders, and thrust out her breasts. Jake was hers for the next hour.

So there.

'Let's use this machine,' he threw over his shoulder, oblivious to the byplay going on behind him.

'Sounds good,' Roma said, increasing her strut to add fire to the flames. Ms Tiny Boobs scowled, and she smiled back sweetly.

'Hop up here, and we'll get started,' he said.

'Whatever you say, boss.'

That, finally, got his attention. He glanced back at her and nearly replayed her pratfall from the day before. He stumbled backwards over his own feet, bumped up against the machine, and nearly went down on his butt.

Damn! Jake thought as he quickly righted himself. What had happened with her? Two seconds ago, she'd been all shy and embarrassed. Now, she was practically a billboard sign for sex. Helplessly, his gaze ran over her. 'Not in strip-down shape', his ass.

With the confident way she held her lush body, he was half-tempted to throw her down on the treadmill and take her right there.

He cleared his throat. Shit. Where was his clipboard?

'Uh, ready to begin?' he asked.

She climbed onto the machine, and a bit of her uncertainty returned. 'What do I do?'

'Relax, it's not going to throw you off,' he said, reading her mind. He looked down at her legs, but that blurred his focus all over again. All he could picture was that stocking creeping up, up, up ... He shook his head to make himself snap out of it. 'You'll want to stand on the side rails until the belt starts moving.'

She widened her stance, and he quickly scanned the room. Sure enough, half of the men were gawking at her.

The lechers.

'This is the start button,' he said, trying to regain command of the situation. 'Over here are the controls for the speed and the incline.'

Her brow furrowed as she listened. He pushed the start button, and the machine beneath her began to move. A flash of fear went through her big lavender eyes.

'Easy. Just step onboard and put one foot in front of the other. You can hold onto this handlebar if it helps.'

She latched onto the bar with a death grip. Cautiously, she lifted her right foot and placed it in the centre of the belt. It immediately drifted backwards, and she automatically stepped with her left foot to keep her balance. Just like that, and she was walking. Proud of herself, she grinned at him.

The grin nearly did Jake in. *Down boy.* She'd asked for his help getting in shape for her reunion. Damned if he wasn't going to make sure she got everything she wanted.

'That's good. Let's up the pace past grandma speed.' He jabbed an up arrow and the belt beneath her feet began to move more quickly. Her fingers tightened around the handlebar, and her face went serious again.

'That's a good steady pace,' he said. 'Once you feel comfortable, you can let go and swing your arms at your sides.'

Her ponytail bobbed as her head snapped towards him. 'Get real.'

'Right. We'll work up to that. How do you feel?'

She nibbled at her lower lip, and he sighed. She wasn't going to make this easy on him. 'Good,' she finally surmised.

'Think you can go for five minutes? Then we'll move on to the strength tests.'

She nodded. 'I can do five.'

Jake shifted his weight uncomfortably. Five minutes was a short length of time, he tried to remind himself. Nothing, really. A pittance. But five minutes of watching her body move? God, when had he become such a masochist? He rubbed the back of his neck. He needed a distraction. 'So tell me more about this reunion. Why all the hype? I didn't get this worked up over mine.'

She let out a snort. 'Why would you?'

'What do you mean?'

She rolled her eyes. 'Don't give me that innocent routine. You're a stud, and you know it. You've got your own business, you've still got your hair and women pant as you walk by. Just look at you.'

Women panted? He glanced back at the wannabe sirens and couldn't help but grin. Was that the reason for her sudden transformation? Was she jealous?

She had said she thought he was a stud.

He filed that titbit of info away for future reference and propped his arms against the control panel. 'You've got your own business, too,' he reminded her. 'And if you haven't noticed, you're creating quite a disturbance for the men in the room.'

She glanced around quickly. 'I am not.'

'Are, too.'

Her breath caught, and her mouth rounded into a tight 'O'. On the sly, she risked a glance down at her chest. 'Is it that obvious?'

Was she trying to kill him? He was doing his best not to look.

'You're fine,' he said, sneaking a peek. She wouldn't think so, but no need to tell her that. 'Explain to me why you're so nervous about seeing your old friends.'

She looked at him as if he were stupid. 'I'm not worried about my friends. It's the enemy.'

The way she said it, you'd think she was gearing up for war. Jake fought not to smile. It couldn't have been that bad. 'You're talking about the girl who picked on you.'

'Well, *yeah*.'

'What did she do to you?'

Roma's face became shuttered. 'I don't want to talk about it.'

Now he was truly intrigued. He looked at the control panel. It was upside down from his direction, but he found the button he wanted. He increased the speed with two pushes.

'Hey!'

'Tell me,' he said.

She began to breathe a little harder as she fought to keep up. 'No. It's embarrassing.'

'It's what brought you here. You said you want to kick her ass.' He punched the incline button. Her fingers turned white around the handgrip as the machine gave a low whirr and tilted so she was walking uphill.

'Whoa! Hey now. Be nice.'

He watched her. Her cheeks were turning pink and her forehead was starting to glisten. 'Tell me.'

48

His finger hovered over the controls threateningly.

'No! Don't. No more.'

He backed off, and she nibbled at her lower lip. She was considering how much to tell him. He could see the gears turning in her head.

'It was little things mostly,' she finally offered.

'Like?'

'Like spreading lies about me and posting embarrassing pictures in the hallways.'

'What kind of pictures?'

Her face flared.

He lowered his voice. 'Tell me or you're never getting off this machine.'

She winced. She was already starting to huff and puff. Cardio-wise, she had a way to go. 'You know how I'm kind of clumsy?' she said.

He nodded. He had the black eye to prove it.

'I'm graceful compared to what I once was. Back then I was always tripping, running into things, or just plain falling down. One day, Mr Carlton, the science teacher, helped me back to my feet. The next day pictures of the two of us were on every poster board in the school.'

'What's so bad about that?'

'From the angle at which they were taken, it looked like my face was plastered in his crotch.'

Jake was taken aback. He hadn't expected anything like that. No wonder she wanted to do some ass-kicking. He was quickly getting on-board with the plan himself. 'She got in trouble, though, right?'

'There was no proof that she did it.'

OK, now he was pissed. 'And that was a little thing? What in God's name was big?'

Roma finally risked letting go of the handlebar and wiped a hand across her red face. She was starting to work up a sweat, but he knew it was the memories that had her most upset. They were getting him worked up, too.

'She got me after gym class one day,' she said.

49

'While I was in the shower, she stole my clothes out of my locker. I was left in nothing but a towel. Ms Gilliam, our gym teacher, found me in the locker room two hours later. She gave me some old basketball warm-ups to wear home.'

'My bra and underwear showed up later in Bobby VanDonselaar's hallway locker.' She glanced away. 'He was the class geek. Six-foot five, acne, a bad sinus condition . . . You get the picture.'

Easy, Jake told himself. He was getting a little too fired up. For her sake, he knew he should drop the whole subject, but he found he couldn't. 'Why'd she do it?' he asked, not understanding.

How would someone be so mean? Especially to someone as bubbly and vivacious as Roma?

Her lips pressed into a straight line. She concentrated on the control panel, and quickly snuck a finger out to decrease the incline. 'She thought I did something.'

'And what was that?' Jake glanced down. Damn, he hadn't meant to work her this hard on her first day. He needed to watch it.

'It was just one of those high school things,' she said between breaths. 'Mountains are made out of molehills. Every little event is the end of the world.'

The light suddenly dawned.

'You stole her boyfriend.'

Roma's head snapped up. 'I did not!'

Suddenly, her foot got too close to the edge of the belt. Her tennis shoe stuck against the side rail, and she tilted crazily. His hand flashed out and closed around her upper arm. She regained her balance and, after a few stutter steps, got herself under control.

'I'm right. It was over a guy,' he said, refusing to be distracted from the topic at hand.

'I was his math tutor.'

'But he had a crush on you.'

'I couldn't help that.'

'No, I suppose you couldn't,' he said gruffly. She

truly didn't understand what that blonde hair and those big lavender eyes did to a guy. The kid hadn't stood a chance.

'I never encouraged him,' she said with a pout.

'But your prankster pal thought you did.'

'She wasn't my pal.' Forgetting her nervousness about the treadmill, Roma let go of the handlebar and flung her hands into the air. 'She called me *Aroma* – like I smelled or something. I couldn't help it that her own boyfriend didn't like her.'

'Slow down,' Jake said automatically. He lowered the speed. Neither of them had been watching the time, and she'd gone for nearly ten minutes.

Damn. He didn't think much of this girl who had terrorised her, but he liked her slimy boyfriend even less. Where had the kid been when all this had been going on? Had he just stood by and let it happen? Irritated, Jake slapped the red stop button on the treadmill. If you asked him, lover boy should be in line for an ass-kicking, too. 'That's enough. Let's move on to the leg press.'

Roma carefully dismounted the treadmill. Jake was unhappy with her, she could tell. He didn't even look at her as he led her into another area of the gym that held the weight machines. All business, he stopped in front of a daunting device that could have come from a medieval torture chamber.

'This is a leg press machine,' he said. 'Sit down there on the seat, and I'll adjust it for you.'

She pulled nervously on her ponytail. He was disappointed in her. 'You think I'm being shallow.'

His blue gaze swung towards her. 'What?'

'You think I should forget about what happened in high school. Grow up and move past it.'

'I never said that.'

'But you're thinking it.'

'Goldie, you don't have a clue what I'm thinking.' He grabbed a spare clipboard from a nail on the wall and started a new tracking sheet. 'Sit down and settle your feet against that big plate.'

'You're right,' she said as she manoeuvred herself into the contraption. 'I'll admit it. I'm shallow, petty and pathetic. I'm going to this thing to have fun, but deep down, I want to impress all my old classmates. I want to set them on their ears – show them that clumsy Roma Hanson made something of herself.'

He moved closer and she got a front-row view of his black eye. It made her feel even worse. 'I'm a terrible person, aren't I? For all I know, Ellie the Witch might have turned out all right. Wouldn't that just be a kicker? For me to be such a superficial ninny and her to be a doctor or a missionary or a preacher ... Huwhaaa!'

He'd pushed a lever and her knees were suddenly digging into her ribcage.

'I guarantee you, nobody like that would turn out to be a preacher,' he said.

'Air,' Roma wheezed.

'Sorry.' He made an adjustment. 'Is that better?'

If you called being bent in half like a greeting card 'better'.

She inhaled deeply. 'But what do all these self-centred thoughts say about me?'

'Oh, I don't know. Maybe that you're human?' He planted his hand against the machine's solid metal frame. 'Screw political correctness. Everyone checks out everyone at a high school reunion. It's what the damn things are for.'

She did a double take. 'Really?'

'Hell, the best part is finding out who got fat, who got arrested, who got knocked up, and who turned out gay. You should have seen how people at my reunion were trying to cover up their weaknesses. Dresses were bursting at the seams, and talk about bad comb overs! The point is that everyone was trying to put his or her best foot forwards. It's just the way people are.'

'Are you saying I'm normal?'

One of his eyebrows lifted. It made the purple hues in his black eye shine. 'I don't know if I'd go that far.'

Roma grimaced apologetically. 'I'm quasi-normal?'

'If that's how you want to put it. Now grip the handles by the seat with your hands and push out with your legs. I need to see how strong you are.'

She assumed the position and pushed. The weight moved easily. 'I am looking forward to seeing my friends,' she commented.

'Well, we've got three months to get you ready for them.' He adjusted the pin in the weight stack. 'If anyone ever deserved to make a splash at their high school reunion, it's you. Try again.'

Roma couldn't believe it. She wasn't a terrible person after all. Apparently, everyone felt this way – vengeful, self-conscious and anxious. How wonderful! With a smile on her face, she extended her legs as he'd instructed. The smile wavered when she felt her legs quiver.

'Watch your form. I don't want to see that cute tush coming off the seat.'

He moved the pin down in the weight stack. *Cute tush*? *Try flabby fanny*. She tried again and, this time, found she had to grit her teeth.

'That's better, but push through the balls of your feet.'

Did he have to keep moving that darn pin? Beads of sweat had popped out on her forehead, and hot fires were burning in her legs. 'You mean I'm still supposed to be able to feel them?'

'Stop curling your toes.' He squatted down beside her. 'You should feel it working back here.'

He brushed the back of her thigh, and she nearly kicked the footplate through the opposite wall. Holy cow! What had that been?

'Good,' he said. 'Let's move on.'

Yes, let's. Hot shivers were spreading up her leg

and settling underneath her. Things were bound to get very embarrassing if she sat here much longer. Clumsily, she uncoiled from her spring-loaded position and started to tag along after him. Something was wrong with her legs, though – something besides the hot handprint he'd left on the back of her thigh. She was walking funny – a bit like John Wayne perhaps. 'Uh, Jake?'

'We'll test your upper body strength on the bench press. Lie down on your back with your head facing the weight stack.'

Self-consciously, Roma climbed on board. Her heart skipped a beat, though, when she rolled over onto her back. With her legs spread to straddle the bench and Jake standing right over her, she felt ... Well, never mind.

'Watch your head. You don't want to be too far up.'

She slid down.

'There you go. This machine is easy to use. Grip the handles there and push straight up. You'll feel the work in your arms and chest.'

Her eyes rounded. He'd better not touch her there!

'Hey, Jake?'

Roma rolled her head on the bench and saw Tito, the kid with the ice pack from the day before. He grinned at her, but turned his attention back to his boss.

'You've got a phone call. Liz needs to reschedule a session.'

Jake glanced down at her. 'I need to take this. Think you can stay out of trouble for two minutes?'

Liz. Wasn't that the name of the woman who'd given him the birthday card? Roma looked at him closely. A break right now would probably be a really good thing. 'I'll try.'

She watched him walk away, and her gaze naturally zeroed in on his tight butt.

Naughty girl, her conscience reprimanded. *That could be his girlfriend on the phone.*

Or it could be just another client wanting to hit on him, her inner devil argued. *Besides, not watching that yummy backside would be a crime.*

Letting out a puff of air, Roma stared at the ceiling. She had no idea what his availability status was. At least without him hovering over her, she had a chance of getting her body under control. He'd been flirting with her – no doubt. But really, one little casual touch and she was reacting like this? Come to think of it, though, it hadn't just been one touch. He'd stripped her in his office. Measured her bust line. Tugged down her panties.

Ms Tiny Boobs walked by with a sneer, and Roma felt her face flush. Oh, God. She hadn't just moaned or anything, had she? Trying to cover her embarrassment, she reached up for the handgrips. She needed to work off some of this sexual energy before he got back – because if he did have a girlfriend, she was in big trouble. Taking a breath, she gave a push.

Nothing.

She let out a grunt. It was tougher than she'd expected. The woman who'd been on this machine before hadn't looked like an Amazon. She slid upwards on the bench to get a better angle. Again, she gave a push, this time with more emphasis.

The bar moved, but the weights clicked when it came right back down.

'Hmmfff.' Not good. She needed to get serious about this. Jake had reminded her of an important fact. She only had three months to accomplish her goal. She slid up on the bench, braced her feet against the floor, and gave a heave.

The weight went up. She gritted her teeth and growled until she managed to straighten her arms.

There! One rep! She let the bar come back down and reversed directions to try a second, but it was just too heavy. It was all she could do to stop the weight stack from banging as it dropped back to its starting position.

How much weight was on this thing anyway? She turned her head to look.

'Ouch!'

Yowza, that hurt. She reached up to the base of her ponytail. What in the world? Hell's bells, her hair was caught in the weight stack!

A little frantic, Roma followed the path of her stuck hair. A good portion of it was jammed between two weights. She wrapped her fist around the ponytail and gave a tug. It wouldn't budge.

She sighed. She was going to have to lift the weights again to get loose. Resuming her position on the bench, she copied what she'd done before. She dug her heels into the floor and gritted her teeth. With an unfeminine growl, she pushed.

Nothing.

She'd used all her energy lifting it the first time. She was well and truly stuck.

Crap! If she didn't do something quick, Jake was going to find her like this.

He'd warned her to stay out of trouble.

She looked around for help. Where was Tito? She winced when she turned her head and saw him at the front desk. Not an option. He was too far away. She stared again at the ceiling. What to do? What to do? Neither her angel nor her devil voice had any suggestions. Out of the corner of her eye, she saw somebody sit down on the machine next to her.

'Excuse me,' she called.

The person didn't respond. 'Could you help me?' she said more loudly.

She turned her head further, suffering through the pull on her hair, and finally caught a glimpse of the guy. Instinctively, she pulled back.

It was a sweaty tattooed man – and a big boy

weightlifter, at that. Talk about imposing. Not only was he huge, but his head was shaved as smooth as a billiard ball. A barbed-wire tattoo wrapped around his massive bicep and another graced the back of his shoulder. From her position, she couldn't quite decipher the artwork, but it looked like some sort of an animal.

He was wearing headphones, so that was why he hadn't heard her cry for help. Did she dare try to signal him again? Well, it was either him or Jake. She didn't know how many more times she could embarrass herself in front of her hunky trainer before she'd be forced to move out to the country and live in a hidey-hole.

She lifted a hand to tap the frightening stranger on the shoulder. It was all the more frustrating now that she'd worked up her nerve, she found she couldn't reach him. There he sat, seemingly in a daze. Her hand fluttered towards him, missing him by only an inch. She tried snapping her fingers, but that didn't work either. His attention was riveted on something else. Braving going bald herself, Roma lifted her head.

Missy was walking by.

She opened her mouth to call for help.

'What in the world have you done to yourself now?'

Jake was standing close when Roma's head whipped towards him. Her eyes were wide with surprise, but they quickly narrowed when her pony-tail pulled tight. She let out a cry and reached up to her head.

'It's not what you think,' she said weakly.

He'd seen her predicament the moment he'd stepped out of his office. 'I think you tried it by yourself while I was gone, and you got too close to the weight stack.'

Her face flushed a million shades of red. 'OK, so it is what you think.'

He shook his head. 'Two minutes. That was all I asked for.'

Dropping his clipboard to the floor, he moved so his legs straddled both her and the bench. The shock on her face told him exactly what she thought of that move. *Interesting.* He wrapped his hands around hers on the handle grips. 'We don't try machines until somebody shows us how to use them properly, OK?'

She looked like a chastised puppy. 'Sorry.'

'You're lucky you didn't give yourself a concussion.' He gave a little pull, and the stack lifted easily. She immediately liberated her blonde strands. He settled the weights back down to their resting position. 'How's your head?'

'Sore,' she mumbled. She started to roll off the bench.

He blocked her with his knee. 'Hold on there. You haven't completed the test yet.'

She looked up at him in disbelief. 'I still have to do it?'

'I'll be here this time,' he said. He leant over her to lighten the load and heard her inhale sharply.

'Could you move, please?'

He could, but he wouldn't. 'I think I'll stay right here to spot you.'

'But you're right on top of me.'

'Just where I want to be.'

Her face flushed crimson, but she wrapped her fingers around the grips. Fierce determination tightened her face, and he could almost feel her heels digging for the foundation of his building. Her back arched off the bench, and he immediately placed his hand, palm open, on her stomach. She dropped flat as a pancake.

'What are you doing?' she said, exhaling like a pricked balloon.

'Don't arch like that. You could hurt yourself.'

He'd liked the look of her straining body, though.

With her stiff nipples, it gave him all kinds of fascinating ideas.

He let out a long breath. Unable to remove his hand, he rubbed her stomach. Damn, he liked touching her. Her skin felt incredible, all warm and soft.

Her teeth bit into her full lower lip, and she glanced down at his hand. When she realised he wasn't going to move it, her eyelids drifted shut. She seemed to call upon some inner strength. Her hands tightened and she pushed upwards on the handlebars. The weight stack lifted, but only a short way.

'Why don't we drop this to something more comfortable?' he suggested.

'Yes, why don't we?' She sighed.

Time and again, he made her lift the weight until he found one that challenged her, but didn't cause any undue stress. He worked as slowly as possible, but eventually, it was time to let her off the machine. Satisfied with her effort, he bent down to retrieve his clipboard.

'Are we done here?' she asked, her pulse pounding visibly in her throat.

'Yeah. That's it.' His heart rate was elevated, too, and he had to concentrate to make sure he marked down her numbers correctly. His pen skidded across the page, though, when he felt her move.

She was like a snake. Apparently unable to stand being trapped by him any longer, she took her one avenue of escape. Instead of rolling off the bench, she chose to shimmy down it. Like a champion limbo player, she went underneath him. He gaped as she slid right through the arch of his legs without even brushing against him.

Quickly, he looked over his shoulder. She slid until she was on her knees on the floor behind him. Then she simply pushed herself up to a standing position and brushed off her hands.

Stunned, he looked at the only other witness to the contortionist display. Hawk sat on the machine next to them, gaping at Roma with just as much wonder. A sly smile crossed his face, and he pulled one side of his headphones off his ear. 'Limber little thing, isn't she?'

Jake shrugged. 'I guess I can skip that flexibility test.'

Hawk shot him a horrified look. 'Are you crazy?'

'Good point.' Jake stepped over the weight bench and crooked his finger at his favourite new client. 'You. Goldie. Follow me.'

Chapter Four

He was watching her again.

Missy could feel Hawk's gaze on her as she walked by. His stare glided over her from head to toe and an uneasy but familiar thrill settled in the pit of her stomach. It began its slow burn, and she licked her dry lips. Every time. Every darn time.

She made herself keep walking, overly aware of the way her hips swayed and her breasts bounced in the confines of her bra. It was always this way with him. He stared and her body would start gunning its engines. He'd never said a word to her – not so much as a hello – but she was more aware of him than anybody else in the gym. How could she not be? That much testosterone was impossible to ignore.

Especially when it was all being thrown in her direction.

And especially when it made her feel so sexy.

Too sexy. The man's blatant carnal interest made her nervous.

Ignoring him as well as she could, she walked to the front desk. She set her backpack on the counter and pulled on her ski jacket for cover. It didn't help. She could practically feel his fascinated gaze slide down to her butt. Her thighs clenched together in unconscious reaction.

'Hey, Tito,' she called anxiously. 'Can I get my cheque?'

Poor Tito. He hadn't seen her coming, and she'd startled him. He jumped so high, he nearly came right out of his tennis shoes.

'Sorry,' she said automatically.

'Keep your pants on, would you?' he said, holding his hand over his heart. 'Jake signed cheques this afternoon.'

Missy tapped her fingernails on the counter impatiently. Keeping her pants on was exactly what she was trying to do.

Unhurriedly, Tito searched through his keys. He unlocked a cupboard behind the desk and pulled out the moneybag that was stored there. He unzipped it and flipped through the cheques until he found hers. 'Here it is.'

'Thanks,' she said, snatching it out of his hands. She put it in the front pouch of her backpack. That covered what she needed for her half of the rent this month. 'Can I see the schedule for next week? Trisha asked me to cover her Pilates class on Wednesday.'

'What's your rush tonight?' he asked as he passed her the clipboard. 'Hot date with the boyfriend?'

Boyfriend. She had one of those – one of the live-in variety, in fact. Why did she seem to forget that every time she set foot in this place?

'Hot date with my kinematics book,' she said. 'I've got a test tomorrow.'

And she was going to have a devil of a time studying for it if she didn't get her thoughts centred. She hooked her hair over her ear and concentrated on the schedule. She inhaled sharply, though, when she felt Hawk's interest focus on the side of her neck. She could almost feel him nuzzling her there, his short moustache and goatee brushing against her skin.

'Something wrong?' Tito asked.

Her hand shook as she passed him back the clipboard. 'Uh, I didn't realise I had three classes on Saturday.'

'Want me to ask Jake if you can switch?'

'No. It's all right. I need the money.'

And she needed to get out of here. She risked a glance at her admirer and found him staring right at her. Their gazes collided and she felt his essence like a punch in the chest.

Tito gave a chuckle. 'That Roma's a pistol, isn't she?'

Missy blinked and for the first time realised what was going on behind Hawk. It looked as if Roma had gotten tangled up in the bench press machine and Jake was giving her the 'what for'. 'I like her. They're going to be fun to watch together.'

'I've got a feeling she's going to give Jake all he can handle.'

Missy knew a thing or two about that. She didn't even know how to begin to deal with Hawk. She glanced at him quickly before her gaze skittered away. He was the kind of man she'd expect to find in a biker bar somewhere — the kind who'd be comfortable because he knew he was the meanest, toughest son-of-a-bitch in the place. Her belly began twittering with excitement all over again. She stopped it by swinging her backpack onto her shoulder and letting it smack her in the middle of the back.

What she really needed was a good smack upside the head. She had no business messing around with a guy like that.

Roma suddenly slipped out of Jake's clutches, and Hawk's attention was diverted to the commotion behind him. Missy saw her chance to escape and she took it. 'Thanks, Tito,' she said as she turned towards the door.

The night air was bitterly cold when she stepped outside, but she inhaled deeply. The sub-freezing temperatures cleared her head and cooled her over-heated body. Stuffing her hands into her pockets, she headed to her car.

The nip in the air quickly became uncomfortable. She ducked her chin and hurried her footsteps. It had been rush hour when she'd arrived, and she'd had to park all the way across the lot. The area wasn't well lit, and she could feel the tips of her ears going numb. Wishing she had a remote starter, she ran the last thirty feet. She unlocked the door, threw her backpack on the passenger seat, and hopped inside.

'Brrrr,' she said, her body giving a dramatic shudder. Winter could leave any day now. She'd had enough of it.

Still shivering, she pushed her key into the ignition. She couldn't wait to get home and make some hot chocolate. Health nut or not, it was her one vice. On a night like this, she was going to imbibe. She might even add a marshmallow or two.

Well, maybe not. She'd hate to get crazy or anything.

She turned the key, and the engine gave a hesitant *whrrrrr*.

'Huh?' She looked dumbly at the dashboard. The lights hadn't even come on. 'Oh, no. Don't do this to me.'

She tried again. The engine coughed, but finally took off. Her shoulders sagged in relief. 'Oh, thank goodness.'

She looked at the gauges. The lighting seemed dim but, more importantly, she was low on gas. That was a problem she could fix.

She rubbed her hands together and blew on them. She hoped the car warmed up soon, because the steering wheel was ice cold. Gripping it with her fingertips, she pulled out of the lot and drove to the nearest gas station. She shivered as she pumped fuel into the tank. By the time she got back behind the wheel, her teeth were clattering. That hot chocolate was sounding better and better.

Ready to go home, she turned the key in the ignition.

And got nothing.

Her heart sank. 'Come on, baby. I know it's cold. Just start for Mama. You'll warm up soon, I promise.'

Sending up a silent prayer, she tried again.

And all she heard was a click. The car was dead.

With a groan, she leant her forehead against the steering wheel. 'Damn.'

The cold soon gave her a headache, and she slumped back into her seat. What now? She looked back into the convenience store, but the only person she saw was a greasy-haired clerk. She shuddered. She wasn't asking him for help. Chewing on her lip, she glanced around. She wasn't anywhere near a bus route. She sighed. She'd have to call Danny to come get her.

'Double damn,' she cursed. He was at his weekly poker game – the one he couldn't afford, but refused to give up.

She reached for the car door handle and gave it a yank. She only had one other option; she'd have to call Jake. He was her boss, but he was also her friend. He'd help her. Climbing out, she slammed the door behind her and headed for the pay phone.

This was just what she needed.

After making the call, she sat in her car waiting for help. Waiting in the warmth of the convenience store would have been more comfortable, but with the way the greasy clerk was looking at her, she'd rather freeze. After a few minutes, a big pickup truck pulled up to the pump in front of her. The headlights pointed right at her, blinding her. She shielded her eyes, hoping that the driver would turn them off while he got gas.

Only the driver didn't head to the pump. Instead, he came towards her. Squinting, Missy tried to make out the man's features. Was that Jake? Already?

The big body was a dark outline as it walked between their vehicles to come up to her window. Hesitantly, she rolled it down a few inches.

'Is there a problem?'

Her hand stopped dead on the window controls.

It was Hawk.

And his voice was so sexy, she thought she might

just melt into the driver's seat. It was deep and smooth, perfect for late-night radio.

'Missy?'

Her hand dropped limply into her lap. The way he'd said her name was like a caress. 'My car won't start,' she said weakly. 'I called for Jake.'

'He's busy with Blondie, so I came instead. Any idea what the problem is?'

Her mouth went dry. The problem? Um ... that he made her nipples stiffen and her belly clench? That he was a man in every sense of the word and she felt young and inexperienced? He had to be in his thirties, and she'd just turned twenty-two. Their leagues were so far apart, they were playing in separate conferences.

'Missy?'

She rubbed her hands on her thighs. Even the way he said her name made her dream of sex. 'I think it's the battery. I turn the key and nothing happens.'

'Sounds like you need a jump.'

She felt her face flush. His eyes flashed, and she had to wonder if the play on words had been intentional.

'Why don't you pop the hood for me?' he asked smoothly.

That sounded like an excellent idea – something she might have thought of if her brain wasn't mush. She pulled the release handle, and he propped the hood up so it blocked her view. She let out a calming breath. That was better.

'Try to start it again,' he called.

The cold air curled down the back of her neck and under her collar. She shivered. 'Please,' she whispered.

She turned the key but, as expected, nothing happened.

'You're right,' he called. 'Let me get my jumper cables.'

She sat on her hands and watched as her breath

turned into fog in front of her face. She hoped this would work. All she wanted was to drive home, get her hot chocolate, study, and return to her safe little life – with 'safe' being the operative word.

'OK, it's all hooked up,' he called. 'Turn the key and see what happens.'

She expected a solid roar this time, but instead, the engine let out a tired *whrrr, whrrr, whrrr . . .*

'Stop.' He made an adjustment and stepped to the side of the car where she could see him. The shadow of his body cast across her, throwing her into darkness. 'Again.'

'Come on, baby,' Missy said, getting a little desperate.

It soon became apparent that it wasn't going to work. She held the key in the start position, but the weak whimper of her engine told her that it was no use. Hawk shook his head and took two steps to place himself at her driver's side door. He propped his gloved hands on the roof and leant towards her. Her shiver this time wasn't due to the cold. He was daunting as he hovered over her.

'Your battery is dead. You need a new one.'

She chewed her lower lip. 'Damn.'

He slapped the top of her car. 'Put it in neutral, and I'll push you back to a parking spot. Then I'll give you a ride home.'

Wide-eyed, she looked up at him. He'd already stepped away, though, and pulled his cell phone out of his pocket.

'Tito? This is Hawk. I'm going to drive Missy home. Tell Jake I'll be back later with a battery. He can help me install it. If he whines, remind him that he owes me.'

Dumbfounded, Missy sat motionless as Hawk unhooked their vehicles and dropped the hood. The bang jolted her, but when she saw him brace his hands against the grille, she quickly put the transmission in neutral. His strength was really something. He gave a shove, and her car started rolling backwards. Her stomach twittered dangerously, and she looked over her shoulder. She guided the car between two yellow parking lines and hit the brakes before the car bumped up against the kerb.

She was still sitting there, mind racing, when he pulled open her door.

He sighed when she flinched. 'Would you stop looking at me as if I were the big bad wolf?'

She grimaced. Was it that apparent?

And was she really so wrong in thinking that he wanted to eat her up? She certainly wanted a taste of him.

'Missy, let me help you.'

She was being ungrateful. His truck was warm, and he'd let others know where they were going. She was safe with him. Still ... There was safe and then there was *safe*. 'If it's too much of an inconvenience, I can call a cab,' she said, stalling.

His big hand wrapped around her elbow. 'Honey, there are a lot of words I'd use to describe you, but "an inconvenience" is not one of them. Now hurry up and get your sweet little ass in the pickup. It's frickin' cold out here.'

Well, when he put it like that ... She knew better than to delay the inevitable. Leaning over, she snagged her backpack, but he took it from her before she could swing it over her shoulder. He waited as she locked her car and followed when she walked to the passenger side of his truck. She could feel him looking at her 'sweet little ass' again when she climbed up into the cab, but he did nothing more than tuck her backpack under her feet. Closing the door for her, he walked through the glare of the headlights around the truck and got behind the wheel.

The moment he closed his door, Missy wondered at her sanity. For as big as the cab of the pickup was, it seemed warm and intimate. He took up more than his share of the space, and she felt tiny and feminine. *Wild and reckless, was more like it.* Unaccustomed to such bold feelings, she curled her hands into fists on her lap.

He saw the nervous gesture and grunted. He turned and began searching behind the seat. When he came up with a ratty pair of work gloves, she looked at them in confusion. Reaching out, he caught her wrist and began sliding one onto her hand.

'You're going to get frostbite running around like that.'

For as grumpy as his tone was, his touch was gentle. She didn't know what shocked her more – that or his consideration. She'd left her mittens at home that morning and had regretted it all day. The warmth felt heavenly. When he held out the other glove, she offered him her hand willingly. Her heart skipped, though, when his finger ran over her red knuckles. The sensation ran up her arm right into her chest.

'Little miss,' he said with a sigh. He quickly tugged the too-big glove onto her hand and settled back in his seat. He shifted uncomfortably before putting the truck in gear. 'Which way?'

Missy's thoughts were a-jumble. 'Fourteenth Street. I live by Folson's grocery store.'

He nodded and stepped on the gas.

The silence that had separated them for months returned, and the ride home seemed to take an eternity. Hawk didn't say a word as he drove towards the west side of town. For her part, Missy had nothing to say, either. The silence was pressing, but she didn't have the nerve to even try small talk. She wouldn't know where to begin. What could they possibly have in common other than the obvious? She certainly didn't want to talk about *that*. He turned the heater on high, and she snuggled into the seat. Her hands clenched into fists to soak up the warmth from his work gloves.

He had big hands. Huge. It was all she could think about.

Finally, he took a left onto her street. 'Where?'

'The apartment complex on the left.' She pointed. 'Turn into that driveway.'

The engine of his truck rumbled louder as he pulled in between the three-storey buildings. She was thrown off guard, though, when he pulled into a marked visitor's spot and parked.

'You can just drop me off here,' she said.

'I'll see you inside.'

No questions. No debate. He leant towards her and her breath caught. It let out on a ragged exhale when he plucked the backpack up from between her feet. She had no choice but to follow him. She caught up with him at the sidewalk, and he looked at her expectantly. 'Uh, this way,' she said, the butterflies in her stomach taking flight. 'I'm in one-hundred-and-four.'

'First floor?' His lips flattened. 'That's not very safe.'

'I have a roommate.'

Her eyes widened when she realised what she'd said. A roommate? When had Danny been demoted? Confused at her own behaviour, she turned and headed up the sidewalk. She had to take off Hawk's glove to search her pocket for her keys. By the time she came to a stop in front of her apartment door, her hands were trembling.

The key refused to go in the lock. Wordlessly, he took the keys from her. He unlocked her apartment and held the door open for her. Missy stepped inside and flicked on the light. The first thing she saw was the mess that Danny had left in the living room. An opened bag of potato chips sat on the coffee table – right beside rings from his soda can. A pair of dirty socks lay on the floor, and the newspaper was spread out everywhere.

She went still when Hawk shut the door behind

him. She could feel his heat radiating against her back and hear his slow breaths.

Her two worlds were colliding.

Her apartment seemed to shrink to half its size, but she made herself turn to face him. 'Thank you for everything. I don't know what I would have done without your help tonight.'

'You don't need to thank me,' he said softly.

Her adrenaline started pumping when his gaze slid down to her mouth.

'But the battery,' she stammered. 'You don't have to replace that. I'll find someone to . . .'

Her thoughts scattered completely when he put down her backpack and reached for her. He caught her by the nape of the neck. His hand was big and warm as he slowly pulled her towards him. 'I'll take care of it.'

She couldn't look away from his dark eyes. They were deep and more intense than she'd ever seen them.

A muscle ticked in his jaw. 'Come here,' he said gruffly.

She watched him, frozen, as the room filled with heat and electricity. Little charges began snapping all about her. She never knew who moved first. He lowered his head, and she went up on her tiptoes. Her hands settled against his massive chest, and his lips touched hers. The electricity suddenly had a path to travel. It coursed through her as if she were a live circuit. It looped around in her chest, shot through her arms and legs, and gathered deep in her core. She became grounded to the floor, unable to step away.

'God, that's good,' he groaned as he came up for air. Their lips clung as he switched to another angle. 'I knew you'd be sweet.'

Turning, he pressed her back against the wall. Nervous excitement threatened to choke Missy. He was big, he was dangerous . . .

And she barely knew him.

Her traitorous body didn't care.

They were both standing upright, but he covered her from head to toe. And he was heavy. His kisses became more intimate and demanding. With jerky movements, he unzipped her coat and pushed his hands under her shirt.

'Hawk,' she gasped when he caught her breasts.

Desire hit her so sharp and fierce, she could hardly breathe. His thumbs found the front clasp of her bra. It didn't take a second for it to pop open and his palms to cup her again.

Flesh on flesh.

'Christ.' He let out a puff of air that ruffled her hair. 'I knew you'd be more than a handful.'

His hold was firm as he took her soft weight. His fingers swept over her, learning her shape and feel. Then suddenly, possessively, he squeezed.

'Ohhhh,' Missy groaned. Her body arched, and he swivelled his hips so she was riding right against him.

'You've been driving me out of my mind,' he said, giving her nipples a deliberate pinch. 'You knew I was watching you, you tease.'

'I didn't mean to,' she said, inhaling sharply. She caught at his forearms and squirmed against the wall as he fondled her aggressively. Had she led him on? Maybe. It was just ... All he had to do was look at her and things happened.

'You knew I was watching and you liked it.'

She had. She'd liked the naughty way he'd stared, but it had teased her as much as him. She'd wanted him to touch. She wanted his mouth, his hands, his cock. She'd take him any way she could get him.

'I watched you, too,' she challenged.

'I know,' he said with a harsh smile. 'I get a boner every time you turn those big brown eyes on me. Feel it?'

'Ahhh.' Her pussy ached as he rubbed more insistently against her. His moustache brushed against

72

her skin as he nuzzled her neck, and it felt even better than she'd imagined. Enthralled, she raked her fingers down his muscled back.

'Want it?'

'God, yes.'

'Then let's fuck.' His hands left her breasts and began to slide down her belly.

Missy fell back against the wall when he unzipped her jeans. His fingers found the edge of her panties and went right underneath them. With the way their bodies were pressed, it was a tight fit. His gaze met hers, and she felt her face flare. His meaty fingers tangled in the curls between her legs, and the intimacy was shocking. Watching her closely, he pushed his hand deeper and cupped her mound.

She was wet. She knew she was slick as a river.

'You're ready to go,' he said with surprise.

A sheen of sweat broke out on his forehead, and his bald head reflected the overhead light. His facial hair gave him an untamed look that made Missy's insides quake.

She wanted him, dangerous and uncivilised as he was. He made her feel like a woman and, secretly, she'd always craved a lover who would make her lose control. Be a little wild. Do new things. Submit.

Catching him by the back of the neck, she yanked his head down so she could kiss him. She pressed her tongue into his mouth and, feeling brazen, she cupped her hand over his. She pushed down hard, taking his fingers deep, and he muttered a low curse.

'Take off your clothes,' he said harshly. 'Everything. I want to see that tight little body as I screw you senseless.'

'And I want to see yours. Get naked. Now!'

Clothes went flying and shoes clattered across the floor. Missy was down to her underwear by the time Hawk got out of his coat and shirt.

'Oh.' She sighed. Her arms dropped, and her bra fluttered to the floor.

It was her turn to ogle. God, she had a thing for bodybuilders. There was just something about the perfect male body, and he was in his prime. Slabs of muscles covered his chest, and their strength and power drew her. Each and every muscle in his body was thick and defined. And his arms. They were as thick as her legs.

Reaching out, she traced the lines of his six-pack abs.

He jerked and caught her hand. Slowly, his gaze ran over her. 'Turn around,' he said softly.

Her nerves jumped, but she obeyed. Her heart began to pound when a rough hand settled intimately onto her bare bottom.

'A thong,' he said with near reverence. 'God, what an ass.'

He squeezed her tightly, and Missy braced herself against the wall. His big hands began to mould and shape her, and she felt the crotch of her panties go wet.

Oh, God. Could he see that?

His hot breaths brushed against her ear as he bent over her. 'Do you wear this when you're working out?'

His fingers slid under the strip of material that disappeared into the crack of her ass and he tugged on it lightly. So much blood rushed to her face, she thought she might pass out. 'I don't wear underwear when I work out,' she whispered.

'Vixen.' The material snapped back so hard, it stung. 'Take it off.'

Missy was so hot, she could barely stand it. He was waiting, though, and with the way he stood over her, he wasn't patient. She caught the thin strips of fabric at her hips. Slowly, she peeled it down.

'That's it,' he growled. He cupped his hand between her legs, and she lurched up onto her tiptoes. 'I can't wait any longer.'

Suddenly, he reached out and pushed away the table that stood against the wall. It went skidding across the tiled floor with a loud scrape. Missy jerked at the sudden noise, and her heart rate took off into the stratosphere. The table hit the edge of the living room carpeting and teetered. Her forgotten mittens tumbled onto the floor.

'Face the mirror.' With his hand at her waist, he moved her to the empty space where the table had been. He untied the string of his exercise pants and pushed them down along with his briefs. 'I want to watch you watch us together.'

Missy's desire took on an edge when she saw their reflection. She couldn't take her eyes off the way they looked together, naked and wanting. Two physically perfect bodies were about to merge. He towered over her, and her memory flashed back to that picture of him in the bar. Her excitement careened out of control and, suddenly, she couldn't wait either.

'Hurry,' she found herself begging. Leaning over, she braced her hands on either side of the mirror.

'Just let me get it inside you.' He caught her thigh and widened her stance as he inched closer.

She felt him line himself up. Impatient, she pushed back, trying to take him into her. All the same, she was caught off guard when he thrust.

'Aaaahhh!' she cried. He was big. Really big. Her head dropped forwards as he burrowed into her.

'So good,' he grunted, his voice strained.

And it was. He filled her to the limit. He began to move, and she gasped as her inner nerve endings fired. Reaching back, she caught his hard ass. Her fingernails bit into his hips as he set up a driving rhythm.

'Yes,' she cried. 'Just like that.'

He began to pump harder and faster. She watched the way they moved together, and her pleasure mounted. His fingers threaded through her curls and toyed with her clit as his hips bumped against her bottom. The double onslaught made her head spin. She closed her eyes tightly as she felt herself start to spiral upwards.

'God, you were built to run, baby. Sweet ass. Full, firm, young breasts. Look at you.'

He was slamming into her, and she couldn't hold onto his sweaty hips any longer. Reaching forwards, she braced her forearms against the wall, fingers spread wide. Her breasts jounced with every harsh thrust.

'That's it,' he said. He caught her about the waist and lifted her right up onto her tiptoes. 'Hold on, little miss.'

Like a piston, he worked in and out of her well-oiled tract. Missy let out a cry when she flew head-long into her orgasm.

He wasn't through with her yet.

He let her crest and began working her up the grade again. The sound of harsh breaths and slapping bodies filled the room. It could only go on so long. The flashpoint came quickly. His cock delved deep, and her pussy clenched around him. He stiffened, and they both came.

When she finally regained her equilibrium, she found them both leaning against the wall for support. The mirror had fogged over, and her body was coated in sweat.

'Damn,' Hawk said, his voice almost shaky.

'Double damn,' she agreed.

He took a deep breath and let it out slowly by her ear. 'All right?' he asked.

'I think so.' Honestly, she didn't know. She'd never done anything like this before. She'd just screwed a virtual stranger. What had she been thinking? They'd never even spoken before tonight.

'Let's move this to a bedroom.'

His pants suddenly started ringing. Actually, they were playing AC/DC if she listened carefully enough. Whatever the sound, it was jarring. It intruded on their little sexual cocoon, and she glanced at him in the mirror.

'Shit,' he cursed. He reached down and pulled his phone out of his pocket. 'Yeah?' he snapped.

His gaze caught hers in the mirror. 'The battery. Uh, yeah. Right.'

Her jaw dropped. It was Jake. Her boss. She saw her face turn red in the mirror.

'Winded? Me?' Hawk said. His gaze flashed to the crookedly placed table. 'Uh, Missy needed help moving some furniture.'

She laughed. Like that would be enough to take his breath away. She closed her eyes and buried her face into the crook of her arm. Even soft, she could still feel every inch of him inside her. With Jake on the other end of that call, it was embarrassingly intimate.

'Give me twenty minutes,' Hawk said with a sigh. He hung up and swore. 'Fuck, I have to leave.'

If he stayed, fucking was all they were going to do. The implications were only now hitting Missy. She'd just had a one-night stand. With a tattooed tough guy.

It was definitely time that he left.

His arms came around her, and he slowly disconnected their bodies. As deliberately as he moved, she felt herself giving him up millimeter by millimetre. It made the act that much more suggestive.

'Where are your keys?' he asked.

'My keys?' She wasn't giving him her keys. Yesterday, they hadn't even known the sound of each other's voice. One little mistake – OK, one huge blunder – didn't mean she was going to give him the keys to her apartment.

'For your car.'

'Oh, that.' His hands hadn't stopped stroking her body. She blamed that for her lack of coherent thought.

'What's your schedule like tomorrow?' he asked.

What did he want to know that for?

'You need someone to take you to your car,' he said, reading her mind.

She ran a hand through her hair. Darn, she wasn't usually this discombobulated. Then again, she'd never been so well screwed. 'Um. I've got a ten o'clock step class and I need to be at school for a test at one.'

'I'll pick you up at nine thirty,' he said. Dipping his head, he brushed a soft kiss against her temple. 'Just do one thing for me.'

The gentle kiss made her go weak all over again. 'What?' she asked hesitantly.

His hand cupped her breast. 'Don't let your "room-mate" touch you tonight.'

Her mouth went dry. Oh, God. Danny. She'd forgotten all about him, yet evidence of him filled the room.

Hawk pinched her nipple hard and gave her one last hot kiss. 'I don't want him anywhere near you. Not tonight.'

Chapter Five

Two weeks later, Roma walked slowly across the parking lot towards the gym. A thaw had finally hit the city, and the warmer weather gave the air a fresh, invigorating scent. Spring was coming. Just the idea of it had everyone smiling – everyone except her, that was. At the moment, she was a bit miffed.

Slush from the melting ice and snow had mingled with dirt and mud to create that lovely mixture called sludge. That would have been a big enough problem by itself. As it was, it made her particular predicament even worse.

She couldn't lift her feet more than two inches off the ground.

'My poor pretties,' she said, looking mournfully down at her new brown leather boots.

Feeling like an old nag, she waded through the grimy gunk. She couldn't remember ever being so sore. It was as if rigor mortis had set in to her body early. A person usually had to die before they got this stiff.

'Ow-ee, ow-ee, ow-eeee,' she hissed as she stepped up onto the kerb.

Oh Lord, she wasn't going to make it for three months. Two weeks and she was already incapacitated. She reached out to open the door and felt a pull between her shoulder blades. This was not good.

'Hey, Roma,' Tito called from his post at the front desk.

'Hiya, Tito.'

'You all right?'

'Oh, sure. Never better,' she lied through clenched

teeth. If she could shuffle as far as Jake's office, she could sit down and stop moving. It only hurt when she tried to move. Unfortunately, moving seemed to be a necessity of life. The good thing was that this was a rest day for her. She was just here to work on the books. No squats. No free weights. No treadmill. The most strenuous thing she had to do was lift a pencil.

'But you're walking kind of funny,' he persisted.

'Blow it out your ear, Tito.'

'Gotcha.' The kid wasn't stupid.

Through sheer determination and quite a bit of internal swearing, she was able to make it to her destination. She closed the door behind her and her shoulders immediately sagged. 'Pain,' she said. 'Oh, big pain.'

How did people do this? The chair. She focused on it like a finish line. Once she sat down, the world would look rosier. Gathering her nerve, she set her briefcase on the desk and shrugged out of her jacket. Just lifting it to the hook on the wall cost her. 'Ei-ya! That hurts.'

She reached for the desk and used it for support as she shuffled around it. With a heartfelt groan, she plopped down. The ergonomic design of the chair made it press into her lumbar region. She let out a long breath and relaxed. Oh yeah, this was better.

Unfortunately, she knew from experience that if she sat still for too long, things would only get worse. With little enthusiasm, she turned to face the piles of paperwork waiting for her.

Oh yeah, this was better, she thought derisively as she looked up, and up, and up. She'd been working on those piles for the better part of two weeks now, but they didn't seem to be getting any smaller. Not ready to face them yet, she swivelled around in her chair. She deserved a treat before she engaged in battle.

She glanced out the office window to see if the

coast was clear. It was. With an eager grin on her face, she grabbed her briefcase and opened it. Pushing back a flap to a secret compartment, she found her prize. A Snickers bar! She tore open the wrapper like a child on Christmas morning. At the first taste of the chocolate delight, her aches and pains were forgotten.

You are so bad.

Stuff it, sister. It tastes too good.

Her devilish side was definitely going to win this argument. She hadn't had anything to eat since lunch, and she'd learnt that when her brain and her stomach vied for her attention, the stomach always won. She'd never get anywhere with the books if she didn't eat something. It was just a coincidence that the only food she had on her was chocolate.

Pure coincidence.

Unfortunately, they didn't make these candy bars big enough. Within five bites, it was gone. She licked her fingers, savouring every bit she could. Somebody walked by the window and she ducked. Hiding the evidence, she crumpled the wrapper and stuffed it back into the compartment.

With a sigh, she sat up straight. It was time to face the menace. She set her briefcase on the floor and started to clear herself a space of desktop, but stopped short when she came across a slip of paper. The familiar pink ink and loopy handwriting made her scowl.

'You've got to be kidding me. Another one?'

She plucked up the note by the corner and held it as if it were poisonous – which actually wasn't that big of a leap. The notes this 'Liz' person liked to leave for Jake were so sickly sweet, they left her ill. Thank you notes, scheduling notes, personal notes … you name it, Liz left them on his desk like it was her personal mail service. Unfortunately, now that it was her desk, too, Roma had come across more than her fair share of the bothersome messages.

'What is it today, Liz hon?' she said with a sigh. 'Flipping out over a hangnail? Need to schedule extra ab work? Complimenting Jake on his new haircut?'

The woman did everything within her power to hit on the poor guy. It was so obvious, Roma couldn't help but be embarrassed on behalf of the rest of the female race. She started to crumple the paper into a ball, but stopped when she realised that this note was different.

Very different.

Can't wait for tonight! Liz.

Roma stared at the five simple words.

Uh, oh.

Pricks of uneasiness settled between her shoulder blades. Had she missed something?

After that first interrupting phone call, she'd done a bit of rudimentary detective work and concluded that Liz was just another one of Jake's clients. A few strategic questions to Tito had left her with the impression that her sexy trainer was single and available. Of course, his blatant come-ons had been another not-so-subtle clue.

But could she have been wrong?

She transferred the note to her other hand as if it had suddenly become a hot potato. Over the past two weeks, she and Jake had been flirting to the point that it might as well have been foreplay. With as much attention as he'd been paying to her, she'd assumed she didn't have any competition. This, though . . . this 'can't wait for tonight' thing had her flustered.

The door suddenly sprang open, and she jerked. Feeling guilty, she let the note drop and grabbed for her pencil.

As expected, it was Jake. 'Busy?' he asked.

'Yes,' she replied, keeping her nose buried in the paperwork. She knew better than to look at him right now. If she looked up, she'd get distracted. And now was definitely not the time for a distraction.

She needed to figure out what this new note from Liz meant. Tonight. What was happening tonight?

Why don't you just ask him? her reasonable side said.

And admit you've been reading his personal correspondence? No way.

'Are you sure you're busy?' he pressed.

'Yes,' Roma said, rubbing her head. It was the only thing that hadn't hurt when she'd woken up this morning. Unfortunately, it was now aching just as much as the rest of her.

'Absolutely?'

Realising she wasn't going to win this battle of words, she put down her pencil and looked up at him. That was mistake number one. He was wearing a tank top. Not only did she get a good view of his muscular arms, she got a great look at his shoulders and that sumptuous chest.

'Did you hear me?' he said.

She blinked and quietly chastised herself. What had she just told herself?

'Hawk is at it again,' he said conspiratorially.

The unexpected news threw her off guard. 'Really?'

'Come look.'

Roma wavered. There was more than one mystery going on at this gym, and she'd been dying for an answer to the Hawk question for days. But the note ... she couldn't help it – the Jake and Liz thing would have to wait.

She hopped out of her chair to go spy on the bodybuilder, but that turned out to be mistake number two. The muscles in her thighs and buttocks clenched, nearly rendering her helpless. Fortunately, Jake was looking over his shoulder and didn't see her difficulties. Skipping across the room on tiptoe power alone, she joined him. 'I can't see,' she protested when he didn't get out of the way.

He opened the door a few inches further and

hooked an arm around her waist. He pulled her in front of him so she had a better view, and her breath caught.

This was not the touch of an unavailable man.

His hand was spread wide across her stomach, and he'd pulled her close against him. A hot shiver went through her. He'd touched her a lot recently – usually correcting her form on free weights – but she'd yet to get used to it. She tended to get all tingly when their bodies came into contact and, at the moment, her back was flush against his chest. It was a regular tingle-rama.

'There,' he said, pointing. 'Look at him.'

Hawk was lifting weights just outside the glass window of the aerobics room. He could see in and Missy could see out. And boy, was the guy working it to the hilt. He was doing military presses straight over his head with impossibly heavy free weights. His muscles would bunch and strain, seemingly ready to pop. After each set of repetitions, though, he'd stop and go through a rigorous stretch.

Roma gawked. He was something to look at, but with the way he was preening, he should have been hanging out with the flirty women on the cross trainers. 'Could he be any more obvious?'

'Missy's not any better,' Jake said close to her ear.

Roma fought to ignore the goosebumps that rose on her neck. 'What are you talking about? She's not even looking at him.'

'That's my point,' he said, rubbing his palm in a slow circle across her belly. 'Every other woman in the gym is. I think she's protesting too much.'

Over the weeks, it had become apparent that Hawk had a vicious crush on Missy. Roma had been the first to notice it, simply because the beast growled at her whenever she blocked his view of the beautiful brunette. When she'd first mentioned it to

Jake, he'd acted like she was crazy. Then he'd remembered the night that Missy's car had died.

Hawk had been out the door to help her before Tito had even relayed Jake the message that she was having car problems. When he'd finally returned from taking her home, he'd been so out of sorts he'd nearly hooked the new battery up wrong.

The guy's mind had definitely been elsewhere.

Roma could relate. She could barely think with Jake's circling caress sending vibrations down to another, more receptive, part of her anatomy.

'Do you really think there's something going on?' she asked, desperately trying to keep focus.

'Hell yeah. There's so much electricity jumping between those two, I'm afraid to see my utility bill this month.'

He cupped his hand over her hip bone, and she nearly groaned aloud. Talk about electricity. They were working up a surge right here.

'Has he said anything?' she struggled to ask.

Jake let out a snort. 'If you haven't noticed, Hawk's not really a talker. What about Missy? Does he have a shot?'

Roma looked at the 'maybe' or 'maybe not' couple. They were just so different. Missy was young and fresh, whereas Hawk was rough and tumble. The only thing they had in common was the gym – but two more perfect specimens you'd never find. When it came to the physical, hormones had to be flying. The possibility made her uneasy. 'Do you think we should warn her?'

'Warn her?' Jake's hand stopped moving, and he cast a curious glance down at her.

'Well, he's kind of scary,' she said cautiously. She knew the two men were friends, but she didn't know how much Jake really knew about the guy. 'You don't think he'd do anything, do you?'

'Do anything?' Jake's forehead rumpled. 'Roma, if

she gives him the go sign, he'll be charging out of the starting blocks, but I guarantee he's not going to hurt her. Hell, he washed and detailed her car before he gave it back to her.'

She turned. 'He washed it? It was like twenty degrees that night.'

'Tell me about it. I was out there freezing my nuts off trying to make sure he didn't blow out the electrical system. It made no sense. The guy's a contractor. He's into that detailed stuff.'

The nuts comment threw her. 'Contractor?' she said absently.

'He builds houses.'

'You mean like with a tool belt? Oh, boy.' She glanced back to the aerobics room. There was just something about a low-slung tool belt that set a gal's heart to racing. 'Missy's in big trouble.'

Jake nudged her. 'What's your problem with him?'

Roma didn't really know. The guy just made her shake in her shoes. Her eyes narrowed as she analysed him from across the room. 'Maybe it's that bald head.'

'Are you serious? You're really afraid of him?'

'Well, he *growls* at me.'

Jake chuckled. When she glared at him, he started laughing so hard people turned to stare. Awkwardly, she extricated herself from his embrace and shooed the exercisers back to work. When he caught his breath, he caught her again and gave her a quick squeeze. 'He's just teasing you.'

She tilted her head back to look at him. 'You call that teasing?'

It was difficult to keep her mind on topic. With the way he was hugging her, the tingling sensation in her body had become a definite zing.

'Goldie, do you know how many times he's saved you?'

'Excuse me?' She couldn't fathom how that tattooed creature could have possibly saved her from anything.

'How many times has he caught you when you've tripped?'

'Well, if he didn't leave his barbells lying around, I wouldn't have that problem.'

'What about when he plucked that extra weight off the stack on the hamstring machine? It was ready to fall on your head.'

'He's the one who put it there in the first place.'

Jake reached down and tweaked her nose. 'He rescued you when you had your bench set up wrong for step class on Monday.'

Impatiently, she swatted his hand away. 'Case in point. He growled at me, physically picked me up, and moved me away. He was just trying to impress Missy. He didn't care that my risers were crooked. He wasn't even there to take the class, for heaven's sake. He was just peeking through the windows like a peeping Tom. Which, in fact, is exactly what he's doing now.'

'Whoa!' Jake quickly pulled back. 'Hurry, close the door.'

With his arms around her waist, there wasn't much Roma could do but move with him. She hiked herself up on her tiptoes and hopped as quickly as she could. 'What's wrong?' she asked through gritted teeth.

'Talk about peeping Toms – I think he caught us spying.' He moved past her to close the blinds. 'Were we too obvious?'

'Oh, please. The man doesn't know the meaning of the word.'

But she did.

When Jake suddenly turned around, she found her nose practically squashed against his chest. Obvious – that would be leaning forwards to lick his rippling pecs. The devilish inclination made her flinch, but even that small tightening of her muscles hurt. She breathed through the pain and became entranced by his clean masculine scent. Was that a hint of musk she detected in his aftershave?

Ooh, musk.

Darn him.

That was why he'd taken so long to pester her after she'd arrived: he'd been showering. Great. That was just the picture she needed in her head when she was supposed to be sorting out his books. Jake with water sluicing down his body. Jake with his hands soaping his chest, his abs, his . . .

She jolted. He'd showered.

He'd showered because he had plans with Liz tonight.

The realisation hurt a little more than Roma could have imagined. Trying to act as casual and as mobile as possible, she backed away. She shuffled around the desk and headed for a tall stack of papers. 'I really should get back to work.'

She reached up too quickly, though, and discomfort had her inhaling sharply.

'Need some help with that?'

She hadn't realised he'd followed so close behind her. She jumped at the sensation of his hot breath against the back of her neck and, voilà, mistake number three.

Her flailing arm hit the stack of paper. It quivered like Jell-O. For a split second, she thought it would regain its tremulous balance, but luck wasn't on her side. In slow motion, the tower tilted.

Forgetting her aches and pains, she lunged for it. She wrapped both arms around the pile, but her momentum got the better of her. She felt herself and her precious cargo falling. Jake's arms wrapped around her, but he, too, was caught off guard. Together, they all fell into the chair.

'Don't move!' she yelped.

He paused for a brief second. 'I wouldn't if you paid me.'

Roma suddenly realised their position. She'd been concerned with the papers. Her arms were wrapped about them high and low, trying to contain them. Even her chin had been put to use. She had it ground into the top of the stack to keep it from disintegrating. Unfortunately, that was the least of her problems.

She was sitting in Jake's lap!

Smack dab, plop in the middle. Her back was against his chest, her thighs were draped over his, and her bottom was settled on a bulge that was growing harder the longer she sat there.

She shifted her weight, wondering if it was possible to stand up and still keep control of the paperwork. Her thighs screamed in protest. Nope, not possible.

'Don't do that,' he growled as she squirmed against him. 'Just ... just hold very still.'

'This is the one pile of paper I've got organised,' she whined. Out of all the thoughts and impressions racing through her head, that was the easiest one to deal with. 'This wouldn't happen if you had more than one filing cabinet in this place.'

'OK, OK, relax. We'll rescue it.'

She could feel the rumble of his chest against her back as he spoke. With his strong thighs underneath her and his arms wrapped around her, she felt surrounded. Temptation curled like a snake within her belly. 'Well, hurry it up!'

'Let me get this top part of the stack before your neck snaps,' he said, laughing.

The vibration ran down Roma's spine, and her thighs clenched tightly. Not good. This was not a good time to be feeling frisky.

He carefully removed about eight inches worth of paper from the top of the stack. She quickly got a better hold with her hands and rolled her neck to relieve the kinks. She went stock-still when his thumbs settled onto her shoulders. He began rubbing his thumbs in deep circles at the base of her neck, and she nearly whimpered in delight.

'Better?' he asked on a low note.

'Mmm hmm. Yup. That's pretty satisfactory.' Her resistance was hanging on by a thread. Liz or not, five more seconds of that and the stack was hitting the floor. 'Can we move on to the rest of this mess?'

'Take it easy,' he said with a chuckle. 'We've got it under control now.'

Control? Was he nuts? She could feel her control slipping away from her fingertips as he spoke. He reached around her to remove more of the pile, and those strong arms brushed against the sides of her breasts. Control be damned!

'I'll just set these on the desk here,' he said.

He reached back and got rid of the papers, but she still wasn't able to move. Her hands clenched the remainder of her precious pile, but her head had found a convenient resting place on his shoulder.

Now, how had she known that that little curve would feel so comfy?

His hands settled on the balls of her shoulders and started massaging the tight muscles. And tight they were. She felt like a coiled spring. She shifted in discomfort, and he hesitated. Cocking his head, he looked down over her shoulder at her.

'Are you sore, Roma?'

Busted.

There was no hiding it. He moved his hands down to the backs of her arms and found muscles as hard as rock – but not in a good way. He dug his thumbs into the tightness, and she groaned aloud.

'Ah, Goldie. Why didn't you say something?'

What was she supposed to have said? Jake, I'm so sore even my hair hurts? It was embarrassing to be so out of shape. 'It's not that bad.'

'Liar.' He quickly relieved her of the rest of the papers, but instead of letting her go, he kept her on his lap. 'Lean forwards so I can get your back.'

Oh, well now. That sounded like an interesting position. 'Um ... I don't know if that's such a good idea.'

'Lean forwards.'

Jake didn't like that she was in pain, but getting his hands on her was a definite plus. He'd been waiting for an opportunity like this, and it had literally been dropped in his lap. No pun intended. He'd been battling his ethics for weeks now, but what was he supposed to do when things like this insisted on happening to them? Even an ethical guy had his limits.

Besides, he'd already rationalised away any reasons why they couldn't get involved. Technically, she wasn't an employee or a client. He wasn't paying her and she wasn't paying him – not that he wanted to get into the nasty aspects of money. It just made him a little more comfortable about the way he felt about her and what he intended to do about it. They were colleagues. Friends even. Friends could easily turn into much more.

Especially when touching her felt so good.

He laid his hands on her and began stroking. The muscles in her back were in the same condition as those in her arms – tense and screaming for attention. He started at her shoulders and moved down. Everywhere he touched, he found knots. She had to be miserable.

'Goldie,' he said with a sigh.

He concentrated on giving her some relief. She groaned when he hit a particularly sensitive spot, and he made the mistake of looking up. She was bent nearly double with her elbows on her knees, and her backside was pressed firmly against his crotch. The position was so overtly erotic, his already alert cock jumped.

'Oh!'

She'd felt that. How could she not with the way she was plastered against him? Her muscles triggered as if to move, but he dug his fingers more firmly into her tense lower back.

'Oooh, that's . . . that's . . .'

His hands drifted lower to work on her gluteus muscles, and her head snapped up.

'That's good,' she said, lurching upright. 'Thanks. I'm feeling much better now.'

'Get back down here,' he said. She started to hop off his lap, but he simply wrapped his arms around her waist and hugged her close. Her breathing went ragged at the close contact and he smiled.

He liked knowing that he got to her as much as she got to him.

'Have you been skipping your stretches?' he asked, his lips close to her ear.

'Maybe,' she admitted.

Her hands settled on his forearms. She shifted on his lap, and they both groaned.

'Why?' he asked. Unable to avoid the temptation, he traced the delicate shell of her ear with his nose.

She tilted her head away as if it tickled and shuddered when he began nuzzling her neck. 'It's the one thing I do well. I figured I didn't need the practice.'

He moved his hands to her thighs. One squeeze had her arching against him. 'Practice has nothing to do with it,' he murmured. 'Those stretches get the lactic acid out of your muscles. They help keep you from getting sore.'

'But it's tax time,' she protested. 'I'm swamped. I'm trying to keep up with my business, your messy books and my workouts. I don't have time to stretch.'

'Make time.' He found an especially tight spot that had her inhaling sharply. Carefully, he applied pressure.

'Oh, please, Jake. Stop!'

His touch eased, but he didn't remove it. If she didn't get these muscles loosened up, she'd be out of action for days. That wouldn't work well with her short reunion time schedule. He pressed his thumbs into her inner thighs, and she came right out of his lap. Her neck arched against his shoulder, and her hips swivelled upwards. He stroked steadily until the muscle gave up the fight and relaxed.

'Holy cow,' she said, sinking back down. 'You really know how to make a girl feel special.'

'Whiner. You brought this on yourself.'

'You're the one who made me do all those squats.'

Because she'd looked so fine doing them! He ran his hands from her knees to her hips, loving the feel of her. 'Don't you like what they've done for your legs and your butt?'

She paused. 'Well, yes.'

'Me, too. Damn, I love this dress.'

She was wearing a long-sleeved sweater dress with a leather belt cinched tight around her waist. The soft material clung to her shape like charged plastic wrap. It was cream coloured and softer than anything he'd ever felt – other than her skin. He couldn't stop touching it. She felt warm, cuddly, and sexy as all get out. Those 1940s sweater girls had nothing on her.

His Roma was stacked.

'You're shaping up like dynamite,' he whispered into her ear.

She ran her tongue across her lips. 'But I feel like I'm eighty years old.'

'You just need a full body massage to put you right.' Experimentally, he stroked up from her knees and under her dress. He'd been right; her skin was unbelievable. 'I'd be happy to oblige.'

She began squirming like a whirligig. 'That's probably not a good idea.'

His hands ventured higher, hitching the skirt up on her thighs. 'It's a fantastic idea.'

Her hands clamped down on top of his. 'But you're easily distracted.'

'So are you.' He had her skirt up to nearly her hips, and his curiosity couldn't be contained. 'What colour are they today?'

Her head snapped towards his. 'What?'

'Your panties.'

'*Jake!*'

She lurched when he peeled the material back to take a peek, but the movement only helped him lift her skirt right up to her waist. His cock twitched almost painfully as he looked down at her. 'Yellow,' he choked out.

Like sunshine. Like her.

She went very still in his lap. Reaching out, he fingered the soft cotton material. Everything about her was soft. Tactile. Touchable. With a groan, he slid his hand between her legs and cupped her. Her hips rolled, and her heat radiated into his hand.

'Oh. Oh, my!' she gasped.

'Goldie,' he said, his voice like gravel. 'You feel amazing.'

He cupped her tighter, and she undulated against him. 'Jake, I –'

The phone rang, and they both jumped.

'Ignore it.' He began exploring with his fingers, running them up and down the thin cotton panel. Her body was hot and pliable. He wasn't going to let anything get in the way of this. 'Roma, let me in.'

'I . . . I . . . Oh, damn.' Her thighs quivered, but then slowly splayed open wide. She leant more heavily against him, and neither heard the persistent phone as it rang and rang and rang.

Jake couldn't remember ever being so turned on in his life – and she was still fully dressed. He'd probably have a coronary if he ever got her naked.

That was a risk he was willing to take.

Watching closely, he spread his hand wide on her lower abdomen. Her belly trembled and her lungs began working hard. Holding her as if she were the most precious thing in the world, he sent his hand back down. They both watched as his fingertips disappeared under the pale-yellow cotton.

Roma's hand suddenly wrapped around his wrist. 'I think my heart rate's above the aerobic zone.'

'Been there. Done that.' His heart was pounding like a freight train.

Her curls were soft and springy. He threaded his fingers through them and searched deeper.

She arched like a bow. 'Uh ... light-headed now.'

'You've had me dizzy for weeks.'

'I ... Oh, damn.'

She was hot and she was slick. He rubbed her, and she nearly purred like a cat. She was so sensual. He wrapped his other arm around her and took advantage of the low-scooped neckline of that killer dress. He caught her breast, and her nipple poked right through her matching yellow bra into his palm.

'That's my girl,' he said as sweat broke out on his brow.

He stroked her more intimately, and her hips rolled. It made her bottom grind hard against his cock, and he gritted his teeth.

Patience. Just a few more minutes. He had to make sure she was ready. Carefully, he pushed a finger into her.

'Ooooh,' she crooned.

'Roma. Christ.'

She was wet and tight as a fist. He pressed his finger as deep as it would go and then began thrusting. He might as well have set off a firecracker. Her body started shaking and she began panting for air. He worked in a second finger, and she let out a yelp.

'Jake! I ... *Oh, damn!*'

Her muscles began to flutter about his fingers and,

next thing he knew, she was coming. Desire racked him from the inside out, but he couldn't help but smile.

Oh, yeah. Getting involved with Roma Hanson was going to be fun.

When she came, she did it like she did everything else. Full bore, one hundred per cent. He pumped her straining body until it went limp. When she finally relaxed against him, she laid her head trustingly on his shoulder.

'Damn,' she said in wonder.

'Seems to be the word of the day.' He strummed his thumb across her clit, and she gasped. 'Want to go for it again? With me?'

A devilish smile spread across her face. 'A girl's got to do what a girl's got to do.'

The fact that she could make him laugh when his cock was ready to poke through three layers of material didn't surprise him.

She blinked and looked at him cautiously. 'Did I say that out loud?'

'You can't take it back now.' His need took on an urgency, and he slid her forward on his lap. His hands shook as he attacked the drawstring of his pants. 'Just give me a second.'

She stretched luxuriously. 'Take your time. I'm good.'

He jerked down his clothes. 'I'm not.'

She glanced over her shoulder to his lap, and her eyes rounded. 'Mmm, that's a big problem you've got there.'

He caught her by the waist and began working her panties down her legs. 'So get back here and help me with it.'

An unexpected knock on the door made them both jerk.

'Fuck,' Jake said, breathing hard. 'Who is it?'

'It's Tito,' came a tentative voice.

Roma threw a frantic look at the door, saw it

wasn't locked, and shot off his lap like a rocket. Jake reached for her, but she was already yanking up her panties and shoving down her dress. The pulse at his temple began to throb painfully.

That coronary might be closer than he thought.

'This better be good, kid,' he snapped.

There came the sound of shuffling feet. 'Uh, Liz is on the phone. She's at the swimsuit shop and she's wondering where you are. She said you were supposed to help her pick one out.'

Liz. Shit. He'd forgotten about that. He dropped his head back against the chair and fought for air. Talk about terrible timing.

'She sounded kind of pissed.'

Roma let out a choked sound. Jake's head jerked up, but before he could see the look on her face, she spun away. With her arms wrapped about her waist, she began tapping the toe of her sexy high-heeled boot against the floor.

Uh-oh.

'She's a client,' he said quickly.

'You're picking out a *swimsuit* for a *client*?' The toe tapped more furiously.

He grimaced. *Brilliant move there, Logan.* He began pulling on his clothes. 'Roma, let me explain.'

'Jake?' Tito called cautiously. 'What should I tell Liz?'

'Tell her he'll be there as soon as he can,' Roma called, her voice strong and feisty.

'Uh, OK. Sorry to interrupt.'

'No big deal.'

Jake came right out of his chair. Moving fast, he caught Roma by the waist and spun her around. 'Don't be mad, Goldie. Let me explain.'

Eyes flaring, she batted his hands away. 'What's to explain? You're a two-timer!'

'It's not like that. You don't understand.'

'You're supposed to be with her, but yet you're here with me.' She gestured wildly at the chair. 'That was two-timing – what with all the falling, the catching, and the *vo-di-o-do!*'

'Listen.' He caught her firmly by the shoulders. 'Liz is a high-end client going to the Midwest Fitness Show. She needs help picking out a competition suit. It's important that she choose the right one for judging purposes. That's it.'

Roma shook her head as if she didn't want to hear any excuses, but the words still hung in the air. She couldn't help but listen. First her brow furrowed. Her eyes widened next, and then her mouth dropped open in surprise. 'The Fitness Show?' she said dumbly. 'She's ... Liz is the client who's competing there?'

He ran his hands down her arms. 'If she does well, it will be good for business here at the gym.'

'Business?'

It was a question. Cautiously, he ducked down to look her in the eye. 'You've got to know I wouldn't stop "vo-di-o-doing" with you unless I absolutely had to.'

She flushed a pretty shade of pink, and he couldn't resist. Leaning forwards, he gave her a long, slow kiss. She tasted sweet. Like chocolate. He was breathing hard when he came up for air. 'Forget it. I'll call Liz and reschedule.'

'No, don't do that.'

'Are you sure?'

She shrugged as if she wasn't entirely certain. 'Keep her happy. This place could use more business.'

And he could use about a week straight of Roma Hanson in his bed.

'Forget the books tonight,' he said softly. 'Go home and soak in a hot tub filled with Epson salts. I'll make it up to you by scheduling an appointment with Paul as soon as I can.'

She cocked her head. 'The masseur with the magic hands?'

She still wasn't happy about the Liz situation.

'Don't go getting any bright ideas,' he growled.

She smiled at the warning.

Relieved, he kissed her again and ran his hand down to her backside. 'Drink lots of water and stretch tonight. I want you warm and limber the next time I see you.'

Her eyes danced. 'Limber for what?'

'Lunges or vo-di-o-do,' he said with a wicked grin. He gave her bottom a quick pat and moved towards the door while he still could. 'We'll decide tomorrow.'

Chapter Six

Chapter Six

Roma was in a confused sexual daze as she walked out of the office and down the hallway to the locker room. A jumble of thoughts crowded her head, each trying to bump the other out of the way. She didn't know what stunned her most – the things she and Jake had done, that Liz was Super Client, or that he'd left her in the middle of sex to go check out another woman in a swimsuit.

Make that a bikini, no doubt!

It was just too much to process. Her brain couldn't take it all in; her body was still humming too loudly. It blocked out everything. Music pumped from the aerobics room, but she didn't hear it. A group of big boy weightlifters posed in front of the mirrors in the free weights room, but she didn't see them. She didn't even feel the soreness in her muscles any more.

Unfortunately, she did feel her big toe slamming into the door of the janitor's closet when it opened suddenly in front of her.

'Ow!' she yelped. Pain snapped her out of her reverie and, instinctively, she reached for her throbbing foot. Her muscles chose that moment to flare back to life, and she let out another yip.

The sound was echoed from inside the closet, and Missy's head popped out from behind the door. When she saw whom she'd hit, her eyes widened and her face turned beet red.

'Roma!' She scooted out into the hallway and shut the door with a bang. Her ponytail was mussed, and her clothes were askew. Self-consciously, she adjusted her Lycra shorts. 'I'm sorry. I didn't see you there.'

'Missy!' Roma felt her face flush nearly as red. She wasn't ready to face anyone just now. What if Tito had seen what had happened inside that office? What if there really was something going on between Jake and Liz? What if the gossip was already spreading? Cripes, she hated gossip. Of course, the rumours that had been spread about her in high school hadn't been true. This would!

She hopped along on one foot, desperate to just keep moving.

'Are you OK?' Missy asked. She hovered around, uncertain what to do.

'Fine,' Roma said tightly. 'Just fine.'

'Are you sure?'

'Mm-hm.' Gingerly, she put her weight on her foot. 'Don't worry about me. Just go back to whatever you were doing.'

Something clattered inside the closet, and Missy flinched.

'Broom,' she explained hurriedly. Ill at ease, she crossed her arms over her chest and leant back against the closet door. A muffled curse came from inside, and she kicked it with her heel. 'I was just putting away a broom.'

Big broom.

'OK,' Roma said, eyeing the closet suspiciously. 'I'll see you later.'

'Yeah. See ya.'

They both turned. When they reached to push open the door to the women's locker room at the same time, they exchanged an embarrassed glance.

'I need a shower,' Missy said, her blush deepening.

Roma knew her colour wasn't any better. Her face felt as if it were on fire. 'Me, too.'

Without another word, they burst into the room and headed to their lockers. Neither dared to look at the other. Roma grabbed a towel and made a beeline to the shower stall on the end. In her current state, she'd prefer to get undressed behind the security of a shower curtain, thank you very much.

Missy had the same idea.

Piece by piece, clothing appeared from behind the curtains and was hung on hooks on the wall. Roma tried to hurry through all the sudsing and rinsing, but Missy was nearly as quick. Her water turned off just seconds later. They glanced at each other abashedly when their shower curtains whipped back as one.

Silently, they got dressed. The tension mounted as, side by side, they brushed their hair. Finally, Missy looked at Roma in the mirror.

'I'm having sex with Hawk,' she blurted.

Roma couldn't take it any longer either. 'Jake just got to third base.'

They looked at each other, mouths agape.

Missy was the first to recover. 'Want to grab a cup of hot chocolate somewhere?'

'Hot chocolate?' Roma snorted. 'This calls for whiskey.'

Missy nodded. 'Let's get out of here.'

They ended up compromising. Missy knew a coffee shop that was only a few blocks away. Roma had to roll her eyes, though, when her friend ordered a hot chocolate without whipped topping. Such a goody-goody!

She got hers with a shot of peppermint schnapps.

'So Hawk?' she asked, deflecting the attention from herself as they found a table in the corner. 'Really?'

Missy draped her coat over the back of her chair and sat down. She glanced around as if she didn't want anyone listening and then leant forwards. 'We can't keep our hands off one another,' she confided.

Roma blinked in disbelief. 'We're talking about the same Hawk, right? Big guy. Shaved head. Tattoos.'

'No, the one with the pocket protector. Of course, the one with the tattoos!'

'Are you serious?' Roma cocked her head. Had Jake been right? Was Missy as much to blame for all that staring and posing? 'You're really into all that?'

Missy bit her lip, but couldn't stop a secret smile. 'I just wrestled him into the janitor's closet, didn't I?'

Roma let out a whoop. She bumbled her cup and nearly lost drops of her precious schnapps. 'I knew that wasn't a broom,' she declared.

'He's not very quiet.'

Ack! Too much information!

Roma busied herself with licking her spilled cocoa off her fingers. Flustered, she plucked a napkin out of the dispenser on the table. Missy and Hawk had been going at it in the closet while she and Jake had been fooling around in his office? It was perfectly scandalous.

'When did this happen?' she asked. 'I thought you had a boyfriend.'

'I did. I do,' Missy said quickly. The grin slipped off her face, and she wrapped both hands around her mug. For a long moment, she stared down into its depths. 'It's complicated.'

'I'll say. Are you still living with him? What's his name again? Danny?'

She gave a small nod.

'Missy!' People turned to look and Roma lowered her voice. 'That's a dangerous game to play.'

'I said that I live with him. I haven't been sleeping with him,' Missy ran a hand through her hair. 'We haven't had sex in a while. He hasn't been interested until last night. I told him I had a headache and moved to the couch.'

Roma took a hit of her peppermint cocoa. She

should have made it a double. 'So this … this *thing* with Hawk. It's serious?'

'It's a serious attraction.' Missy shifted uncomfortably in her chair. 'All we have to do is be in the same room, and the air snaps. It's almost chemical – although the physical has a lot to do with it, too. I mean, come on. Have you seen him without his shirt?'

'Yes.' And there had been a bit of drooling involved.

'You should see him without his pants.'

'Missy!'

This time half the coffee shop turned.

'Well, he's hung,' the brunette hissed. 'He's hung like the state of Florida.'

Roma coughed as her drink went down the wrong pipe. She patted her napkin over her lips and wheezed until she caught her breath. Well, as they said – in for a penny, in for a pound. 'That's fine and dandy, but is he any good with it?'

Missy let one eyebrow lift. 'You'd have to do him to believe it.'

Oh, God. Her and Hawk? Roma reached out and caught the arm of the waiter who was walking by. 'I'm going to need another shot of schnapps in this. Pronto.'

The waiter walked away, and Missy let out a tortured sigh. Shakily, she ran both hands over her heated face. 'I don't know what's gotten into me. I can't seem to help myself. That body. It just makes my fingers itch. And that bad-boy appeal. All he has to do is look at me and I'm tearing off my clothes and bending over for him.'

They really were going to have to talk about this information overload thing.

'But what do you guys have in common?' Roma asked, trying to be the voice of reason. 'What do you talk about?'

'We never seem to get around to the talking part.'

Roma leant back in her chair as the waiter doctored her drink. Well, that was something. She mulled it all over in her mind. Hawk certainly did have that bad-boy thing going for him – it just sent her running to a corner somewhere. Missy, on the other hand, must have a thing for danger.

Of course, if he was as good with his big weenie as she said he was . . .

'You think I'm out of control.'

'I think you're out of your mind.' Roma felt bad when her younger friend looked stricken. She scooted her chair closer and dropped her voice to nearly a whisper. 'It's just lust. Pure, unbridled lust.'

'Is that bad?'

Yes! Roma's puritan side declared.

'Hell, no,' she found herself saying. That devilish side was winning more and more often. 'Just be careful. Enjoy it while it lasts, but don't be too upset when it peters out.'

Missy sighed and swirled her hot chocolate. 'That's just it. I think it's getting stronger.'

'His peter?' Roma exclaimed.

'The attraction.'

'Oh, yeah. I knew that's what you meant.' Casually, she sat back and crossed her legs. Could she help it if all this talk about peters and weenies was making her think of Jake? 'Well, you can't keep going on like this. Sooner or later you'll have to do something about Danny.'

'I know,' Missy said quietly. She thought about it for a while, but then her gaze slid slowly upwards. She nailed Roma with a look. 'So third base, huh?'

Uh-oh. Roma picked up her mug and slammed the hot chocolate back. She signalled to the waiter. 'Another round over here.'

'You're not going to avoid me that easily,' Missy said, nudging her with her foot. 'I just spilt about Hawk.'

'And you've got a thing or two to learn about the sharing of private information.'

'Tell me what happened between you and Jake, and we'll be even.'

'Oh, you're a tricky one,' Roma said. She eyed Missy carefully. It was tempting to play along. She really did need to talk to somebody, especially about this whole Liz thing. Jake's special 'client' had really screwed things up for her tonight.

She tapped her fingers on the table. She could use a girlfriend's advice on this. 'OK. It started out innocent enough. You see, there was this stack of papers. It fell over and we both tried to catch it. To make a long story short, I ended up sitting on Jake's lap.'

'Mm. Convenient.'

'Sitting led to touching, which naturally led to fondling. Anyway, we got to third base before we were interrupted. I mean, I think it was third base.' Roma's forehead crumpled in confusion. 'How does that work? He made it to third, but I kind of, well, scored.'

'Hey, hey!'

'But how do you count that? Because he never actually slid into home, if you get what I mean.'

'All that matters is that nobody struck out. Shh, here comes our waiter.'

The man appeared from out of nowhere. With the way he slinked around the place, he was lucky he didn't get an earful. Carefully, he lowered his tray and set their drinks in front of them. 'One plain hot chocolate and one with a double shot of peppermint schnapps.'

Roma rolled her eyes. 'Oh, for heaven's sake. Get that girl some whipped cream.'

'Of course, ma'am.'

'No. Wait,' Missy said, holding up her hand to stop him.

Roma nearly growled. She wasn't going to overload on sugar and gossip by herself.

'Make it marshmallows instead.'

'Atta girl!' Roma raised her mug in salute. 'Carb heaven, here we come.'

Laughing, they enjoyed their warmed cups of cocoa. Roma felt herself relaxing for the first time in weeks. She'd been so intent on work, the gym's books, and her workouts, she'd forgotten how good it felt to have a little girl time.

'So are you going to ask Jake to your reunion?' Missy asked.

Roma frowned grumpily. Now why had she gone and brought that up? 'I was thinking about it, but now I don't know.'

'What do you mean you don't know? You two just got to . . . Well, you played some baseball.'

'Yes, but he ran off to another woman as soon as she snapped her fingertips.'

Missy set down her mug with a thump. 'Another woman? Jake is seeing someone? I didn't know that.'

Roma crossed her ankles underneath her chair and leaned her elbows onto the table. She drilled Missy with a look. If anyone knew the deep, dark secrets of the gym, it was her. Or Tito. She just couldn't face the kid yet.

'Who is this Liz person?' she asked.

'Liz?' Missy cocked her head as if considering the possibility. 'You think that Jake has something going on with Liz?'

'He left before rounding the bases, didn't he?'

'I don't think we've figured that one out yet.'

Roma slapped her hand firmly against the table. 'He left. OK? That's the point. We were . . . running the bases . . . when she called. He stopped running.'

'Did you?'

'I ran right off the playing field when Tito unexpectedly knocked on the door.' Roma's eyes rounded as she realised something. 'Oh, my God! I didn't stop play between you and Hawk, did I?'

'No,' Missy said, shaking her head. 'We both scored. Twice.'

'Aha. Lucky you.' Roma ran her finger along the rim of her cup. So Jake was the only one who hadn't crossed the plate tonight – as far as she knew. The schnapps began to swirl in her gut. There was no telling what was happening between him and Liz right now. At the very least, his fervent admirer was flashing some flesh. 'Tell me more about her. Jake said she's an important client.'

'She is. She's drawing a lot of attention in the world of women's fitness.'

Roma sunk further into her chair. 'She's that hot?'

'She has a hard body, that's for sure. Her muscle definition is incredible.'

Roma winced. Her muscles didn't define anything. 'Where's she been all this time? I haven't seen anyone like that at the gym.'

'She usually works out during the day. Jake blocks out most of his mornings just so he can work with her.'

Wasn't that special? Jealousy started to gurgle through Roma's veins. Did he train Liz like he trained her? The Jake she knew was a toucher. He was always spotting her or correcting her form. He seemed to use any excuse he could find to run his fingertips across her skin. Was he the same with Ms La-di-da Liz? Was that part of his technique?

Missy continued, unaware of the chaos she was causing. 'They've done a fantastic job preparing. If she does well at the competition, the gym is sure to draw in a lot more of the higher-paying clientele.'

'Hmmmph,' Roma grumbled. 'Higher-paying clientele.'

Just what was that woman paying for anyway?

'You've seen the rates. Clients who work with trainers pay more than the people who just come in to work on the machines,' Missy said. 'But it's worth it. Look at you.'

Roma shooed her off with a wave of her hand. Coddling was the last thing she needed.

'I'm serious. You look great.'

'I look OK.' She'd thought she was looking pretty darn hot until this hard-bodied Liz had come along.

'Would you stop worrying about her? Jake's into you, and the entire gym knows it. Believe me, after the competition's over, he'll forget about Liz entirely.'

Roma shifted on her chair. She wished she could forget the woman that easily. Her saccharine notes, too. That pink ink had to go.

'Enough of that nonsense. Back to your reunion,' Missy said, sitting up straight. 'Let's get down to the important stuff. What are you going to wear?'

Clothes? She wanted to talk about clothes? Jake was out there helping another woman pick out a bikini. 'I don't know,' Roma said. 'I hadn't thought about it much yet.'

This time, it was Missy who nearly blew a marshmallow out her nose. 'Are you kidding me? It's only a little over two months away. You've got to get started.'

'Yeah, but . . .' But what? Reality started to set in, and Roma's sore muscles stiffened all over again. 'Oh, my God. You're right! What was I thinking?'

'Easy. Don't panic,' Missy said. She laid her hand on top of hers and they both breathed deeply. 'I'll help. We'll go shopping together. We'll start this weekend.'

'What if we don't find anything? Worse yet, what if I pick something and it doesn't fit once reunion day rolls around?' Roma looked at her hot chocolate and shrieked. She pushed it away as if it were poison. 'What if I fall off the wagon and get fat?'

Missy caught her by both shoulders and shook her. 'You won't get fat. Jake and I won't let you. Now pull yourself together, woman. I need your help, too.'

'You do?'

Missy looked around carefully. That waiter tended to appear at the most embarrassing times. 'I need you to help me pick out lingerie,' she whispered.

'Excuse me?' Roma squeaked.

'I'm tired of Hawk wrestling with my sports bras. I want to surprise him and look sexy for once.'

Roma couldn't help it – she started to laugh. 'Honey, have you looked in the mirror lately?'

At the mention of a mirror, Missy flushed to the colour of fuchsia.

Roma knew that look.

'OK, OK. Hold back that info – whatever it is.' She rubbed her brow. Her head was beginning to hurt all over again. Whether it was all this talk about Liz or the schnapps she'd drunk, she couldn't tell. 'Fine. We'll go on the hunt for a dress for me and naughty underwear for you.'

'Aren't you going to need some naughty underwear, too?'

This time, it was Roma's turn to flush. 'Jake does have a thing for my coloured panties.'

Missy playfully clapped a hand over both ears. 'Information. Too much information.'

'Right.' The more Roma thought about it, though, the more she liked it. She did need help picking out a dress, but fancy lingerie could come in handy for more than just the reunion. She'd put her panties up against Liz's bikinis any day. 'You're on. Saturday, we hit the stores. They won't know what hit 'em.'

Missy grinned. 'Neither will Hawk nor Jake.'

Missy parked her trusty Honda in her assigned spot in front of her apartment building. She turned off the engine and affectionately tapped the steering wheel. The thing hadn't given her a bit of trouble since Hawk had replaced the battery. She had a feeling he'd worked on some other problems, too, but she hadn't asked and he hadn't fessed up to anything.

She wished he would.

She got out of the car and slammed the door behind her. Her talk with Roma tonight had been fun, but it had also unsettled her. Her friend had raised a lot of questions she'd been trying to avoid. What was really happening between her and Hawk? It had been going on too long for it to be a fling. Were they in a relationship? Was it an affair?

It was hard to tell, because they didn't talk – not like lovers should. When it came to the physical, they communicated perfectly without words. Anything else and they were like two awkward seventh graders at their first school dance.

What did she really know about the guy? Was he worth the risks she was taking?

She inhaled deeply and felt the bite in the spring night air. For all the questions Roma had raised, she was glad she'd confided in her. When it came to Hawk, sometimes she felt like she could just burst. Keeping it a secret much longer would have killed her.

'Missy.'

Her footsteps stopped mid-stride, and her gaze flew to the visitors' parking area. A black truck took up nearly two spots. Almost as if she'd conjured him, a big man stepped out of the shadows. 'Hawk!'

A sizzle went down her spine, charged by both excitement and alarm. She glanced quickly to her apartment. The blinds were closed, but the lights were on.

Danny was home.

Oh, God.

She hurried over to see what Hawk wanted. As always, they couldn't get within three feet of each other without touching. She reached out to lay her hand at his waist, and he brushed the backs of his fingers against her cheek. The gentle caress made her air puff out in a cloud. How could he do so much to her with such a simple touch?

'You shouldn't be here,' she whispered. She threw a worried look at the apartment, but didn't step away.

'Neither should you.'

She looked at him sharply, but found that he was looking at her apartment, too. Her heart gave a stutter-step. It was the first time he'd acknowledged Danny's existence since he'd given her that infamous ride home. It made her uneasy.

'Why did you come here?' she asked. 'I just saw you at the gym.'

'That was over two hours ago.'

Heat unfurled in her belly when he caught the hand at his waist and put it over the crotch of his jeans. He stiffened underneath her hand. 'You're insatiable,' she hissed.

'And you love it.'

'Hawk,' she said, feeling herself already starting to weaken. 'Please tell me you're not here to cause trouble.'

'I'm not.' He shifted, though, as if he'd given it some thought. 'I saw you head out with Roma. Does she know about us?'

'Yes.'

'Does that bother you?'

'No.'

'Good.'

She looked up at him, somewhat surprised. 'I thought that you didn't want anyone to know.'

'I didn't – not while you're still with the slug.' He jerked his head towards the apartment.

'Oh,' she said softly. He'd been trying to protect her reputation? The idea was strangely touching, although perplexing at the same time. He hadn't hesitated one second about putting her in this position. Boyfriend or not, he'd come on like gangbusters.

Now he was concerned about what people thought of her?

'You need to leave him,' he said firmly. 'Soon.'

'Leave Danny?' Her mouth dropped open. 'I can't do that.'

'Yes, you can.' He leaned down and kissed her hard. 'Come home with me. Spend the night.'

Leave Danny? Spend the night? He had her head spinning – and she had a feeling he was doing it on purpose. For a guy who didn't use many words, he sure knew how to choose them.

'You don't have class until tomorrow afternoon,' he said. His fingers tangled in her hair as he ran his tongue down the side of her neck. 'Think about it, little miss. You. Me. A bed.'

A bed. Her knees wobbled. They'd done it against the wall, in the cab of his truck, in her aerobics room on a stack of padded mats. They'd even done it after hours on a weight bench, but a bed?

She looked guiltily towards the apartment. Danny would be sitting on the couch watching a basketball game. A can of beer would be at his side, along with a jar of peanuts. She knew, because she knew him as well as she knew herself.

Danny was safe. Danny was home.

Hawk was a fleeting adventure.

If she needed to dump anyone, it was him.

He turned suddenly and backed her up against the pickup. Her arousal flared when he thrust his growing erection into her hand. 'Give me one night,' he said in a low voice. 'No more of these hit and runs. I want to take my time. It's time you let me.'

A shiver ran through her. What they'd been doing hadn't been enough for him? What did he want out of her?

And what was she willing to give?

'Missy,' he whispered. 'Please.'

With one little word, he got her right where it counted. He looked so rough and tough, yet he sounded vulnerable. It was a chink in his armour she hadn't expected.

Still, she wasn't a bad girl by nature. She knew what her answer should be. Home called. Home was comfortable.

But the sofa wasn't.

She hadn't let Danny touch her. There had to be a reason why.

She looked Hawk in the eye. His stare was so intense; it nearly burnt her. 'OK,' she whispered.

He didn't smile. If anything, his look became even fiercer. In no time, he bundled her up into the truck and passed her his cell phone. 'Call him.'

Her stomach dropped. 'What do I say?'

'That you're with me.'

'Hawk,' she said softly. 'I can't.'

His hand fisted on top of the steering wheel. 'Do you have caller ID?'

'We can't afford it.'

'Then it doesn't matter what you tell him, does it?'

The cab of the pickup got very quiet. Missy wished she could do this in private, but Hawk sat there, intent on listening to every word. She dialled and felt sick when Danny answered. Her palms got slick and, for a split second, she thought about telling him the truth. When she opened her mouth, though, she lied.

'Danny? Don't wait up for me tonight. I'm going to stay over at my friend Roma's.'

'Who?'

Her boyfriend sounded distracted. She heard the TV and knew she was interrupting the game. It made her feel even worse. 'Roma from the gym.'

'Yeah. OK.'

'I'll see you tomorrow.' She fiddled with the zipper of her backpack. Tomorrow – after she'd spent the night in another man's bed.

'All right. Later.'

She opened her mouth to say more, but he hung up. One moment he was there, and the next the phone was dead. Shocked, she pulled back and stared at the display screen. That was it? That was all he had to say to her? She was cheating on him. Didn't he care enough to notice? Silently, she passed the phone back to Hawk. His hand brushed against hers. She looked up to find him watching her closely.

He was waiting for her to back out.

All she had to do was say something.

And she might have if she hadn't seen the tension in his body. His hand gripped the steering wheel as if it were a weighted barbell. His jaw was set, and the tendons in his throat were tight. It was the glimmer of hope in his eye, though, that made her heart start to pound.

He wanted her to pick him.

'One night,' she said softly. 'That's all I can give you.'

His fingers tightened around the steering wheel. 'That's all I need.'

Missy could have sworn he added 'for now' as he turned the key in the ignition.

He pulled out of the parking lot and drove to the outskirts of town. With every mile they went, the butterflies in her stomach increased. He was taking her to his home. She was finally going to see a personal side of him and, for the first time, it would truly be just the two of them. They wouldn't have to worry about any boyfriends coming home, any exercisers stumbling into a dark aerobics room, or any accountants deciding to take on janitorial duties.

Missy felt herself becoming more nervous than the first time he'd taken her home.

He didn't make matters any better. He didn't say anything during the drive. Not one word. With the tension level as high as it was, it was almost as if he was nervous, too.

Finally, he turned down a dark road. No city lights ventured out this far, and the homes were spread far and wide. By the time he pulled into a long driveway, Missy's palms were wet. The house came into view, and her nervousness momentarily gave way to surprise.

'Oh, my God. Hawk, is that yours?'

He pulled at his seatbelt uncomfortably. 'Yeah.'

'It's gorgeous!'

The ranch-styled house was modern but sturdy, with a beautiful stone facing lining the bottom half. Whoever had designed the place had taken nature into consideration. The home sat at the edge of a tree-lined creek and bent to follow its path. The asymmetrical shape gave the house character.

'Are you going to just sit there staring, or do you want to come inside?'

Missy was surprised to find him standing at her door side. She could have sworn she saw a smile on his face. She scrambled to undo her seatbelt, and he opened her door. He hadn't bothered to park inside the three-car garage. Instead, he let her walk up the front steps.

Once inside the entryway, Missy couldn't move. The place was masculine, with heavy wooden tables and supple leather furniture. It was also spotless. That told her something about him – something she wouldn't have expected from someone she'd originally thought of as a biker-bar rebel. 'I love it,' she whispered.

This time, he did smile. It changed his face entirely. With a playful growl, he swept her up into his arms. 'Wait till you see the bedroom.'

She let out a laugh and held onto his wide shoulders as he took a direct path through the house. He didn't even bother turning on the light as he entered the master bedroom. Moonlight streaming through the windows showed it off better than any man-made light ever could.

Carefully, he set her on her feet. He wrapped his arms around her and pulled her back tight against his body. 'What do you think?' he asked.

The bedroom was just as masculine, and it made her feel feminine and sexy. Turning in his arms, she reached up and wrapped her arms around his neck. 'I think I might not make it to class tomorrow at all.'

His eyebrows rose, but then she was tugging him down for a kiss. As always, it burnt out of control. Hands started groping and clothes started flying. Soon, they were both stripped and ready. Hawk started to back her towards the bed, but Missy stopped him by pressing both hands against his chest.

'Wait,' she said softly.

They always went so fast, and he was so dominant. *Not that she was complaining.* He'd never left her wanting. This time, though, she wanted to touch him.

It was her turn to drive him crazy.

Leaning forwards, she kissed the spot over his heart. She could feel it pounding against her lips. 'Just let me do this.'

He flinched when her hands began exploring. 'Do anything you want, baby. I'm not going to stop you.'

And he didn't. He stood as still as he could under her attentions. She kissed and stroked, taking real pleasure in the beauty of his male body. His muscles were so hard and so well developed. He was like a Roman sculpture – only he wasn't made of cold marble. He was hot, and his skin was smooth.

'Hey!' he protested when she circled around behind him.

He went quiet when she wrapped her arms about him.

Gently, she brushed her lips across his back. She was delighted when his strong muscles quivered. From her angle, it looked as if the hawk on his shoulder was trying to take flight. 'What came first?' she asked softly. 'The tattoo or the name?'

'The tattoo.'

'What did they call you before then?'

'Does it matter?'

It did. She wished he would tell her, but now was not the time. Lifting herself up on her tiptoes, she flicked her tongue over the drawing. 'I like it,' she whispered. 'It turns me on.'

Everything about him turned her on.

Intently, she slid her hands down his six-pack abs. He inhaled sharply when she wrapped her hands around his cock.

'I like that,' he grunted.

He was about to like it even more. With a soft touch, she traced her finger across the bulbous head. She knew his thickness and his length. She'd been introduced to both up close and personal.

She wanted to get more personal. She took a shaky breath. 'Hawk,' she said softly. 'I want to go down on you.'

He went still.

'I know you like to take the lead,' she said in a rush. 'But you brought me here so we could take our time. I . . . I want to do this.'

He took a ragged breath and slid his hands down so they covered hers. 'We can go as slow as you want, little miss.'

The butterflies fluttered up from her stomach right into her throat. The only other man she'd ever done this with was Danny. Suddenly, she felt nervous. She didn't know how many calming breaths she had to take before she slowly circled back in front of him. Their gazes connected. Unsteadily, she dropped to her knees.

His hand caught her at the nape of her neck. 'We'll stop whenever you want.'

She didn't want to stop. She wanted to taste him. Timidly, she reached out for him. He was hard and hot. She wrapped her fingers around his thickness and felt it pulse in her hand. Slowly, she leant forwards.

A grunt left his lips as he aimed his raring tool at her mouth. 'God, you look beautiful like that.'

The head of his cock bumped against her lips. She kissed him softly and slid her hand down to cup his balls. She opened her mouth, and he carefully pushed his hot, smooth, pulsing rod inside. It filled her mouth and rasped against her tongue. He was big, though. Really big.

'You can take it,' he said, pulling back slightly. 'Open wider and loosen up. Relax.'

Fighting her reflexes, she eased the tightness in the muscles of her throat. Her mouth was filled with his hot flesh, and she realised she liked it. Curious about his taste, she let her tongue curl around him.

'Oh, that's good,' he said, groaning. 'Real good. Try sucking it.'

The request made her pussy clench. She had a mouthful of cock. It felt hot and hard, but his texture was fascinating. She suckled experimentally and was enthralled when she felt the soft pulsations running through his flesh.

He jerked. 'Fuck!'

Unable to hold still, he thrust. 'God. That's right, baby. Suck it hard.'

His hands fisted in her hair, and he began pumping in and out of her mouth. His balls were drawn up tight. He was going deep down her throat. A moment of uncertainty gripped her when she realised just how much she was submitting – but then she realised something else. She loved it. Her flare of nerves quickly turned into a flare of arousal. Reaching around, she caught his buttocks and squeezed tightly. He jolted at the touch, and she gagged when he went a little too deep.

'Sorry,' he said harshly. 'You just feel so fucking incredible.'

So did he.

Missy was so excited, her hips were squirming. She laved him with her tongue and went at him harder. Reaching down, she touched herself. She was wetter than she'd ever been in her life.

Hawk was close. Harsh words were coming out of his lips, and his fingers tangled in her hair. He wasn't letting her go as he fucked her soft mouth. The motion of his hips became quick and jerky. She shuffled forwards on her knees, and he thrust harder.

He swelled and, within three more thrusts, was ejaculating. Hot come filled Missy's mouth, and she swallowed as quickly as she could. His pleasure made her happy. It made her realise she hadn't submitted at all. She had as much power over him as he did her.

Finally, he pulled out. As strong as he was, his stance was unsteady. 'God, baby. You can take the lead whenever you want. You're awfully good at it.'

'Am I?' she asked, smiling up at him.

'You know you are,' he growled.

His eyes sparked. Reaching down, he caught her under the armpits and lifted her off her knees. His muscles bunched, and he tossed her onto the bed. Missy let out a laughing shriek when she bounced. He caught her by the ankles and spread her legs wide.

'Now it's my turn to show you how good I am.'

Her laughter stopped short. Her heart began to pound as, like a sleek panther, he crawled onto the bed. With his hands still holding her ankles, he bent her legs until her thighs were pressed against her chest. The position left her toes pointed straight up in the air and her pussy lifted like a sacrificial offering. Her fingers anxiously clutched the bedding beneath her.

Watching her closely, Hawk dipped his head.

She bucked when his mouth settled on her.

'Good?' he murmured.

Any better and she'd have jolted right off the bed. Unable to answer, she reached down and cupped his head. It felt sleek and smooth under her fingertips.

His tongue was adept. Keeping her legs splayed open wide, he investigated every nook and cranny of her pussy. And his tongue ... it would lick and soothe, only to plunge deep when she least expected it. With each intimate touch, her pleasure wound tighter and tighter. When his lips finally puckered around her clit and began to tug, she went off like a firecracker.

She was still floating back to earth as he crawled up on top of her. She took his weight as his cock determinedly slid into her wetness.

'Ohhhh,' she groaned as her body was pressed deep into the mattress.

'This time, I'm going to show you what a bed is for,' he said, his voice tight.

The box springs began to creak, and the headboard began to totter.

'A bed,' Missy said with a sigh.

It was a very, very good thing.

Chapter Seven

The next day after work, Roma pedalled the stationary bike at the gym as if she were racing in the Tour de France. She couldn't help it; she was a bit frazzled. How was she supposed to react when she saw Jake today? It was, after all, the morning after. Or the evening after. Yesterday, they hadn't even dealt with the uncomfortable minutes after. He'd just hopped out of his chair and ran once precious old Liz had called.

Liz.

The stationary bike cranked up to a higher rpm.

Just who was this paragon of physical fitness anyway? The woman even had Missy in awe of her. Missy, goddess of the female form! Men in the gym practically fell at the beautiful brunette's feet – especially one beefy brute, but that was an issue for later. What must this 'high-end client' of Jake's look like? And just what kind of a relationship did they have? Obviously, they were close enough for him to help pick out the bikini that best showed off her assets.

Ass being the important part of that word.

Roma put her head down and cranked away when the bike went into hill mode. If she had to try on a bikini right now, she'd run screaming in the opposite direction. The styles got skimpier every year, which brought up a disturbing thought. Just how much taut, toned skin had Lizzipoo shown last night?

The Lizard!

Her forehead crumpled in concentration. She needed to find out more information about this woman, but how? She'd searched the membership database, but there were so many Elizabeths it was useless. She'd tried talking to people around the gym. To say they'd gushed would be understating it. Tito, in particular, had gone on and on and on and on.

Ay yi yi. Roma's head began to hurt. She didn't have time for relationship roulette right now. She could barely keep things straight as it was. Her and Jake. Jake and Liz. Missy and Hawk. If that wasn't enough, tax season was at its peak. It would only get more stressful as 15 April approached, and then there was the reunion!

Every time she thought about that, she got woozy.

Should she ask Jake? Was he available or wasn't he? She'd learnt long ago not to step on another woman's turf – especially one who could pummel her into the ground with her pinkie. Even ignoring the Jake factor, there were so many other things to consider. How many people were actually going to show at the thing? After all her hard work, would Ellie even be there? What about her old boyfriend, Brian?

And what should she wear?

Missy had put that wonderful question into her head, and it just wouldn't go away. Whatever outfit she chose, it had to be stunning – but what would be best? A dress? Pants? A clown suit? Even if she did find something, how was she supposed to know what size to get? What was her body going to look like in three months?

Ugh! As Missy had so kindly reminded her, it was more like two months now.

Sweat began to drip down her temples as she started peddling like a fiend.

Two months!

The front door to the gym opened.

'Hey, Goldie.'

Roma jerked. Oh, crud. It was Jake. Morning-after

time had arrived, and she still didn't know what to say or do. Why had she let herself get sidetracked?

'Sorry I'm late,' he said as he headed her way.

'It's all right,' she said, continuing to pedal furiously. It was true what they said about exercise. It did help with stress.

He grinned. Before she could prepare herself, he leant down and planted a big kiss smack dab on her lips right in front of everybody. And it was no ordinary 'nice-to-see-you' kiss. It was a 'this-girl-is-mine' sort of kiss – the kind directors put at the climax of a romantic movie. His lips sealed against hers, and her toes curled inside her tennis shoes.

Then he used his tongue.

Sproing!

'Oh!' Roma pulled back sharply. The bike! The bike was attacking her!

Whistles and catcalls filled the room. Jake smiled at their audience but, behind him, Roma yanked frantically on her captured foot. It was stuck.

He turned his attention back to her and ran a hand comfortingly down her spine. 'Are you feeling better? Have your muscles loosened up from yesterday?'

Momentum had the pedals spinning around endlessly. On each rotation, the heel of her tethered foot got smacked. It hurt like the dickens, but she didn't want him to see. She'd already single-handedly shut down half the equipment in his place. 'A little,' she said, smiling painfully.

'Are you up for what we talked about?'

With the bike out of control, it took a second for her to catch on. When she did, she slammed on the brakes. The whirring sound of friction pierced the air.

Vo-di-o-do or lunges. He was talking about vo-di-o-do or lunges!

He winked. 'Come meet me in the office.'

Her jaw dropped, and she looked at him wide-eyed. That was how he wanted to handle the morning after? What about Liz and her bikini?

He grinned and tapped her on the chin. 'I've got something for you.'

Oh, Lordy!

She finally got the pedals stopped, but her heel throbbed. As nonchalantly as she could, she looked around the room. Nobody seemed to be staring or eavesdropping – except for one overgrown pool cue. Hawk chose that precise moment to wander by. He looked down, saw her predicament, and let out a laugh.

Jake had stepped away, but he stopped when he saw her frozen on the bike. Reaching out, he gave her ponytail a playful tug. 'Don't you want to see?'

Her mouth went dry. He was so casual about it – as if they just had some ordinary, everyday business they needed to finish. Everything about his demeanour said 'Liz who?' Roma shifted on the bike. Well, she could be casual, too. She was a consenting adult. She'd be so casual, he'd never believe it. Of course, first she had to disentangle herself from this man-eating machine.

'I'd love to,' she said, stalling. Her brain whirled frantically for an excuse. He was being all clever and seductive. She didn't want to spoil the mood by being all klutzy and goofy. 'Give me a few more minutes on this. I want to put in a full thirty minutes.'

'All right,' he said, his gaze moving over her face. 'That will give me time to get things ready.'

Get things ready? What did he have? Props? She felt herself overheating all over again.

'I'll be right there,' she said in what she hoped was a scintillating voice.

He turned and walked from the room. The moment he was out of view, she turned a furious gaze on Hawk. 'Well, don't just stand there laughing, you big muscle head. Help me!'

She pulled on her shoe, but it wouldn't let go. Frustration made her want to scream. Darn it! A girl didn't get an invitation like that every day. He'd had a shot with a toned hottie, but he'd chosen her.

'Hold still,' Hawk growled as he lowered himself down beside her. Even kneeling, the man was huge. 'Your shoelace is wrapped around the axle.'

'Then undo it!' She twisted her foot and hissed. Bad idea. The lace pulled tighter and cut off her circulation. 'I'm losing the feeling in my toes.'

'Tito, help us out here,' Hawk barked over his shoulder. Looking again at the problem, he followed her shoelace from her shoe back to the machine. He shook his head. 'Boy, you've done it good this time.'

Tito approached with a pair of scissors, but Roma pulled back. 'Wait. I need this shoelace.'

The kid smiled broadly and held up a spare. 'We've got back-up plans for people like you.'

'You mean this has happened to others?'

'Uh, no,' he said, his smile wavering. He put an OUT OF ORDER sign on the bike's display screen. 'Usually people just break their shoelaces when they're tying them.'

'Yeah, you have to be special,' Hawk grunted.

Roma's eyes rounded when the big guy took the scissors. She didn't know if she trusted him with those things. 'Be careful there, Hoss.'

He let out a snort. 'What? You think I'm the dangerous one?'

He efficiently freed her from the bike, but Jake chose that precise moment to poke his head around the corner. 'Hey, Goldie. What's the hold up?'

Hawk pivoted and blocked his view. 'Keep your pants on, Logan.'

Jake's eyebrows rose. 'You're one to talk,' he muttered.

He looked at them strangely, but eventually backed out of view.

'Hurry!' Roma hissed. Time was wasting. She snatched the shoelace away from Tito, and the kid went back to his desk. She began working on her shoe, trying to rid it of the useless lace, but she'd ridden the bike like a madwoman. The moment she bent over, all the blood rushed to her head.

'Ah, hell. Do I have to do everything?' Hawk grumbled.

He pushed her back upright on the seat and steadied her until the light-headedness passed. Once he was sure she wouldn't fall off, he turned his attention to her shoe. The broken shoelace was tossed aside, and he started replacing it with the newer one. For such a big man, he did have deft fingers.

'I don't know why I'm doing this,' he muttered. 'He'll have it off of you within thirty seconds.'

Roma gaped. 'Hey!'

He looked up at her, perplexed. 'What? It's the truth.'

'Maybe, but . . .' She bit her lip when she realised what she'd nearly admitted. 'You don't say things like that out loud to people.'

He threaded the shoelace through the last holes and began cinching it up. 'Why not?'

'Because,' she sputtered. 'There is such a thing as decorum.'

'Decorum? Shit. That's just a big word for "dancing around the facts".' He tied the bow securely and looked her dead in the eye. 'If two people want to get it on, they should just do it. Keep it simple and straightforward, and everyone stays happy.'

Her mouth opened and closed three times before she could form a response. She couldn't believe she was having a talk about her sex life with Hawk of all people. 'You don't know what's going on between Jake and me.'

'No?' He stared blatantly at her chest. 'You look pretty happy to me.'

Roma nearly fell off the bike when her nipples peaked. Whoa. She suddenly understood what Missy had been talking about. When this guy looked at a woman – really looked – she could feel it right down to her core. Self-consciously, she crossed her arms over his chest. Darn Jake for banning her flamingo shirt! 'So what's it to you?'

Hawk shrugged and uncharacteristically patted her on the knee. 'I like to see my friends happy.'

Roma shook her head to try to clear it. *What?* He thought of her as a friend? Or was he talking about Jake? Before she could ask, he stood and walked away. She pushed herself off the machine to go after him, but Missy walked into the room. Hawk's attention focused on her, and Roma could feel the blast furnace of attraction from where she stood.

It made her stop and think. Maybe there was something to his point of view after all.

She glanced towards Jake's office. Simple and straightforward, huh? She had a tendency to overthink things – hence her tizzy over the Liz situation – but she could try.

She could try right now, in fact.

Screwing up her nerve, she went in search of her trainer. She found him standing in the doorway of his office, waiting impatiently. Her palms began to sweat. Was there a difference between straightforward and overeager? Because after that pep talk from Hawk, she was ready to jump his bones.

'Close your eyes,' he said.

Oh, God. She obeyed and ventured closer. He caught her outstretched hands. To her surprise, he started guiding her down the hallway. Her sense of direction was terrible with her eyes open. With them closed, it took only a few turns before she was completely lost.

'No peeking,' he warned when she started to cheat.

She clamped them back shut but, just then, he stopped.

'OK. Stand right here. Now open them.'

Roma opened her eyes and saw ... the massage room. Soft, relaxing music floated through the air. Candles were lit, and the table was prepped. Her insides got all tingly and, this time, it wasn't due to peppermint schnapps. With effort, she turned her gaze on Jake.

'Paul wasn't available,' he said. 'But I am.'

Jake watched as Roma's pretty lavender eyes widened. Self-consciously, her hand came to the nape of her neck. It was damp from exertion. She looked down at herself and her nose curled.

'But I can't. Not like this. I need a shower.'

He took a step towards her. 'You're fine as you are.'

She looked at him as if he were crazy. 'No, I'm not. I'm sweaty and stinky and ... just wait. I'll be back in a flash.'

He reached out to stop her, but she was a wily one. She grabbed a robe from the wall and was gone before he could catch her. He started to follow her, but made himself stop. She'd said she'd be right back.

But who knew how long a flash was in female time?

He raked a hand through his hair. He didn't know why she was so fussy. They were just going to get hot and sweaty all over again. And that didn't even take into consideration the lotions and massage oils. Oh yeah, oil was definitely going to come into play once he got her onto that table.

Busying himself, he strapped Paul's belt of assorted lubricants around his waist. He had to adjust the bottle of almond oil when it rode just a little too close to his crotch. He'd been dealing with half a hard-on ever since he'd left her yesterday. The cold showers he'd taken last night and again this morning hadn't done the trick.

Not even close.

'Idiot,' he said to himself for what had to be the thousandth time.

He never should have left her like that.

If he'd had half a brain, he would have rescheduled with Liz. By leaving Roma and showing up late, all he'd ended up doing was irritating both women. Liz had been grumpy from the moment he'd stepped into that swimsuit store, but he'd understood. This competition was important to both of them. He'd made it up to her by paying for the bikini. The cost for such skimpy pieces of fabric was mind-blowing, but then again, so was the way they'd looked on her.

Talk about sizzling. The judges weren't going to find anything wrong with that.

He shook his head. Now it was time to make it up to Roma. And he would – just as soon as she got her cute little butt back in here.

Her cute little butt.

Damn. He wiped the back of his hand across his brow. Just thinking about how she'd felt sitting on his lap made him break out in a cold sweat.

A flash was too long.

He was just heading towards the door to go get her when it squeaked open. Roma slipped into the room, and his senses jumped. Her hair was wet from the shower, and she looked all pink and cuddly. She was wearing the robe she'd swiped, only it was at least two sizes too big. She acted uncommonly shy as she gathered the lapels together. It made him wonder what, if anything, she was wearing underneath it.

He cleared his throat roughly. 'Ready?'

His cock nearly jumped out of his pants when she took a deep breath and reached for the belt of her robe. She was taking it off! The vee between her lapels widened, and he looked in fascination at her smooth skin. He'd just caught a glimpse of well-rounded breasts when her gaze focused on his crotch.

The intimate look nearly sent him off.

'What are you wearing that for?' she asked bluntly.

He couldn't really help it!

He glanced down. *The belt*. She was talking about Paul's tool belt.

He gritted his teeth. 'For your rub down.'

Her eyes went huge as she looked from him to the table and back again. In an instant, she whipped the lapels of her robe together so tightly, she nearly strangled herself. 'You're really going to give me a massage?'

'Well, sure. What did you think?'

She blushed redder than he'd ever seen her.

'Oh.' He glanced around the room. '*Oh!*'

Well, hell. He liked her idea a whole lot better. He took a step towards her, but she backed away. Nervously, she rubbed one bare foot on top of the other.

'A massage,' he said, holding up his hands. 'Whatever you want.'

She licked her lips, and his willpower wavered. If she kept doing that, he'd be hard pressed to keep his promise.

She glanced at the table one more time. Finally, she levelled a look at him.

'My legs hurt. That misogynist who runs this place makes me do lunges.'

He couldn't help it; he laughed. 'The bastard.'

'Yeah, the bastard.'

He grinned and, although it cost him, he turned his back. 'Climb up there on the table, and I'll see if I can help.'

She paused for a moment, but then he heard rustling sounds. They only infused his curiosity. Was that her robe falling to the floor? His cock swelled, and he had to shift his tool belt once again. He heard the sound of cotton slipping against cotton and knew she was crawling between the sheets on the table.

His fingers flexed. She was naked underneath that sheet. She was naked and waiting for him to touch her. *Slow*, he reminded himself. Pouncing was unacceptable.

'You'd better be good,' she said, trying to tease, but still showing her nerves. 'If you gyp me, I'm demanding to see Paul.'

Oh, she wasn't going to get gypped. He'd be so good she'd forget all about Paul and his so-called magic hands.

Slowly, Jake turned. Just looking at her in the candlelight made his fingers ache. He approached the table carefully.

'How does your neck feel?' he asked, tapping the padded ring in which she rested her face. 'Is this adjusted all right?'

'It's fine.'

'OK, Goldie. Just relax.' With a deep breath, he reminded himself to do the same. Soft, sultry music played in the background as he painstakingly removed the sheet from her right leg and tucked it aside. His gaze automatically clapped onto her curves. Damn, she had the best legs in town. He wished he could take some credit, but those lunges she complained about had just helped to tone what was already damn near perfect.

He rolled his shoulders. She wasn't the only one who was tense. 'Any problem areas?' he asked.

She lay very still.

'My calves are tight,' she finally admitted. 'I made the mistake of wearing those high-heeled boots yesterday.'

He'd seen those boots. 'Those weren't a mistake.'

To his amazement, he found his hands shaking as

he squirted a liberal amount of almond oil into the palm of his hand. He warmed it before settling his hands onto her foot.

Her head instantly popped up out of the support ring. 'Oh!'

'Tender?'

'No, it's just that . . . Well, Hawk was right.'

'Right about what?' he asked as he pressed his thumb into the arch of her foot.

She groaned. 'Nothing. Shoes . . .'

He dug his knuckles into the ball of her foot, and she settled back down into a relaxed position.

'It doesn't matter,' she said with a sigh.

No, it didn't. In this room, the only thing that mattered was him taking care of her. With the candles glowing and the music playing, he massaged her foot and each one of her toes. Working deliberately, he moved up her leg. Her skin just begged to be touched, and his fingers couldn't get enough of her silky smoothness.

At least she wasn't as cramped as she'd been the day before. She must have followed his advice, but her muscles were still tight. He started out slowly, using long strokes to warm her muscles and encourage them to loosen on their own. The more stubborn ones warranted more acute attention, though, and he gave it to them. He worked deep, drawing out the pain, but kept up the sweeping, soothing motion that would draw the toxins away.

Except she wasn't as soothed as he would have liked.

By the time he got to her hamstrings, high on the back of her leg, she was squirming.

'Relax,' he whispered.

'Trying,' she said tightly. 'It's just that . . . oh!'

His hands slipped to her inner thighs, and her body arched like a bow. The tension in the room thickened. When she didn't say anything, the temptation became too much. He started to edge his hands up under the sheet.

Her head popped out of the support ring again.

'So how did shopping with Liz go last night?' she blurted. 'Did you find her a swimsuit?'

His hands stopped mid-motion. She wanted to talk about Liz? Now?

Danger signs flared in his head. He should've known she wouldn't let him off that easily. 'Yeah, we found something that will work. Lie down now.'

Her leg shifted ever so slightly under his touch. 'Tell me about this bodybuilding competition.'

He swore under his breath and moved his hands back down to a less dangerous spot. 'It's not bodybuilding; muscle mass isn't the goal. It's a fitness competition.'

He covered her leg with the sheet and moved to the other side of the table. The music and candles weren't doing the trick any more. She was tenser than ever when he started working on her other leg. He barely touched her, and her muscles jumped.

'So what does Liz have to do? Run an obstacle course?'

He sighed. She was going to make him work for this. He should have pounced when she'd first started to strip for him. 'It's harder than that. The fitness round is a high intensity, choreographed routine that displays both strength and athleticism. Competitors are also judged in swimsuit and evening gown rounds.'

'Evening gowns?' Her head slowly turned, and the candlelight reflected off the blonde highlights in her damp hair. Her eyes narrowed. 'So the Lizard isn't a muscle-bound freak with veins popping out of her neck?'

The Lizard?

He let the comment pass. Reaching up, he cupped the back of Roma's head and coaxed her back down.

'Judges don't go for that type of thing. They're look-ing for tone, symmetry, strength, flexibility and endurance.'

He ran his finger down her leg. 'Something like this, in fact.'

She let out a harrumph that wasn't even halfway muffled by the headrest. 'So, basically, Liz is a ramped-up beauty queen. That's great. Just great.'

Jake had had enough. He didn't want to talk about Liz or work. He needed her concentration back on them – and he knew exactly how to get it. Deter-minedly, he spread his hands over her bottom. Before she could say another word, he squeezed.

Her hips came right up off the table. 'Jake!'

The position was pure hedonism – ass lifted, head down. Jake felt his cock harden as the music swelled and the candlelight danced.

'If you put your mind to it, you could be my star pupil next year.' Unable to help himself, he began kneading her luscious curves. 'What do you say, Goldie?'

'Me?' she gasped.

Her fingers dug into the sheet beneath her, but he didn't ease up. He'd given her way too much time to think already.

'With these lines? Sweetheart, you'd blow the competition away.' He leant down and whispered in her ear. 'I'm willing to put in the hours if you are.'

'Oh,' she groaned. Helplessly, she rubbed her bot-tom against his hands.

That was more like it.

Before she could regain her self-control, he moved up the table and pulled the sheet loose from around her shoulders. Carefully, he folded it down low on her hips. Her back was beautiful, all soft and sleek. He trailed his finger down her spine. 'Now relax and let me make you feel good.'

She inhaled shakily, but went quiet. Music filled the room. Watching her intently, Jake oiled up his hands. They both sighed when he cupped her shoulders. Something incredible happened whenever their bodies came into contact. It was a phenomenon he wanted to investigate in more detail.

He used a firm touch, and her skin warmed in response. He worked his magic, staying in one area before sweeping up and down, looking for another. When he pressed his thumbs to the base of her neck, she moaned as if she'd died and gone to heaven.

It was his turn for a little bit of heaven, too.

'Roll over, Roma,' he said hoarsely.

When he didn't lift the sheet up to cover her, she went stock still. The music played on, though, and eventually her hands slowly came up from her sides. Bracing her palms against the table, she turned.

Jake's breath caught in his throat. God, she was incredible.

Her lavender eyes were huge as she looked at him, but he couldn't say anything. It was all he could do to breathe. He watched her full breasts sway as she rolled onto her back. She settled down, but her breasts stood proudly with her nipples perking up into the air.

Light from the candles flicked over her until he had to touch, too.

Reaching out, he cupped one big breast in each hand. She gasped and shifted, but he flicked her nipples with his thumbs and she arched into him. 'Like that?' he whispered.

'God, yes.'

Two quick squirts from the bottle at his belt resupplied him with oil. He reached for her again, and the slickness of his touch made them both groan. Her nipples stiffened as he played with them, and her eyes clouded over with desire.

'My turn,' she said a little desperately. Reaching out, she began tugging at his T-shirt. 'I want to touch you, too.'

'It's your massage, baby.'

She yanked the T-shirt up and laid two hot hands on his chest. It was all the argument Jake needed. Letting go of her for the briefest of seconds, he pulled off his shirt and threw it across the room. He shuddered, though, when she caught at his tool belt. She found the oil and soon her hands were hot and slick upon him.

The touch nearly brought him to his knees.

They caressed each other, daring to find who had the most dangerous hands. It was a toss-up, but as much as he loved her legs, Jake was a breast man. He knew how to work them, and her nipples were the most responsive he'd ever seen. He plucked and pinched until they glowed like two bright-red beacons.

'Jake,' Roma said, her voice tight. She was squirming so wildly, she was in danger of falling off the table.

He was feeling the urgency, too. Reaching down, he flicked back the sheet. 'Panties,' he said in surprise.

She was wearing pretty peach panties.

He let out a shuddering breath. 'Goldie, is there a colour you don't own?'

He slid his oiled fingers down her middle and her belly quivered. As much as he liked her taste in underwear, he wanted them off. Leaving her abruptly, he rounded the table until he stood at her feet. Reaching up, he caught her panties with both hands. 'Lift,' he ordered.

Her teeth bit into her lower lip, but then her hips swivelled. It made his mouth go dry. Without much finesse, he pulled her panties off her and caught her ankles. Boldly, he spread her legs.

And promptly forgot his own name.

Uncomfortable under the scrutiny, Roma bent one leg at the knee and propped herself up onto her elbows. Her breasts bounced seductively. She was breathing heavily, but she wasn't backing down. 'Are you just going to stand there and look?'

'Not on your life.'

Jake began tearing off his clothes. He'd planned to finish the massage first, but his plans had just been shot to hell. *Thank God*. His shoes went, then his socks. He pushed his pants down his legs, taking his briefs with them. He kicked them all aside and vaulted onto the table with her.

It teetered dangerously, and Roma gasped.

'It'll hold,' he promised.

For how long, he didn't know. With what he had in mind, it might give way halfway through.

Like that would stop him.

'Hurry,' she said, reaching for him.

He crawled up the table and knelt between her spread legs. There was barely room for her to keep her heels on the narrow table. He reached for the oil in the belt still cinched about his waist.

But she beat him to it.

Sitting up, she lavishly filled her hands with the slick liquid. Before he had anything to say about it, she caught his raring cock.

He jolted, and the table groaned ominously.

'I told you I wanted to touch you.'

Jake gritted his teeth. 'Do you hear me complaining?'

She had a wicked touch, and she wasn't shy. She pumped both hands up and down him, but her fingers were curious. They traced up the length of him and tickled his sensitive tip. His hips bucked and, devil that she was, she did it again.

'Goldie,' he warned.

'You got to play yesterday,' she said. 'I didn't.'

'You played fine,' he growled. Reaching down, he got his own supply of oil. Circumventing the hands that were busy on his private parts, he found his way to her pussy. She was plump and wet. Still, she squeaked when he brushed her clit.

Leaning forwards, he kissed her hard. Using his weight, he pressed her back down onto the table.

Their mouths mated as their touches became more and more intimate. She cupped his balls. He thrust his fingers into her. She rubbed her thumbs into his pubic hair. He plucked at her clit.

'You're going to slide home today,' she whispered against his lips.

That sounded good to him.

He explored deeper between her legs and rubbed his middle finger over the bud of her anus. She shook like an earthquake and drew her legs towards her chest. Her hands left his cock and wrapped around his back. 'Time to score, big guy.'

He kissed her again and aligned their bodies. Her ankles crossed behind his back, and he thrust. She was so hot and tight, he just about exploded right then and there. Settling deep within her, he fought for air.

'Oh, God,' she groaned.

She flexed her hips, and the heat was almost too much for Jake to bear. He began to move, and the candlelight danced with them. Their bodies were so slick with oil, there was nearly no friction. Just hardness against softness, heat and thick pleasure.

'That feels so good,' Roma said. She urged him on, murmuring desperate sounds.

Jake thrust harder and faster.

He was going deep, but the weight around his waist kept him from fucking her like he wanted. The damn tool belt. He'd forgotten to take it off. He reared upright, and her arms and legs clenched about him. They didn't let him get far.

'Let go, babe. Just for a moment.'

She opened her hazy eyes, but saw the problem. 'Damn props,' she muttered.

Their hands batted against each other as they fought with the buckle riding low on his hips. It finally gave way and the entire thing – belt, bottles, tubes and all – hit the floor with a thud.

Catching her about the waist, Jake sat back on his

haunches. He tilted her hips up to meet him. 'Now, let's get down to business.'

She let out a peep. 'You mean we weren't before?'

He moved more intently. Without the tool belt, his hips could swing free.

'Ooooh,' she groaned. 'We weren't.'

The table creaked out of time with the music as he set up a harsh rhythm. Roma's upper body twisted and her legs wrapped around him once again. He reached up to catch her juddering breasts.

'Jake!' she cried.

She went a bit frantic underneath him and, suddenly, everything inside of her clamped down. Her fingers bit into his shoulders, and her heels dug into his back. Her pussy clenched tight, and she surged up against him.

'Damn, Roma!' Jake clung to his control, fighting not to join her. It was too soon. He wasn't ready for it to end yet. He'd just gotten started.

Gritting his teeth, he held out. He kept his thrusts deep and steady as he watched her. The pleasure on her face was almost as erotic as the connection of their bodies. He fucked her until she sagged back against the table.

It took only seconds for her to realise that he hadn't joined her. Her eyes snapped open, and he would have smiled if his jaw weren't so tense.

'Oh, no, you don't,' she growled. 'You're not going to do this to me again.'

Reaching down between their bodies, she let her oiled fingers play. She rubbed his drawn-up balls, and he swore as pleasure, razor sharp in its intensity, seared him. Ready or not, he began to come.

It seemed to go on forever until he fell heavily onto her. She let his weight press her into the table and their bodies clung.

'I had more in mind,' he murmured into her soft hair.

'No reason to use up all your tricks in one day.'

Contentment swept through Jake. He'd had to wait, but damn, it had been worth it. Sighing, he placed a kiss on her temple. 'I like vo-di-doing with you.'

'Yeah,' she said softly. 'Me, too.'

He shifted atop her so she'd be more comfortable and cupped his hand over her breast. Being with her was so comfortable. For a long time, they just enjoyed the feel of each other. Her fingers trailed up and down his spine as his played softly with her nipple.

'Simple and straightforward,' she whispered.

He lifted his head and found her lost in thought. 'What?' he asked.

Her lavender eyes flared when she realised that she'd spoken aloud – and that he'd caught her. 'Oh, nothing.'

He gave her a nudge. 'What's simple and straightforward?'

She swallowed hard. 'It's just that Hawk said ...'

'You seem to be talking with him a lot these days.'

'Jake, I need a good-looking man on my arm when I walk into that reunion. Will you go with me?'

He grinned. Well, hell, she should talk to Hawk more often. 'It's about damn time you asked me that. Goldie, it would be my honour.'

Chapter Eight

Roma wasn't ready when the doorbell rang. Today was shopping day, but she'd gotten wrapped up in other things. Putting down the box of photos, she hurried to the door. 'Hey, Missy,' she said, smiling. 'Come on in.'

Missy looked around, her eyes wide. 'Wow. It looks like a cyclone struck in here.'

'That would just be me on one of my tears,' Roma said. She swiped up a yearbook from a chair and encouraged her friend to sit down. Her normally tidy living room was strewn with photographs, banners and various other high school mementos. 'The schedule of reunion events arrived in the mail this morning. It really got me going.'

'Looking through your old stuff?'

'I couldn't help myself. I'm starting to get excited about this whole thing.'

'Well, it's about time,' Missy said, snatching the yearbook back. She sat down with a plop and eagerly began flipping through the pages. 'Reunions are supposed to be fun, you know. You'll see all your old friends. Talk about old times. *Eat*.'

She was beginning to know her too well.

'They've got cheesecake on the menu,' Roma said, licking her lips. 'Do you know how long it's been since I had cheesecake?'

'Last night, if Jake's T-shirt on that hassock is any indication.' Missy's smile was impish as she looked up. 'Oh, wait. That would be beefcake, right?'

Roma stuck out her tongue. 'Smart ass.'

They stared at each other for all of two seconds before bursting into giggles.

'Where is he today?' Missy asked. 'I didn't see him at the gym this morning.'

'He's spending the weekend in Chicago.' Roma picked up the shirt and folded it neatly. It was all she could do not to hold it to her nose and inhale. 'He's visiting his sister and her family before taking an early look at the venue for the Fitness Show. He wanted to see the auditorium, the warm-up areas, the dressing rooms. Those types of things.'

'That's smart. They'll have enough to worry about when they get to the competition.'

'He's got it figured out from every angle.' Roma hugged the T-shirt to her chest. 'I've got to tell you, the accountant side of me loves that.'

Missy grinned before turning her attention back to the yearbook.

'So where are you in this thing?' she asked, trying to find Roma's high school photo. She thumbed through the pages, but stopped when she saw a group picture at a football game. 'Hey! Is that you in the flirty little skirt? Were you a cheerleader?'

Roma rolled her eyes, wounded to the core. 'Puh-lease. My arch-enemy, Ellie, was the head cheer-leader. She was always bounding around doing backflips and handsprings.'

'Show-off.'

'I refused to even try out.'

Missy ran her finger along the edge of the photo-graph. 'So what's the uniform for? Were you on the drill team? I was on the drill team.'

'Well, that explains your amazing dexterity when it comes to step aerobics.' Roma wandered back to the couch. Absently, she began gathering up photo-graphs and putting them back into their shoebox. 'Drill team really wasn't my thing.'

'Oh, come on. You're getting more coordinated.'

'And you're a terrible liar.'

'Flags,' Missy said, snapping her fingers.

'I tried, but I whapped Jeannie Smothers in the head and got tossed off the squad.'

'Then what? What's left?'

Roma finally turned. 'I held the school sign, OK?'

Missy looked perplexed.

'You know when the band is in a parade, they're led by two people carrying the school sign. When we performed at half-time, Myrtha Snodgrass and I stood at the edge of the field facing the grandstand.'

'Myrtha?' Missy choked.

'Snodgrass,' Roma said sympathetically. 'Poor thing.'

'Hey, at least you two were out in front. That's cool.'

Roma cocked her head. 'You're right. I never considered that.'

'You should have. You look cute as a bug.'

Roma moved so she could peek over her friend's shoulder. She did look rather adorable in the shot. Even more, she looked slim. Maybe she hadn't been as chunky back then as she'd thought. 'Want to know a secret? My goal with this whole weight-loss and fitness thing is to fit back into that skirt.'

'You still have it?' Missy asked, her head swivelling around.

Roma pointed to the chair on the other side of the room. Her uniform was draped across it as if on display. The white sweater had a big green 'W' on the front and the short swirly skirt matched with green trim on the hem. 'Washington High Wolverines,' she said proudly.

Missy hopped out of her chair to investigate. 'They let you keep it? I didn't get to keep my uniform.'

'They knew they were purchasing new ones for the next year, so they let us keep them if we wanted.' Roma fingered the skirt lovingly. 'I wanted. We had so much fun going on band trips.'

'See,' Missy said, nudging her. 'That's the sort of thing you should be concentrating on with this reunion – not some bouncy cheerleader on a power trip.'

'I know,' Roma said. 'I'm trying. With every day that passes, I'm looking forward to going more. I can't wait to see everyone – *or have them see me.*'

'I don't suppose Jake has anything to do with that?'

Roma couldn't help the grin that spread across her face. 'Can you imagine how people will react when I walk in with such a fine-looking stud? But seriously, he's more than a trophy date. Look what his training has done.'

She wiggled the loose waistband of her jeans. There was a gap of nearly three inches between it and her tummy. 'These are supposed to be my skinny jeans. Even they're getting baggy on me!'

Missy let out a whoop and, together, they did an impromptu happy dance.

'We'll have to add jeans to our shopping list today.'

'But the dress,' Roma said. She reached out and grabbed Missy by the shoulders. It was imperative that she listened. 'We've *got* to find the dress today. It's the third time we've been out looking. We're running out of time.'

'Don't worry. Today's the day. I know it. I'm feeling lucky.'

'Oh, really.' Roma wiggled her eyebrows suggestively. 'I don't suppose *Hawk* has anything to do with *that*?'

'Hush,' Missy said, blushing. Turning, she snatched up her purse and headed to the door. 'Let's get going. You have about a hundred purchases to make, and I need a new teddy. Preferably red.'

'I thought you bought one of those last week.'

'I did, but it's in shreds now.' Missy let one eyebrow arch before stepping out the door. 'Don't ask.'

There were days when shopping could reduce a woman to tears. Styles were unflattering, fits were all wrong, or colours were just gross. Hours could be spent looking for that illusive buy, with each store becoming more depressing than the last. For Roma, that had been the case for the past three weeks.

Today, though, things were different. Missy had been right. It was one of those rare occasions when everything was coming together. The planets had aligned, and Lady Luck was smiling down. Yes, it was one of those days when shopping could propel a woman into the stratosphere.

Roma was currently somewhere over the moon.

'A size smaller. Can you believe it? I just bought jeans an entire size smaller!'

'I know,' Missy said, smiling indulgently. 'I was there.'

'But I haven't been able to buy a size smaller in . . . well, ever! It's always a size bigger.' She gestured with her cup of Starbucks coffee to the other women prowling the mall's corridors. 'You ask any one of these ladies. I'll guarantee you that being able to buy jeans in a smaller size is unprecedented.'

'Yes, it's never been done before,' Missy said. 'Remind me to tell Jake to lower your caffeine intake.'

'It's not the caffeine,' Roma said, taking another big swig. 'It's life. I'm high on life.'

'You're high on something.' Missy laughed. She tossed her own empty cup in a trash bin and pointed to a store across the way. 'Want to go in there?'

Roma scowled. 'The dresses there are too froufrou. I want something bold. Something sleek and sexy. Something totally opposite of clumsy Roma Hanson.'

'Right. No bows,' Missy said, remembering their disastrous shopping trip from the week before. 'Let's wander for a while.'

'Sounds good to me.' Roma felt fine just strutting up and down the mall's hallways. She was, after all, wearing jeans one size smaller. She glanced at her reflection in a store window as they walked past. It was spring, and she and Missy were similarly dressed. Their outfits of jeans, stacked boots and fashionable tops were simple, but attention getting. For that, her smile just wouldn't fade. She was quickly learning that a good body could make anything look great.

And she had a good body.

A fantastic body.

A size-smaller jeans body.

Ha!

'Do you think I should start tanning?' she asked, nodding at the Tropic Topic store as they sauntered by.

'God, no,' Missy said, giving a dramatic shudder. 'Liz does that, and it looks so phoney. You don't want to show up at your reunion looking that way.'

Roma perked up, if that was at all possible. 'Liz? You mean Jake's Liz.'

'He'd hate it if you did that. It's been a constant argument between the two of them.'

Jake and Liz argued? Double ha!

''Nuff said,' Roma murmured happily. She took another swig of her too-strong coffee and savoured it on her tongue. Life was getting better and better.

'A haircut might be a good idea, though,' Missy said. She stopped in front of the Styles and Smiles shop and looked at the products they had on display.

Roma's high-riding mood dipped. 'What? Does it look bad?'

Automatically, her hand went to her hair. 'Am I

behind the fashion trend again? Damn, that always happens.'

'Oh, stop it,' Missy said, bumping her with her hip. 'Natural blonde is always in. I'm just thinking that you should get your hair cut about two weeks before your reunion. That way it won't have that "just cut" look and you won't be too shaggy.'

Roma's shoulders slumped in exaggerated relief. 'Where did you learn all this stuff? I swear you're a fashion guru.'

'Well, you're the expert when it comes to lingerie.'

Roma snorted. 'Honey, when you've got boobs as big as mine, you learn quick.'

Missy glanced down at her own chest. 'I guess that explains why I'm a slow learner.'

'Oh, give me a break. Your knockers are top of the line.' Roma hooked her arm through her friend's and started walking down the walkway once again. 'They're full and perky, just like they should be.'

Missy watched herself jiggle as she walked in her high-heeled boots. 'Hawk does seem to like them. Quite a bit, in fact.'

'Whoa,' Roma said. 'Information!'

Missy started to laugh, but stopped mid-breath when she looked up. She came to a halt so suddenly, she nearly jerked Roma's arm out of its socket. 'Oh, my God. There it is!'

Roma struggled not to slosh the last precious drops of her coffee onto the floor. 'Hey, careful.'

'Look! That's it. That's the dress.'

'*The* dress?' Roma's head snapped so hard to the side, she nearly gave herself whiplash. What she saw made her forget about her coffee entirely. A mannequin in the store window directly in front of her was wearing a dress so pretty, it made her eyes sting. And it was *the dress*. 'Ooooooooooooh,' she sighed, all her air leaving her lungs at once.

'Watch it,' Missy warned, grabbing the coffee cup as it slipped from her hand.

Roma stood motionless as her friend tossed her coffee into the trash. She couldn't stop staring. It truly was a thing of beauty.

'Don't just stand there. Let's go try it on,' Missy said excitedly. She caught her by the arm and gave a tug.

Roma followed, but craned her neck to keep an eye on the pretty confection until it was out of sight. When she finally snapped to, she found herself at a rack holding at least a dozen of them. 'Out of my way,' she said, diving in.

She chose two – one in her normal size and one a size smaller. Who said it couldn't happen again? Turning on her heel, she made a beeline to the dressing room.

Missy was close on her heels. She stood outside tapping her toe impatiently as Roma whipped off her newly minted favourite jeans. 'How's it look?' she asked.

'Mmmphhh,' Roma said, her words muffled as she pulled off her shirt. She tossed it towards the hook on the door, but it sailed over the top. Missy caught it before it hit the floor.

'Let me see,' she said. 'Let me see.'

Roma pulled the material over her head and reached back for the tab of the zipper. The dress took shape as the zipper cinched up – and what a shape it was. Stunned, she stared at herself in the mirror. 'Somebody pinch me,' she whispered. 'Is that really me?'

The stretchy fabric clung to her curves as if it had been made for her.

Missy pounded on the door. '*Let me see!*'

Roma whipped it open and looked at her friend helplessly. 'Tell me I'm not dreaming. Tell me it's for real.'

Missy took a step back, and her jaw dropped. 'Oh, heavens! That's gorgeous.'

Roma spun back towards the mirror. It truly was – and it made her look gorgeous, too. The dress was Grecian style with one thick strap going over her right shoulder. The bodice was snug, showing off her full breasts and trim waist. At her hips, it flared lightly into an asymmetrical skirt. It angled from mid-thigh on her right leg to somewhere mid-shin on her left. The colour, though, was what set everything off. It was a deep purple, nearly blue in intensity. She wasn't one to wax poetic, but the colour brought out the lavender of her eyes and made her hair shine like spun gold.

Best of all, it was the smaller size.

Roma felt like she just might faint.

'You look incredible,' Missy said in awe. 'You'll be lucky if Jake doesn't tackle you before you get to your reunion.'

Roma turned to see her profile. Oh, yeah. Jake was definitely going to like this. From the side view, she looked unbelievably curvy. Even more amazing, the asymmetrical skirt made her legs seem long and lean.

'Ring it up,' Missy declared. 'We've got to hurry back to Burgette's. I swear I saw a pair of cute purple sandals on sale there. Then we need to find you a strapless bra. Oh, my God. Your classmates will be stunned.'

Roma smiled into the mirror. Oh yeah, the day just kept getting better and better. This was exactly what she'd wanted that first day she'd stumbled into Jake's Gym. Perfection – or as close to it as she could get.

Reunion, watch out!

'Bring it on, Ellie,' she whispered in challenge. 'I'm ready for anything you've got.'

* * *

The shoes Missy had seen at Burgette's were a perfect match and thirty per cent off to boot. It had been a challenge, but the outfit they'd finally found for Roma's reunion dinner was stylish, seductive and kick-ass all at once. Missy wished she could be a fly on the wall when her friend made her grand entrance. Tongues were certainly going to be wagging.

They had one last purchase to make, though, and it was the store she'd been waiting for all day. *Lingerie.* Once they set foot inside the door, Roma headed for the strapless bras. Missy took time to stop and look around. As always, she could hardly choose where to begin. She just hoped the shopping fairy would look down on her, too.

'Do you have anything new in red teddies?' she asked the sales clerk.

The woman pointed to the far corner, and she started moseying in that direction. It was funny. Just a few months ago, she'd walked by this store without giving it another glance. Back then, she hadn't seen the point in buying delicate undies. As a college student and aerobics instructor, they weren't practical. She just couldn't rationalise spending the money.

Now she could – and this store was her favourite.

A little zing settled in her belly as she walked between the racks of bras, panties, nighties and hosiery. So many colours. So many pretty things. So much sex!

She rubbed her damp palms on her jeans. It didn't matter what she looked at, visions of Hawk's reaction would appear in her head. Red was definitely a trigger for that man. When she'd stripped down to that teddy the other night, it had been like waving a flag in front of a bull. A very, very horny bull.

The frothy fabric hadn't lasted long once he'd gotten his hands on her. Afterwards, he'd been sorry, but she hadn't. *God*, she hadn't. He'd insisted on giving her money to buy a new one, only he'd made a special request.

The new one should have an open crotch.

She licked her lips and tried to tamp down her excitement. The idea of buying something so naughty should have shocked her.

It didn't.

She had a sex life. A wonderful, glorious, active sex life. She'd be a fool not to revel in it.

Fighting a smile, she headed towards the far wall. She wasn't even halfway there when a teal-coloured bra suddenly caught her eye. Her breath caught. The blue-green colour was her absolute favourite. She stopped to look and, like Roma with her dress, simply stared. Carefully, she ran her finger over the lace trim. She loved the frillier things. Lace, satin, bows . . .

'That's beautiful,' Roma said, coming up to stand by her side.

'It's push-up,' Missy said, still entranced. She swept her fingers along the inside of the cup. It was padded and comfortable.

'It's demi-cut,' her friend warned. 'You'll be spilling out all over the top. That could be a good or a bad thing, depending on how you look at it.'

It was a good thing. Definitely good. She sorted through the bras until she found one in her size. It was rather expensive, but with her discount card, she could swing it. Another discovery made the decision for her. She sighed happily. 'Oh, look. Matching thongs.'

Roma laughed. 'You'll be spilling out there, too.'

'It's perfect,' Missy said. She picked out a pair of the underwear and held the bra above it, trying to envision how the combination would look on her.

'I don't know how you wear those things,' Roma commented. 'I tried once, and it felt like butt floss.'

'You get used to it,' Missy said. She'd never admit it, but she liked the sensation.

'Then try it on.'

'I will.' She glanced at her friend. 'What did you find?'

Roma screwed up her nose. 'They didn't have any purple.'

Missy frowned sympathetically. Her friend had a thing for colour and, apparently, so did Jake. 'It would have been hard to match anyway.'

'So what do you think?' Roma held up two possibilities. 'White or black?'

That was an easy call. 'Definitely black. That dress is dark enough that the white would show like a spotlight if you had any slippage.'

'My thoughts exactly. Shall we hit the dressing room?'

'You go. I'm not done looking.'

'The red teddy?'

Missy felt her cheeks heat. She hadn't told her friend everything. 'It was a very specific request.'

Roma rolled her eyes. 'That man is a machine.'

Missy grinned. 'From what you've told me, Jake can hold his own.'

'And then some.' With a flounce, Roma pivoted and walked to the dressing rooms.

Missy turned her attention back to the teal set. The brief coverage of the thong was a bit shocking. It was more of a T shape than a V. The zing in her belly got a little stronger, and she pressed her thighs together hard.

Red. She couldn't forget the red.

It took a while, but she finally found what she needed. The racier garments were kept at the very back corner of the store, away from where the more timid shoppers might venture. Good thing. The teddy she found not only had a convenient opening in the panty panel, two ribbons held together the fabric covering her breasts. Two little tugs, and Hawk would have access to whatever he wanted.

She'd have to try this one on when Roma wasn't looking.

The stalls in the dressing room were nearly empty when she walked in, but she knocked on the door where Roma was changing. Her friend opened the door and she slipped inside.

'What do you think?' Roma asked. She squared her shoulders and stood up straight. All she was wearing was the black bra, a pair of light blue panties, and the new purple sandals they'd bought to match the dress.

'Interesting colour combination,' Missy said as she started to strip.

'I have black panties at home.'

'Oh, splurge for once would you, Madam Accountant? How often does your reunion roll around?'

Roma looked at herself in the mirror and bit her lip. 'You're right. I'll buy the panties, too. I think the bra is a good fit.'

She pivoted to and fro, looking at her reflection. The change in her figure was really dramatic. Jake had done a fantastic job of getting her in shape in a relatively short time period. All that remained was a bit of toning work.

Missy wiggled out of her jeans and pulled her top over her head. She glanced at herself in the mirror. She'd been teasing about her figure. She liked the way she looked, and why shouldn't she? She worked her ass off to get this way.

Reaching back, she undid the hooks of the bra she was wearing and let it fall down her arms. Her breasts weren't as big as Roma's, but they had a nice shape. They were full and firm, and Hawk couldn't get enough of them. She saw whisker burns near her nipple and turned before her friend could see.

She undid the teal bra from its hanger and put it on. Roma helped with the hooks at the back, and they both were a bit stunned as they looked at the effect in the mirror.

'Wow!' Roma said.

Missy ran her tongue across the back of her teeth. 'Wow' was an understatement. The teal colour was the perfect match for her pale skin and dark hair, but the style . . . Yowza. 'I look as busty as you!'

'And then some. Zheesh, that's an awesome optical illusion.'

'Illusion? These are all mine.' Missy shimmied to see what would happen. Not much movement there. The push-up bra was doing its job, but the demi-cut made it look like it was a frilly nothing.

'Try on the thong.'

She was already reaching for it. Remembering the store's rules, she pulled it up and over the black one she was already wearing.

Roma gasped. 'There's nothing to that.'

Missy cocked her head. It was a little spare, but she liked the idea of being daring. She'd been so safe for so long. 'I'm buying it,' she declared.

She whipped the tiny strip of fabric off, along with her own thong. As long as she was buying it, she might as well try it on for real. She swivelled her hips as she pulled the lacy teal into place. The strips of fabric settled over her hips and into the crevice between her cheeks. It cupped her perfectly.

She stared at herself, amazed at the sensual creature that stared back. She looked so good, she was turning even herself on. By the time she got together with Hawk, she was going to be ready to tear off all *his* clothes.

Roma joined her at her side, grinning as she stared at their scantily clad bodies. 'Look at us. Have you ever seen two such hot babes?'

'Never. And tonight, I'm going to crank up the heat.' Missy turned and peeked over her shoulder to see how she looked from behind. 'When Hawk gets home, he's going to find me lying on the couch wearing nothing but this. He'll never know what hit him.'

'Home?' Roma said, keying in on one little word. Her eyes narrowed. 'Wait a minute. When did his place become home?'

Oh, damn. Why had she let that slip?

Her friend caught her by the shoulder and turned her so she could look her in the face. 'Have you moved in with him?'

'No,' Missy said defensively. 'I've just been spending a lot of time there.'

'As in nights?'

'Maybe.'

'What about Danny? Has he figured it out?'

She really didn't want to get into this. Not now. She was having such a good time. 'Maybe,' she admitted. 'I think so.'

'You think so? What has he said?'

God, what was this woman doing as an accountant? She should be an interrogator down at the police department.

'Not much,' Missy mumbled. She adjusted the strap riding on her hip, suddenly uncomfortable.

Only the discomfort wasn't external.

Oh, God. Here it came. She could feel it bubbling up inside her. She was not good at juggling two men, and she didn't like doing it. She hated that she was hurting both of them, and she hated even more that she was hurting herself.

Frustrated, she flung her hands into the air. 'I don't know what's going on with Danny. I've been with him since I was a sophomore in high school. That's eight years as a couple, but all he can say when I head out for the night is "later". *See ya later.* Doesn't he care? Isn't he suspicious? Why doesn't he at least check up on me?'

Roma took a step back, surprised at the sudden outburst. 'Where have you been telling him you're going?'

'To your place.'

'*My* place?' She blinked. 'Well, you're right. He hasn't called.'

Missy picked up her jeans from the floor and tossed them onto the dressing-room bench. 'That's probably because he's taking advantage of my being gone and heading out with the boys. I swear all he does any more is play poker, watch TV, or hit the bars.'

Roma scowled. 'How old did you say he was?'

'Twenty-two. Like me.' Missy ran a shaky hand through her hair. This had been festering inside her for a while. She'd been racked with guilt for cheating on him, but was it really cheating when the other person had already checked out of the relationship emotionally?

She'd told Hawk once that Danny was her roommate. It hurt a little to realise she'd been telling the truth.

'I don't know what happened to us,' she said, suddenly angry. 'We used to be so happy.'

'Oh, honey,' Roma said, rubbing her on the shoulder. 'It sounds like you've just grown apart. You were so young when you started dating. You've matured, but Danny hasn't gotten there yet.'

'He's not even close.'

'Well, that doesn't mean you can't make it work. Do you have similar interests?'

'I'm into health and fitness; he's into being a couch potato.'

'Well, what about friends?'

'We don't have that many in common any more.'

Roma crossed her arms under her breasts. One blonde eyebrow rose. 'Have you slept with him since you started seeing Hawk?'

And she's moved in for the kill, Missy thought.

'No,' she admitted softly.

She rubbed her hand across her belly. That really was the crux of the matter. Not only had she stopped having sex with Danny, she'd been sleeping on the couch. If you could call it that ... It was hard for her to sleep any more without Hawk at her side.

Roma's voice went soft. 'Then I think you've already made up your mind.'

'I have,' Missy said. If she was honest with herself, she'd made up her mind a long time ago. She'd made it up on the night she'd accepted a ride home from a man she hardly knew. 'Danny doesn't know it yet, but I'm moving out of the apartment at the end of the month. I'm paid up in rent until then. After that, I'm gone.'

Roma nodded as if that was a good idea. 'Are you going to move in with Hawk?'

'No.' She was a little embarrassed when the word came out so strong.

Her friend held up her hands as if sorry she'd asked. 'Why not?'

'Because he hasn't asked me,' Missy said with irritation. There were a lot of things he hadn't asked her. There were a lot of things he hadn't told her.

'Have you talked about it at all? Does he know your plans?'

Oh, that was rich. 'Talk? Please. You know Hawk. He's more action than words. I hardly know any more about him now than I did when we first got together.'

'Well ...' Roma said hesitantly. 'I know a little.'

Missy's head snapped to the side. She'd been dying to know more about the man she was sleeping with, but there was only so much snooping she could do. 'Like what?'

'He builds houses.'

'He what?'

'He's a contractor. Jake told me so.'

She gritted her teeth together. 'No wonder I got a smile out of him when I told him I liked his house. He must have built it. That pig-headed jerk! Why didn't he say something?'

Roma rubbed her hands together nervously. 'It goes both ways. Have you ever asked him anything about himself?'

'I don't even know his real name!' she snapped. 'How can I be falling in love with the big galoot when he won't even tell me his name?'

Roma's mouth rounded into a big 'O'. When Missy realised what she'd just admitted, she clapped a hand over her mouth. Her eyes went wide, and she felt the blood drain from her face.

Roma pointed at her and wiggled her finger accusingly. 'You said you *loved* him.'

'Falling in love,' Missy quickly clarified. Her shoulders slumped. 'Oh, who am I kidding? I'm already there.'

She was crazy about the guy; that's why he made her so upset. He was about as open as a clam, but he was sweet to her in his own way. He kept her car in top condition, made her breakfast, made sure she got to class on time ... What really got to her, though, was the way he held her. It didn't matter if they'd just made love or not. He always held her like he didn't want to let her go.

Tears started to well up in her eyes. 'I love the big muscle-headed jerk.'

Roma started to get weepy, too. She waved a hand in front of her face as if that would fight back the tears and sniffed loudly. 'Well, if you feel that way about him, you need to knock him upside the head. Get him out of his shell.'

Missy smiled weakly. 'It's a little late for that. We kind of jumped into the deep end of this relationship. I can't go back and ask him his name *again*. God, how embarrassing would that be?'

'You two,' Roma said, rolling her eyes. 'Fine. If you won't do it, I will.'

'You'll do what?'

'Put that man straight.'

Missy let out a laugh and wiped her eyes. That

was a picture. Little terrier Roma nipping at the heels of a Rottweiler like Hawk.

'But you've got to get off your duff, too,' her friend challenged. 'Talk to him. Ask him questions. Badger him.'

'I don't even know where to start.'

'I do,' Roma said. She rubbed her hands together as if the plan was already forming in her head. 'Simple and straightforward? *Ha*! Just let me at him.'

Chapter Nine

Roma spotted Hawk the moment she stepped in the gym door on Monday after work. Then again, he was kind of hard to miss. He was doing lateral raises with the free weights on the other side of the room. The scowl on his face was menacing as he stared at his reflection in the mirrored wall in front of him. He was in the zone, blocking out anything and everything around him as he concentrated on his form.

Perfect.

Her eyes narrowed. Her plan was a surprise attack. Get in, make her point, and get out – hopefully before he could catch her in a headlock. Squaring her shoulders, she headed towards him.

Her chances of getting through this unscathed were much higher if he was tired.

Intent on her target, she closed in. He finished the set and began to put the weights down to rest. Now!

'Haw—'

The 'k' was cut off unexpectedly when she suddenly found herself swept up in a kiss. Strong arms wrapped around her, and a hard body pressed against hers. The kiss was hot and sweet. The arms tightened, lifting her until her toes dangled towards the floor. When she was finally allowed to come up for air, she found herself a bit dizzy.

'Hey, Goldie. Miss me?'

'Jake!' she said in surprise. 'I didn't see you there.'

'I noticed. I'm trying not to take it personally.'

She rubbed her lips together. They tingled like crazy. 'I was trying to talk with Hawk.'

'Talk with him later,' he said as he tugged her to the office. 'Make out with me first.'

'Well . . .' She glanced again at the bodybuilder. She was on a mission, but she wasn't stupid. 'OK.'

Together, they stumbled into the office. Roma kicked the door shut with her heel and shrugged her shoulders as Jake pushed off her jacket. Impatiently, she urged him backwards to his desk. He sat down and pulled her between his outstretched legs.

'God, I missed you,' he said as he kissed her hungrily.

She struggled to get closer. 'Not as much as I missed you.'

'These are new,' he said as he slid his hands into the back pockets of her jeans. 'I like them.'

'Me, too,' she said as she nibbled on his lower lip. 'They're a size smaller.'

'Congratulations,' he said. He kissed her soundly to stop her teasing. 'What did Missy have to use to peel you off the ceiling?'

'The dress.'

'*The dress?*'

She sighed happily. 'It was a great weekend. It will go down in the annals of shopping history.'

He pulled back. 'That good, huh? When do I get to see it?'

'Later,' she said with a mischievous smile. She wove her fingers through his blond hair. 'How was your trip to Chicago?'

'Productive.'

'Did you figure out all the details like you wanted?'

'Most of them.'

'Did you remember to bring something back for me?'

For a moment, he looked panicked – as if he'd forgotten to get her a present. When he saw the expectant look in her eyes, though, he let out a chuckle.

'You're twisted,' he said, shaking his head. With regret, he extricated his hands from her back pockets and reached into his own. He pulled out his wallet and opened it. 'Most women want jewellery.'

'Receipts, please.' She held out her hands as he pulled out white slips of paper. She frowned when she saw how folded and crumpled they were, but she took them eagerly. She'd learnt she needed to get information like this out of him quick before it disappeared entirely.

'Now get back here,' he said.

She stepped back, nimbly escaping. 'I told you I have to talk with Hawk.'

'Can't it wait?'

She shook her head. 'I need the element of surprise.'

'Uh-oh.' Jake's eyebrows lowered. 'I don't like the sound of that.'

She glanced with interest at his filing cabinet. 'You don't happen to have his real name in there, do you?'

'What do you need that for?'

'Ammunition.'

'Oh, God. What is this about?'

She shrugged. She didn't see any reason she couldn't tell him. 'I promised Missy I'd have a talk with him.'

'A talk about what?'

'What do you think?'

He turned a bit pale.

'Goldie,' he said in warning. 'Let those two work their problems out on their own.'

She rolled her eyes. Wasn't that just like a man? 'And just how are they supposed to do that? They're humping like rabbits, but neither can work up the courage to talk to the other. Somebody's got to give them a nudge.'

'It doesn't have to be you.'

'Jake, they're our friends.'

He let out a bark of laughter. 'That's the point. I'd like to keep them that way. Hawk would have my head on a plate if I gave you his name.'

'Oof. You're no help.' Miffed, Roma scooped up her jacket. She hung it on a hook on the wall and circled around to the back of the desk. 'Where's your sense of romance?'

'Standing on the other side of this desk.'

He started to follow her, but she stopped him by pointing at an imaginary line. 'Hey, stay on your side.'

She put down the receipts. She hadn't planned on doing this now, but she might as well get it out of the way. 'Since you're here and you're so cold-hearted, we might as well do some business.'

'Cold-hearted?' He looked back to the spot where they'd just been engaged in a heated clench. 'Did that feel cold-hearted to you?'

'Your tax forms are ready for signature,' she said proudly. She had everything sitting in a neat pile on the corner of his desk. Since he'd stopped her momentum, they might as well get things taken care of now. She was going to have to screw up her courage all over again before she went after Hawk. She plucked a pen off the desk and passed it to Jake along with the forms. 'Sign here and here,' she instructed, pointing with her finger.

'Now who's cold-hearted?' He leant across the desk towards her. 'Come on. Give me another kiss.'

The way he said it, all low and seductive, made her waver. He just looked so delectable. His hair was tussled, his eyes were sparkling, and that dimple in his chin wouldn't stop. Roma could feel herself succumbing. What would one little kiss hurt?

Her plans! If she let him kiss her again, she'd never go after Hawk. With Jake, one kiss always led to two. Two led to three. Three led to fondling. Fondling led to groping. Etcetera, etcetera . . .

Oh, Missy was going to owe her big time.

'Hey!' she said, slapping her hand on the table. She was behind the desk. Ergo, she was the one in charge. 'No vo-di-o-do until we finish this. I've already had to file for one extension. Come on, Jake.'

He jumped at the loud *whap*! 'Spoilsport.'

She sighed. 'I did this for you. I thought you'd be happy to get it finished.'

His hands dropped limply to his sides. 'I am. I just didn't get to see you all weekend.'

'I'm not going anywhere.' She tilted her head, letting her blonde hair sway. She was wearing her killer boots, sexy jeans and a rather tight knit top. She emphasised the fact by pulling her shoulder blades together and thrusting out her boobs. For good measure, she wiggled her shoulders. 'Help me get these loose ends tied up, and we can go make out all you want.'

His eyes lit up, and he started towards her. She held up her hand, though, and his shoulders slumped. He dropped into the chair, looking like an uncomfortable fourth grader who'd been called into the principal's office. He didn't like being on that side of the desk, she knew. Numbers and finances were as painful to him as lunges, dips and running were to her.

Just the thought of it made her devilish side laugh. *Weren't paybacks a bitch?*

That doesn't mean you have to be one, her angel chastised.

Roma sat down in her chair, refusing to waver. He never did.

'This is what you owe for state,' she said, using the pen as a pointer this time. 'And this is for federal.'

He finally looked.

And he turned a little green.

'That can't be right.'

She bristled. 'Excuse me?'

His gaze quickly lifted.

167

'I'm not saying it's wrong.' He held up his hands defensively in case she came across the desk at him. He'd made that mistake once before.

Just once.

'I guess I'm a little surprised,' he admitted.

'You wouldn't be if you'd listened to what I've been telling you.' Feeling bad, she started to unfold and flatten the receipts he'd given her. She hated this part of her job. 'I've been trying to warn you.'

'I know.' He raked a hand through his hair, tussling it even further. He scowled as if looking at the numbers hurt. 'I didn't realise it was that bad, though. That's ... That's downright ugly.'

'I know,' she said, commiserating. She rubbed her palm over a crumpled gas receipt.

She truly didn't like being the messenger of bad news. She much preferred to be the hero. There was nothing like telling people they were in for a refund. Refunds brought flowers, kisses and sometimes chocolate. A balance due, however, could bring weeping, teeth gnashing and sometimes puking. She had a trash can at the ready, just in case.

She tried to ease the shock. 'It's pretty steep, but I've come up with some tax strategies to stop you from getting "surprised" in the future.'

He turned a woeful look on her. 'Let's use them now.'

'Sorry. Too late.' She cautiously slid the company chequebook across the desk. 'Don't dwell on it. Just write the cheques. Do it fast – like pulling off a bandage.'

She remembered all too well how that tactic had worked for her.

Jake winced as he signed his name, and she couldn't watch. Busying herself, she began unfolding the hotel receipt. He'd folded it into nearly a little ball in order to fit it into his wallet. It formed a little tent on her desk when she finally got it opened. He cursed, and she knew he was through. Reaching over, she plucked the cheques away before the ink could dry. Quickly, she tucked them into their respective envelopes.

'I'm sorry,' she said.

'I need that kiss now.'

That sad, puppy-dog look made him even harder to resist – and he was such a good kisser. She felt herself weakening.

'Just one more thing,' she said, less forceful this time.

'But that hurt,' he said, honing in on her weakness. 'I'm in need of comfort.'

'I know. You'll probably need it even more after this.' She settled her elbows on the desk and folded her hands. As company owner, it was his job to manage the business. As his accountant, it was her responsibility to let him know when things weren't working. She took a deep breath. 'We need to talk about your cash flow. It's getting a bit tight.'

She braced herself for a response.

One never came.

There was no sharp intake of breath, no whiplash of the neck and no protests that it couldn't be true. There wasn't even an admission that he was aware of the fact.

Her brow furrowed. 'Jake. I just told you that it's getting hard to pay your bills. Don't you think you should do something about that?'

He let one eyebrow lift and smiled like the cat who'd caught the canary. 'Now who hasn't been listening?'

Roma blinked. 'What? Who me?'

'Yes, you. I'm working on a marketing strategy. I've told you about it several times.'

She quickly searched her memory banks. She prided herself on her nearly photographic recall, but this so-called marketing strategy rang no bells. 'You've told me of no such thing.'

Proud as punch, he relaxed back in his chair. This

time, there was no discomfort in his slouch. It was more like a king settling into his throne – even if he was sitting on the wrong side of the desk. 'Liz,' he said simply.

'Liz?'

The Lizard struck again. Irritation seeped into Roma's system. She'd had just about enough of that woman. Liz this ... Liz that ... 'I don't see how she's going to help with your company's finances unless she's got an MBA tucked inside her athletic bra.'

He shook his head and made a tsking sound. 'Think outside the square box, accounting queen.'

'Jake,' she growled in warning.

'OK, OK.' He bounded out of his chair, obviously excited about his master plan. 'We've been drawing fewer new members since the big chain gyms have come to town. They advertise like gangbusters, and sheer volume allows them to undercut our membership rates.'

'I know,' Roma said succinctly. She'd seen half a dozen commercials for their competitors last night as she'd been watching her favourite evening soap opera. Loyalty had made her stick her tongue out at every one of them. She'd become quite attached to their little gym.

'One on one, we can't compete,' he conceded.

'But the all-powerful Liz can?' Roma squashed the propped-up receipt under her palm, trying to get it to lie flat. 'What do you expect her to do, Jake? Beat them up?'

'In a way.' He folded his arms across his chest and leant back against his filing cabinet. 'Liz is our marketing tool.'

Roma scowled. She'd known that woman was hot. 'You're going to use her as a spokeswoman.'

He shook his head. 'Not quite. The plan isn't to target the whole consumer market, just the most profitable niche. We'll start at the Midwest Fitness Show. When Liz competes, all her gear is going to be stamped with the Jake's Gym logo. When she's out there doing backflips, handsprings and one-armed push-ups, she'll be wearing Jake's Gym clothes.'

So Liz was going to sell out. The publicity slut.

'You're going to try word of mouth.' Roma couldn't help it if she didn't sound all that excited. She'd seen that technique used before. It rarely worked. Irritated, she grabbed the phone book and dropped it on the crinkly piece of paper. It landed with a satisfying thud.

Jake wiggled his finger at her as he approached the desk once again. 'You don't understand the fitness world, Goldie. Hard-core fitness freaks and bodybuilders like to talk. Got any idea what they like to talk about the most?'

Uh, let her think. Could it possibly be ... *Liz*? God, she'd heard just about as much about that woman as she could stand. Roma's gaze slid down to the receipt she'd been fighting. The corner had gotten folded under. With a growl, she slid her finger under it to straighten it out.

Jake planted his hands on the desk and leaned over her, looking cocky as hell. 'They want to know who's getting results, how they're doing it, and where. It's the perfect set-up for us.'

Roma hardly heard him – because she suddenly felt set-up herself. Distressed, she stared at what she'd just uncovered. Someone had scribbled on the corner of the hotel receipt.

In pink ink.

Suddenly, she found it hard to breathe. She recognised that ink. She'd seen it on this desk enough times before – but always on notes.

Intimate, lovey-dovey notes.

Oh, God. How stupid could she have been?

Jake was too wrapped up in his grand plans to notice her change in mood. 'That's when we strike. We sell ourselves as a small, exclusive, intimate gym. We'll hype our training programme and our ability to give individualised attention. Believe me, the word will get out fast once we have some credibility behind us. The high-end market is going to want us bad.'

Roma's eyes were going dry as she stared at the pink loop-de-loops. Apparently somebody else wanted him bad, too. Liz's handwriting was on his *hotel* receipt. He'd taken her to Chicago with him.

'So what do you think?'

She thought she could go over this desk to strangle him.

'Roma?' He looked at her expectantly.

She turned a hard look up at him. 'Individualised attention,' she said numbly.

It was the only thing she remembered of what he'd said.

'That was why you came here. Right?'

She felt so used. So that *was* his modus operandi with his female clients.

'You wanted personal attention.'

She had. She'd just thought it was an exclusive arrangement.

'You wanted a competent trainer.'

She'd wanted *him*.

He rapped his knuckles against the wood, jolting her. 'Well, that's the plan. We hit the high-paying, elite training market, and we hit them hard. It just all keys off of Liz.'

Liz, Liz, Liz.

Roma's head hurt. Liz and Jake were a team – in every sense of the word. And why not? They were both prime, fit athletes. What had he even been doing with her? Slumming? 'That's why she needs to do well at the show,' Roma said flatly.

He smiled. 'I knew you were listening.'

She'd listened to the parts she wanted to.

He leant forwards. 'Come on, give me that kiss now.'

Was he crazy? She felt more like grabbing that trash can.

Reflexively, she jumped out of her chair. 'I need to find Hawk.'

Jake stopped short. 'Now?' he said in surprise.

'Right now.'

Roma's legs felt weak, but she stormed by him.

Seeing the look on her face, he automatically stepped back. 'Roma?' he called as she yanked open the door.

She kept right on going. She needed to think, and she couldn't do that when he was hovering over her. In her fevered mind, all she could see was red.

Make that pink.

The thoughts and emotions were overwhelming, but one thing was clear. She was spoiling for a fight.

She began her search in the weights room. Hawk wasn't there, which was unusual. The muscle-head. Where was he? She had more than enough courage to face him right now. She needed to blow off some steam.

She walked down the hallway to the aerobics room and saw Missy. 'Hey, Miss!' she called. 'Have you seen . . .'

Her question died on her lips when her friend brushed right on by as if she hadn't even seen her. She darted into the women's locker room, and the door shut with a bang. Roma's eyes narrowed. It looked as if she wasn't the only one having a bad day. She started to follow her friend, but instinct made her turn towards the janitor's closet instead.

Missy's hair had been mussed.

That Neanderthal!

With her hands clenched into fists, Roma marched up to the door. She caught the handle and gave it a turn. She'd barely opened it a crack when, suddenly, she was caught. The world went dark as she was pulled inside. She stumbled and landed against a hot

173

wall of muscle. Thick arms of steel wrapped around her waist, and she found herself sealed against a male body.

'I knew you'd come back.'

Before she could utter a peep, a hand fisted into her hair and a hot mouth found hers in the darkness. At that point, Roma could have sworn the world turned upside down. The body against hers was hot and urgent, and so was the kiss. A tongue swept deep into her mouth and, with her emotions so raw, her senses came alive. In the darkness, there was nothing but touch.

And she was surrounded by it. She felt tiny and feminine as a male hand caught her bottom and tilted her hips. She let out a soft sound as a huge, excited erection ground against her.

'I'm sorry for whatever I did.'

She started to say something, but then he was kissing her again. As kisses went, this one about knocked her socks off. A sizzle shot through her belly, and she shivered violently.

A growl erupted from the man holding her, and the hand on her bottom squeezed tighter. Roma went right up onto her tiptoes at the sensation. Suddenly, the world spun again and she found herself pressed up against the wall. The big male body leaned into her, letting her take its weight. She found herself clutching his back as his mouth ate at hers avariciously.

Oh, Lordy. It was like a whirlwind she just couldn't hold back.

And he wasn't slowing down.

She flinched when a big hand came up to catch her breast. It covered her possessively and ground her in a slow circle. Roma couldn't stop her body's instinctive reaction. Her nipple pressed into his palm, and a fire erupted in the pit of her belly. The embrace was so carnal, she couldn't stay immune.

Unable to help herself, she raked her fingers down his back. 'Hawk,' she moaned.

He went still. Slowly, his tongue dipped to evaluate her taste. The hand at her butt squeezed tentatively, and the one at her breast measured her size.

Like a flash, he backed off. She heard him scrambling around, and then the light was suddenly on. Its glare made her eyes clamp shut.

'Roma!' he barked.

She winced as she forced her eyes open a slit. The poor guy looked poleaxed.

'Yeah, it's me,' she said as she wiped the back of her hand across her lips. 'Maybe you should check the next time you yank someone in here to maul them.'

'Oh, fuck!' He backed away from her as far as he could get, but the space was limited. 'Jake's going to kill me.'

Wide-eyed, they stared at each other.

'What are you doing in here?' he finally asked.

'Looking for you – but not for that,' she quickly clarified.

Silence permeated the tiny room. Roma, for one, was trying to get her thoughts centred. She'd been in a lather when she'd stormed in here, but that kiss had been a rather effective 'get-yourself-together' slap across the face. She ran her tongue across her lips. They still tingled. Say what she would about the man, he certainly could kiss. From the other limited moves he'd made, he had quite the talent in other arenas, too.

'Don't do that,' he said, tearing his gaze away from her mouth. He ran a hand across his bald pate. He looked as green as she felt. 'I thought you were Missy.'

She grimaced. 'I noticed.'

'Why didn't you say something?'

'I couldn't. Your tongue was halfway down my throat.'

He swallowed hard, and she took a quick peek below his waistband. He really had thought she was Missy.

'Hey!' he snapped, catching her. 'Eyes up.'

Her gaze popped up to meet his. She found slashes of red colour lighting his chiselled cheekbones.

'This never happened,' he declared.

'Never,' she agreed. She wiped her damp palms on her thighs. Nobody could ever find out that they'd been necking in the closet – even if it had been a mistake.

Although, she had to admit it was an intriguing mistake. Her legs felt like spaghetti, and the fire in her belly still smouldered. Whew! No wonder her young friend hadn't been able to resist.

Hawk pointed towards the door. 'You leave first. I'll wait a few minutes so nobody sees us together.'

Roma nearly bolted, but thoughts of Missy made her remember her mission. Besides, she had no desire to go back and face Jake. The traitor. The cheating two-timer. Feeling her ire return, she crossed her arms over her chest. 'I need a few answers out of you first, Barney.'

'We can talk later,' he said, catching her by the shoulder. He started to usher her out when he realised what she'd called him. The double take he did was so emphatic, he nearly gave himself whip-lash. *What did you call me?*'

'Barney,' Roma said, feeling feistier than she should. 'That is your name, isn't it? Or is it Herman?'

He looked at her strangely.

'I figure it must be something embarrassing, otherwise you'd tell Missy.' She cocked her head and let her hair swing forwards. 'So what is it? Archibald? Fred? Harvey?'

'You're crazy.'

'Oh, come on. You can tell me. Kisser to kissee.'

'Hey,' he said, looking somewhat panicked. 'We

agreed that never happened. Missy's upset with me enough as it is.'

Roma's eyes narrowed. She'd thought Missy had looked a little ragged. 'What did you do?'

He shrugged uncomfortably. 'I don't know.'

Ignorance was no excuse. Jake had just cut her to the quick, and now she found out that this big lummox had hurt her friend? Reaching out, Roma poked him with her index finger. 'Tell me the truth.'

'Ow! *I don't know.*' He rubbed the spot on his chest, and all the muscles in his upper body seemed to clench and release. 'I wish I did.'

The sadness in his voice sounded authentic. Even more, the worry lines on his forehead couldn't be faked. Pensively, Roma glanced to the door. Maybe this guy was telling the truth. How novel. 'Was she just in here with you?'

He swallowed hard. 'Yeah. That's why I thought you were her. I thought she'd come back.'

'Did she say anything when she left?'

'No!' he said, the word bursting from his lips. He was obviously upset. He lifted both arms and laced his fingers behind his neck. The position made a riot of muscles pop out in his chest and arms. 'She just looked at me with those big brown eyes and shook her head.'

Roma hesitated. 'Were you two ... you know?'

'What?'

She rubbed her hands together. Why did she always seem to end up talking sex with this man? 'Were you getting down to business?'

'Well, yeah,' he said, blunt as always. 'We snuck in here like we always do. Things were getting pretty hot and heavy when she decided to stop. She's never done that before. I don't know what I did wrong.'

Roma knew. 'It's not what you did. It's what you didn't do.'

'I'm not in the mood for riddles, Blondie.'

She looked at him crossly. He really didn't have a clue. 'I hate to tell you this, Hawk, but your strategy is flawed. Relationships aren't simple and straightforward.'

She was learning that better than anyone.

'Missy wants more.'

'More?' His arms dropped slowly. 'What do you mean "more"?'

'I mean more than just sex,' Roma said. She could be just as blunt as he could. 'She wants a boyfriend, not just a lover.'

'She has a boyfriend,' he said bitterly. 'That lazy ass . . .'

She blew out a puff of air. 'Oh, please. Danny is yesterday's news.'

Hawk's look focused on her so hard, it nearly knocked her over. 'Say that again?'

Roma could have kicked herself. 'Crap. I wasn't supposed to say anything.'

He came at her, and she backed up until she was pressed against the wall. The toes of his shoes bumped against hers, and she had to crane her neck back to look up into his face. 'What do you know?' he demanded.

'Nothing.'

He planted a hand on each side of her head and leant closer until his nose was scant inches from hers. 'What . . . do . . . you . . . know?'

Roma squeaked. She was beginning to remember why she'd been nervous about doing this. He was a big, scary man. 'She's leaving him at the end of the month. She's going out on her own.'

His head snapped back. 'Her own?'

She pressed her lips together stubbornly. She'd already said too much.

'Why didn't she tell me? She can move in with me.'

She couldn't let that pass without comment. 'No, she can't.'

His eyes narrowed dangerously. 'Why not?'

'She's not happy with you either!'

He looked stricken. Absolutely stricken. The tough guy act vaporised, and he stood before her a wounded man.

'She's not?' His hands dropped slowly to his sides, and his gaze went to the door. 'But things were going so good.'

Boy, that sounded familiar. Roma had thought the same about her and Jake. 'In the sack, maybe,' she said bitterly.

Apparently that was all men thought about.

Hawk pulled back from her with his hands clenching and unclenching at his sides. 'Well ... What does she want? How do I fix things? *Do I even have a chance?*'

That was a good question. A great question, in fact.

'I don't know,' Roma said. 'Are you willing to talk to her?'

'We talk.'

She rolled her eyes. 'She doesn't even know your name. She doesn't know what you do for a living. How can you expect her to move in with you? Have you asked her? Women aren't mind readers, you know.'

If they were, she would have known what was going on between Jake and Liz a long time ago.

'Neither are men,' he barked. 'How am I supposed to know all this?'

'Ooof,' Roma growled in frustration. 'No wonder she walked out on you. Aren't you even the least bit curious about her? Do you know what she's studying in school? What she wants to do once she gets her degree? Come on! What does she like on her hot chocolate?'

He paled. 'Something in the medical field, I think. I've seen her schoolbooks. And she likes the little marshmallows!'

So he had been paying attention. 'Do you want to

know more?' Roma asked, honing in on the heart of the matter.

'Of course, I do. I want to know everything.' He ran a hand across the top of his head. 'I just ... I just don't know how to get her to tell me.'

The confession hit a little too close to home.

'You open up. You let her get close, and you'll get closer to her. It's called intimacy,' Roma said with a sigh. She wished she was as good at taking her advice as she was at giving it. 'Get used to the concept or get used to standing in this closet alone.'

Alone. The one word hit them both hard.

Hawk looked particularly unsteady on his feet, and Roma instinctively reached out to catch him. She didn't know what she planned to do. If he went down, she was going to tumble right along with him. The guy had to be pushing two hundred and thirty pounds.

She patted him on the arm. It was like patting a rock. 'I don't know why, but I'm actually rooting for you, you big brute. So get off your butt and straighten things out with her. I like to see my friends happy, too.'

It would be nice if someone around here could make a go of it. She'd just thought it would be her and Jake. Feeling depressed again, Roma turned for the door.

'Wait!'

Hawk surprised her when he reached out and caught her. Scowling, she peered over her shoulder. He had her by the loop at the back of her jeans. She had to stutter-step backwards as he pulled her towards him. 'Hey!'

'Give me specifics.' His fingers tightened, refusing to let her go.

'Specifics?'

'I need to know what to do. Step by step. You tell me, and I'll do it.'

The sincerity in his voice stopped Roma in her

tracks. She looked into his dark menacing face and saw something that nearly set her on her tush. Vulnerability. He looked almost scared. 'Are you serious?'

He merely glared. It was enough to make her shake in her boots.

'OK,' she said soothingly. He really was an intimidating man – but she was hardly the expert at this. She tapped her toe nervously, trying to figure out where to start. 'Just don't jump her first thing you see her. Try something novel like asking how her day went.'

'I can do that.' He nodded as if making a mental note. 'What else?'

She shook her head in amazement. 'Romance her, Hawk. Buy her flowers. Take her on a date.'

He turned an even whiter shade of pale. 'You're going to have to help me with that. Coach me or something.'

'For a date?'

He pinned her with a look. 'Blondie, I've never been with someone like Missy before. She's a classy, educated lady. The kind of women I've been with in the past were satisfied with a six pack of beer and a romp in the back of my truck.'

Roma blinked. With him, that actually sounded like fun. She wondered just what moves he was capable of making in the bed of that pickup. She shook her head to clear the image. 'I can help you do better than that.'

He nodded hurriedly. 'I'll do whatever you tell me.'

That was an intriguing concept. 'Anything?'

'Anything. I want her.'

She scowled. 'You want her in your bed.'

'I want her every way I can get her.'

At least he was honest – and she couldn't help but feel a kinship with him. He had Danny to deal with. She, unfortunately, had Liz.

'All right. It's a deal,' she said, sticking out her hand. 'I'll help you get the girl.'

He caught her hand in a nearly bone-crushing grip. His eyes narrowed. 'What do you want in return?'

Such an uncivilised man! She looked up at him as haughtily as a woman nearly a foot shorter could. 'I want you to treat her right. If you hurt her, so help me, I'll hunt you down.'

A smile suddenly appeared on his face. It made such a difference, Roma felt her heart rate pump up a pace. Whew, if the guy grew some hair and smiled every now and then, he'd be a heartbreaker.

'You don't scare me.' He gave a tug on their enjoined hands, and she found herself plastered against his front.

She was stunned when he kissed her again. This time, it was under a hundred watts of artificial light, and he didn't rush it. His arms circled around her, and her breasts plumped up against his massive chest. His lips were curious this time, more exploring. He nibbled on her lower lip, and she gasped when he began to suck on it.

He took the advantage to go in deeper. Her knees betrayed her first. She relaxed against him and felt bold enough to reach up and cup the back of his bald head. He ground his erection against her, and she shuddered. Oh yeah, bald could be sexy.

Slowly, he pulled away. He shook his head as if their chemistry surprised him, too. 'That's not like kissing my sister at all.'

Stupefied, Roma wiped her thumb across her lower lip. She was pressing her legs together so tightly, she was standing nearly knock-kneed. 'If we were related that would be illegal.'

'But a lot of fun,' he said, patting her on the bottom. 'Thanks for the heads-up and the offer to help. I need it.'

She stepped back gingerly. She wasn't so sure of

that. He seemed to do fine on his own. 'We'll come up with a plan to win her. Don't worry.'

'I won't.' He nodded, this time more confidently. The lines of stress were gone from his forehead. 'You're a keeper, Roma Hanson. If that trainer of yours ever does you wrong, you come to me.'

He cupped her chin and looked her dead in the eye. 'I'll set him straight.'

The idea was tempting. 'I just might take you up on that offer.'

Hawk's eyes narrowed. 'What's the problem?'

'Pink ink.'

Chapter Ten

Jake was working on the schedule with Tito when he saw Roma coming down the hallway. As one, all his senses went on the alert. He still couldn't quite figure out what had happened back in his office. They'd been getting along fine until, all of a sudden, she'd seemed to snap. When she'd stormed out on him, she'd been practically breathing fire.

For the life of him, he couldn't figure out what he'd done. Or what he'd said. Hell, maybe it hadn't even been him. Maybe this thing with Hawk was more serious than he'd thought.

She'd certainly been gone longer than he'd expected. He didn't know if that was a good thing or not. At least she seemed to still be in one piece. The expression on her face, though, was somewhat dazed.

Oh, boy. He could just see those two going at it. Talk about a mismatched pair. Hawk was big and tough as steel. Roma didn't have size on her side, but she was stubborn and feisty. Once that woman got something into her head, there was no holding her back.

He'd hate to even hazard a guess what had gone on between the two.

So help him, though. If Hawk had hurt her feelings, they were going to have words.

'I think Hawk won,' Tito whispered.

Jake hated to admit it, but the kid was probably right. 'At the very least, it was a tie.'

He watched Roma as she slipped back into his office. Something was wrong.

Very wrong.

His gut clenched. Anxiously, he pushed himself away from the counter. 'I've got to find out what's going on.'

'Yeah,' Tito said. 'It's a tough job, but somebody's got to do it.'

'Get your own good-lookin' blonde, little man,' Jake said as he walked away.

'You could help,' the kid called. 'Why don't you try sending some of the cardio babes my way?'

Jake waved. That actually wasn't a bad idea. The girls were somewhat lost now that he was 'taken'.

And he was definitely taken with the little dynamo who'd crash-landed in his gym. He couldn't quite remember what life had been like before Roma Hanson. Probably less funny, more boring, and a whole lot safer. She certainly kept him on his toes.

Not to mention the other parts of his body that were on constant alert whenever she was around.

This mercurial mood, though ... This was different. It wasn't normal, and it wasn't her. Something had set her off. He needed to find out what was wrong so he could fix it. He didn't like seeing her this upset.

His steps quickened towards his office, but he noticed that the shades were shut. It made him hesitate. Maybe her confrontation with Hawk had gone worse than he'd thought. Damn that man. If he'd made her cry, he was going to pay. She'd just been trying to help.

Jake tamped down his anger. He'd deal with that bully later. Right now, his Roma needed him. He tapped on the door lightly and opened it. 'Hey, Goldie,' he called softly.

Paperwork shuffled, and she sprang up from behind the desk. When she saw it was him, she slammed her briefcase shut with a bang. She was as protective of that thing as he was of his filing cabinet.

'Sorry. I didn't mean to surprise you. Is everything all right?'

She skittered away from him and shoved her hand behind her back. 'Fffnnn.'

Was that supposed to be 'fine'? Because she didn't look fine. He paused briefly in the doorway, trying to figure out what to do. She looked ready to cry, and that made him nervous as hell. He'd never seen her cry, not even close.

'What did Hawk say?' he asked, coming into the room and shutting the door behind him.

'Nuffing.' She swallowed hard and waved him away with her one free hand. 'Leave me alone.'

'Like hell.' He stomped towards the desk. 'What did he do?'

'Nothing,' she said more clearly. 'Hawk did nothing.'

'OK. Then what did I do?'

Her eyes threw sparks. 'Don't play stupid, Jake. It doesn't work on you.'

He planted his hands on his hips. He'd never claimed to be able to figure out what was going on inside that head of hers, but this time she had him totally baffled. On the one hand, she seemed to want a fight. On the other, though, she was backing away from him and acting like she wanted to hide.

'You're going to have to give me a clue.'

'A clue? You want a clue?' With her free hand, she grabbed the corner of a piece of paper that was tucked under the phone book. It let out a squeak as she yanked it free.

'How's this for a clue?' she snapped. 'You went to Chicago with Liz!'

He stopped dead in his tracks. Oh, shit.

'Don't try to lie,' Roma fumed. 'Her ink on this thing is more incriminating than lipstick on your collar.'

He glanced at the hotel receipt that she waved in

front of his face. A bright pink scribble shone up in the corner.

Hell.

He was caught. Then again, he never should have kept the truth from her in the first place.

'You're right,' he admitted. He held up his hands to placate her when she let out a screech. 'Liz called me on Saturday morning saying she wanted to go with me. I thought it was a good idea. It's her competition. She's the one who needs to be comfortable with things there.'

'Well, I'm not comfortable with things here!'

'I knew you wouldn't like it.'

'So you lied to me?' Roma roared.

She shook the receipt so hard, the paper snapped. 'You've been lying all along, haven't you? You two-timing snake. There's only one hotel room charge on this thing.'

Jake was starting to get a little hot, too. She had no reason to be jumping to conclusions like that. She should know him better by now. 'That's right. There's one charge – for her room.'

Roma tilted her head. 'And where did you stay, pray tell? On the sofa? Give me a break.'

'Yeah, I stayed on the sofa – the sofa at my sister's house.'

She went silent, but she met his gaze head on. 'I don't believe you. If you'd planned on doing that, you wouldn't have reserved a hotel room in the first place.'

'This is getting old real fast,' he growled. 'You don't believe me? Maybe you'll believe "the other woman".'

Stomping towards the phone, he hit the speaker button and got a dial tone. Before she could say another word, he punched in a phone number. He watched her steadily, and she was the first to look away.

The call had made her wary.

'Hi.'

Jake's head snapped back to the phone. That wasn't quite the other woman he'd expected. 'Marly?'

'Who is this?'

'It's Uncle Jake.'

'Uncle Jake!'

'What are you doing answering the phone, peanut? Where's your mom?'

'She's out back. Tommy turned on the hose and her flowers got all wet. Do you want to talk to her?'

'No,' he said quickly. One disaster in the family at a time was plenty. Besides, nobody got to the heart of the truth like a four-year-old. 'You'll do just fine. I want you to talk to my friend, Roma.'

'Roma?'

'You remember. I told you about her.'

'Oh!' Marly said dramatically. 'The lady who got her hair stuck.'

Jake shot Roma a look. She looked embarrassed and somewhat uneasy.

'That's right.' He crossed his arms over his chest and watched her unflinchingly. 'She wants to hear all about what we did together this weekend.'

'When you stayed with us?'

'That's right – *when I stayed with you.*' Bless the little pipsqueak. He hadn't even had to prompt her. 'I think she's a little jealous.'

It might have been his imagination, but he could have sworn Roma turned green.

'Jealous?' his niece asked. 'Because she didn't get to come to my tea party?'

Roma's gaze flicked towards him, and he shrugged. What could he say? He had a weakness for cute blondes.

'Tell her about the fort, Marly,' he encouraged.

Giggles sounded from the other end of the line. 'Uncle Jake slept on the couch and we built a fort around him. He forgot about it when he got up the next morning, and he stubbed his toe. Mommy pinched his ear because he said some bad words.'

Jake watched as Roma sagged like a puppet just cut loose from its strings. She dipped her head and bit her lower lip. He didn't need any more proof that he hadn't lied.

'Does it feel better now, Uncle Jake?' his niece asked sweetly.

'Lots better, peanut. Thanks for asking. I'd better go now.'

'Me, too. Tommy just ran through the living room with mud on his shoes. I think Mommy's going to pinch his ear, too.'

'Be good, kiddo.'

'OK.'

Click. The line went dead without so much as a goodbye. The dial tone hummed, and Jake reached out to disconnect.

'In case you hadn't noticed, my sister's place is a nut house,' he said succinctly. 'That's why I hadn't planned on staying there.'

Roma looked thoroughly chastened.

He caught her chin and made her look at him. 'Nothing happened between Liz and me. I told you before, she's just a client.'

Unable to stay angry with her, he gently rubbed his thumb across her lips. 'You're not,' he said gruffly. 'You're more.'

Her eyes went all watery. 'Why didn't you just tell me?'

'After that swimsuit fiasco? I thought it would be better not to.' He shrugged. 'I was wrong.'

She blinked rapidly. 'So was I.'

Shakily, she backed away until she was standing in front of the filing cabinet. Using that one hand, she wiped her eyes. 'I'm sorry. I'm such a spaz when I overreact.'

'I'm sorry, too. I should have been up front with you.' He cocked his head. 'Are we OK now?'

She nodded mutely.

He approached her cautiously. 'What about Hawk? I'm not going find him torn into little pieces some-where, am I?'

That, finally, got a Roma-like response. She let out a nervous laugh. 'He is a little the worse for wear.'

Jake felt like he'd been through the wringer, too. Reaching out, he touched her hair. Slowly, he leant forwards. The kiss they shared was gentle, but emotional. He pulled her into his arms and held her close.

She jerked, though, when his hands started to slide down. Trying to cover her reaction, she patted his chest as she stepped away.

He didn't let her get far.

'What are you hiding, Goldie?'

Her eyes went wide. 'What do you mean?'

'I mean, "What are you hiding?". You shoved something behind your back the moment I stepped inside the door.' He'd tried to be subtle, but that had gotten him nowhere. He reached for her hand again, but she twisted away in a move that would have done Chubby Checker proud.

'It's nothing,' she said.

He had a good grip on her wrist, but that was it. With that flexibility of hers, she was able to twist and contort in unimaginable ways to avoid him.

'Come on. Just show me,' he coaxed. 'Did Hawk give you something?'

'No! *Hawk didn't give me anything*. We didn't *do* anything.' She rolled her hand in circles and bent her arm in a way that would have separated his shoulder if he'd tried.

'Give me a peek.'

'No. It's ... It's secret accountant stuff.'

'I won't tell.' He tugged on her arm, setting her off balance. She took an involuntary step forwards and crashed into his chest. Smiling in victory, he wrapped his arms around her and reached for her hands.

She wasn't going down without a fight. When his hands ran down, she hopped up on her tiptoes. When his hands ventured upwards, she dropped to a squat. She was basically rubbing herself all over him, and it shot his concentration all to hell. Before he could come to his senses, she bounced on her toes again. Only this time, she headbutted him in the chin.

'Oops. Sorry,' she said, still struggling to evade his wandering hands.

Jake saw stars – actually it was more of an explosion of white-hot lights. She'd clipped him in just the right place to weaken his knees. He felt them crumple and, on the way down, he remembered the reason why he hadn't gone into boxing.

He had no chin.

The two of them went tumbling but, through his hazy senses, he tried to protect Roma. They landed with a whoosh with her right on top of his lungs. He gasped for air.

'Jake!' she cried. She planted her hands beside his head and levered herself off of him.

Still disorientated and oxygen-deprived, he was unable to respond.

His eardrums shuddered when she screeched his name again.

'Jaaaaaaake!'

'Stop screaming at me,' he wheezed. 'I'm right here.'

'Are you OK?' She patted her hands down his shoulders and arms. 'Oh, my gosh! I've done it again. I didn't mean to hurt you.'

'I'm all right,' he said, closing his eyes to try to get his equilibrium.

'No, no! Don't fall asleep.' She slapped his cheek. 'Jake!'

'Stop hitting me,' he said grumpily.

When he opened his eyes, he saw that hers had gone wide with regret. In a flash, the slap turned into a caress. Her fingertips glided over his cheekbone and down the line of his jaw. With a touch as light as a feather, she traced the red spot on his chin that marked the place where she'd hit him.

'I'm sorry,' she whispered. 'For everything.'

There was just so much a man could take. Her blonde hair was spilling like a curtain about him. Her eyes were wide and gentle. Most importantly, her body was lying on top of his like a blanket. He reached up, cupped the back of her head, and pulled her down.

'I deserve that kiss now.'

At the touch of their lips, he knew this wasn't just going to be a peck. This was one kiss he wanted to savour. She felt too good. She tasted too good. 'Sweet,' he murmured.

He adjusted his head for a better angle and found it. With a groan, Roma turned from a soft, well-used comforter to an electric blanket cranked on high. She squirmed on top of him, and his arms tightened around her. Her fingers slid into his hair, and he was suddenly happy that the shades were closed.

With a growl, he grabbed her and rolled. He settled her underneath him and dragged kisses from her lips, to the point of her chin, and down to the soft skin of her throat. Groaning, she wrapped one leg around the back of his thigh. Determinedly, he rocked against her. With them, one kiss always led to two. Two led to fondling. Fondling led to groping . . .

He found the pulse at the side of her neck and licked. Her neck arched, and her head ground against the floor.

In that moment, though, she froze.

He felt her withdrawal and he froze, too. 'Roma?'

She didn't respond. He pulled back quickly to look at her. She had the strangest look on her face – one he couldn't even begin to interpret. Ever so cautiously, she lifted her hand to feel the back of her head.

Her hand stilled, and she let out a long groan. 'Oh, nooooo.'

Oh, God. Had she banged her head?

'What is it, baby? Are you OK?' Following her hand, he gently investigated the back of her scalp. His heart lurched when he felt something – only it wasn't wetness like blood. Confused, he rolled her on her side and looked at the gooey mass. The light quickly dawned.

'A Snickers bar?'

She gasped dramatically. 'Chocolate? Here in the gym? No! It couldn't be.'

His eyes narrowed, and he looked at her accusingly.

'Who put that there?' she said with an innocent look plastered on her face.

He settled back onto his haunches. He'd known he'd tasted sweetness in her kiss. 'My suspicions point to that secret accountant stuff.'

He was off of her and moving towards her briefcase before she could scramble to her knees.

'No!' she cried. 'That's got ... um ... confidential information in there. You can't look.'

'Huh.' He flipped back the lid. 'Maybe you should have locked it then.'

She darted towards him, but he held her away with a straight-arm move from his football days.

'What have we here?' he said. He plucked an incriminating wrapper out of the inside of her briefcase. 'And you thought I was cheating.'

Her eyes sprang open wide. '*I didn't cheat!*'

He waved the wrapper in front of her.

'Oh, you mean that. It's not mine,' she said quickly. 'I was just holding it for somebody.'

'Sure. That's what they all say.'

He felt around the inside of the briefcase and

triggered open a secret panel. Inside he found two more wrappers – both containing illegal candy bars. He shook his head and made a tsking sound. 'Roma, Roma, Roma. Refined sugar. You know this isn't on your diet.'

'I was upset,' she said, taking a new tactic. 'I couldn't help myself.'

His head swivelled towards her. 'So this is my fault?'

'No, no. It was just ... I'm a chocolate addict,' she admitted, throwing herself at his mercy. 'I need rehabilitation. Yeah, that's it.'

'Rehabilitation?' He let out a snort. 'What you need is a spanking.'

The one, simple word brought her head up. Their gazes connected, and the air snapped.

'You wouldn't dare,' she said in a scandalised voice.

Normally, he wouldn't. But with her ...

'You think not?' Moving slowly behind her, he gave her bottom a swift tap. 'You deserve twenty lashes. At least.'

His touch lingered. Those lunges had done wonders for her gluteus maximus.

She let out a shriek of laughter and spun around, holding her bottom. Her eyes were dancing as she looked at him. 'You're not going to spank me.'

'After all the grief you've given to me today? Damn straight I am.' He'd gladly spend some one-on-one time with her tight little ass. She'd given up all her 'behind-the-desk' power when he'd discovered that candy bar.

She giggled uncontrollably. She blinked, though, when he moved to lock the door. At the sound of the click, the look on her face was absolutely priceless. There was shock, curiosity and excitement all at once.

He folded his arms over his chest and waited. The next call was hers.

Her gaze went from him to the locked door and back to him again.

'OK,' she said finally, taking him up on his dare. She bent over the desk and wiggled her hips at him saucily. 'Never let it be said that I didn't take the punishment I deserved.'

The pose stopped Jake dead in his tracks. The teasing had all been in fun, but seeing her splayed out like that ... thrusting her tush at him ... ready for him to spank her ... Holy shit.

He swallowed hard. It was suddenly getting very hot in here.

Roma wiggled her butt, watching his reaction closely. 'Come on, big boy, make me pay.'

His hard-on nearly jumped out of his pants.

She was challenging him. It was one of the things about her that turned him on the most. Over the past couple of months, her muscles weren't the only things that had been honed into shape. Her confidence had grown by leaps and bounds. She'd always been a hottie. The difference now was that she knew it.

And she liked to test her new-found sensuality out on him.

How lucky could one man get?

'Oh, you're going to pay,' he growled as he stepped up behind her. Before she could brace herself, he gave each of her rounded cheeks a sharp rap.

She flinched, but started giggling again. 'That tickles.'

The next one didn't.

Roma's fit of giggles turned into a surprised gasp when Jake's flat palm connected just a bit harder. Even through the denim of her jeans, she could feel the hot imprint of his hand. It burnt and pulsed, drawing all her attention down to that one spot.

'Three down,' he said sternly. 'Seventeen to go.'

'Seventeen?' She shifted, suddenly a bit uncertain.

That last one was smarting a bit more than she'd expected.

He waited, giving her the opportunity to call the whole thing to a stop. She didn't. Her curiosity was too strong. She'd heard of people who did this sort of thing. She'd certainly never tried, but with Jake ... She trusted him, and the sting was turning into a peculiar warmth.

She stayed put and was rewarded with three rapid-fire smacks on the butt. The sensation was startling. Groaning, she leant more heavily onto her forearms.

'Are you still willing to pay?' he asked, leaning over her.

He gave her another quick spank, and she jolted.

'Oh!' The heat was spreading across her bottom, into her crevice, and down between her legs. She pressed her thighs together. 'Oh, damn.'

She liked it.

'Roma?' he asked, waiting for her response.

She dropped her head in submission. 'Yes.'

He exhaled shakily. Reaching out, he ran his hands down her hips, tracing her shapely new curves. Even that gentle touch drove her crazy. The spankings had left her bottom hot and overly sensitive.

'God, these new jeans show off your ass to perfection.'

He caught her square on her right cheek, and she bucked. Her groan of pleasure filled the office.

'Why would you think that I'd cheat on you?' he asked. 'Look at you.'

'I'm sorry.' Her old hang-ups had gotten in the way. 'It won't happen again.'

She panted for air as he spanked her again.

'It better not,' he said. 'And no more cheating for you, either.'

She nearly panicked before she realised he was talking about the Snickers bar, not Hawk.

'It just happened,' she said. Both the chocolate *and* the kiss.

'Naughty girl.'

The words made her wiggle before him. She'd always wanted to be a bad girl – within reason, of course. Before she'd met him, the angel on her other shoulder had won too often. *The priss.* She should have experimented with her more adventurous side a long time ago.

I told you so, her devilish side said gleefully.

I am not a priss, her angel side huffed.

Roma's hips shifted left and right, trying to avoid the inevitable sting. He caught her at three different angles in quick succession, and she grabbed for the sides of the desk. 'What if I told you I've been smuggling those candy bars in for the last two-and-a-half months?'

He laughed. 'Greedy little thing, aren't you?'

She thrust her bottom up towards him, practically begging for the next lashing. Instead, he peeled her off the desk. Her knees were weak, so she leant back into him and gripped his thighs for support. He wasn't quite steady, either. He pulled her top off her and tossed it aside. He wrangled with her bra next. Like a slingshot, it flew towards the corner of the room.

Roma moaned when he reached around and thumbed her nipples. They were already hard.

'Back down in position,' he whispered into her ear. 'That confession just upped your punishment.'

She shivered in delight.

Compliant, she went down. She jerked up, though, when he reached around her for the tab of her zipper. Whoa! She rather liked that layer protecting her bare skin. It wasn't doing that good a job, but flesh on flesh might be a bit too brisk.

'Down,' he said calmly.

With a hand between her shoulder blades, he

gently pushed her back into position. She lay still as he unzipped her jeans. He pulled off her boots and worked the denim down over her hips. She gasped as the rough fabric abraded her sensitive skin.

He stopped and cupped her. 'The pink,' he said appreciatively.

She was wearing the pink panties she'd worn the first day she'd come to the gym. She still didn't know how he'd seen them, but they'd become somewhat of an obsession for him. He took a shaky breath and fingered them delicately.

'Can I keep them on?' she asked.

'No.'

She hissed as his fingers spread wide over her curves. His hand fisted in the material, and he pulled them off her. At last, she lay bent over before him with nothing on but a pretty pink blush.

'Ready?' he asked softly.

'Yes.'

She trusted him completely.

She had seven to go, and he didn't cheat her out of one. With nothing between them, the contact was shocking and so much more intimate. By sixteen, Roma was moaning and shifting. Papers from the files were crumpling under her feet, but she didn't care. Pencils and the stapler had been knocked off the desk. Neither of them stopped to pick them up.

'Eighteen,' Jake said, his breath coming hard and fast.

He stopped, but her bottom still pulsed. The heat now felt like fire; she couldn't think of anything else. She didn't even notice his fingers venturing else-where. When they dipped between her legs, she let out a moan that echoed off the walls of the small room.

She was wet.

He couldn't wait any longer. He gave her the last two swats with one hand as he pulled down his pants and drawers with the other. The sting was still vibrating through her red cheeks as he thrust into her.

'Oh! Oh!' she cried, coming right off the desk.

He rocked backwards a step and wrapped his arm about her, low on her hips. He was already pumping fast and hard. Their bodies were slapping together as he went deep with every thrust.

'Ah!' Roma hissed. She wanted him, but the way their bodies were coming into contact, her butt stung like the dickens. She couldn't stand it. 'Sore bottom. Sore bottom!'

She reached back to push at him. 'Stop!'

Everything inside Jake was saying 'go, go, go', but he slammed on the brakes, halfway through a stroke. Gritting his teeth, he forced himself to stay half in and half out of her. 'Are you saying you can't?'

She paused for nearly a full minute. 'Not this way,' she finally admitted.

He was going to die. Plain and simple. Die.

He jerked out of her and bent over with his hands on his knees. His cock thrust randomly in the air, looking for her. Shutting his eyes, he struggled for control.

Roma was looking around the room frantically, waving her hands. 'There. On the floor where we were before. On your back.'

He'd stand on his head if he had to. He pushed his pants off the rest of the way. She came over to yank at his T-shirt. He caught her and pulled her to him. The T-shirt fell at his feet as they kissed voraciously.

'Ah!' she hissed against his lips. 'Not the bottom.'

His hands had wandered. 'I thought it felt good.'

'It did before. Now, not so much.'

She pushed at his chest. Together, they dropped to the floor. Jake couldn't remember ever being so hard. His balls were pulled up so tight, he was practically puckering. If she didn't hurry, she was going to be out of luck. Quickly, he lay on his back and pulled her on top of him.

'Find whatever works,' he said, desperately.

She straddled him, and he felt her line their bodies up. Unable to stop himself, he thrust upwards.

'Oh!' she cried. Her head fell back.

Damn it. He froze. 'No good?'

'No. *Great.*' Her hands fisted on his chest and she lowered herself, taking him deeper. 'Oh, that's fantastic.'

Jake's neck arched against the hard floor, and he felt a peanut poke into his skull. 'Faster,' he demanded.

She began to ride him hard. Out of habit, he caught her by the hips. She lurched upright and caught his hands. She peeled them off of her backside and settled them over her breasts instead. 'Here. Do whatever you want here.'

Oh, hell yeah.

She was his kind of woman.

He thrust as well as he could, but she took on most of the work. She began bouncing up and down on his rampaging cock. Her breasts juddered, and he pinched and squeezed her. Suddenly, she reared back and grabbed her heels. The position ground her down on him hard and stars exploded behind his eyes.

Good stars this time.

'Roma,' he said a bit frantically.

She arched forwards and braced her hands on his heaving chest. Her hair swung back and forth as she pumped up and down. Up and down. Finally, Jake couldn't take any more. Unable to stop himself, he grabbed her bottom and squeezed hard.

He erupted, and she let out a cry. His fingers bit deeper, and an orgasm hit her hard. She went rigid on top of him, and then collapsed.

Together, they lay on the floor of his office gasping for oxygen.

'Holy shit,' he said.

'Oh, damn,' Roma said with a sigh.

'What was *that*?' he asked, stunned.

'Really good make-up sex.'

She lay draped across him, totally limp. He rubbed her bottom gently, and she winced.

'Is it really that bad?' he asked, feeling guilty. He hadn't meant to hurt her.

She eased his conscience with an intimate grin. 'It's all a matter of perspective.'

The scamp. He grinned back. 'Damn, you're a lot of fun when you're not paranoid.'

'You're a barrel of monkeys, too.'

Jake relaxed back. He was relieved that they'd gotten past that, because she was more than just fun. She was smart, sassy, daring, caring and lovable all at once. He wondered, not for the first time, what he'd done to deserve her. He wasn't going to question his luck, though; he was simply going to enjoy it. Just lying with her like this made him happy, even if he was in a pile of chocolate goo.

He had to chuckle when he found the glob in her hair.

'Turn your head,' he said. 'Let's see how bad this is.'

She grimaced and obeyed.

'Damn, you've got caramel all over.'

He tried to pluck it out with his fingers, but it was a sticky mess. He should know. He could feel it on the back of his head, too.

He sighed. 'You'd better go take a shower before it hardens. I'd hate to have to cut it out.'

Her head snapped back around so fast, she damn near clipped him on the chin again.

'Cut it out?' Her hands clapped over the back of her head. 'You can't go hacking away at my hair. I just got it cut for the reunion.'

She pulled away from him as if he'd suddenly become poison. He grabbed for her, but she'd already disconnected their bodies and climbed off him. He propped himself up onto his elbows and watched as she scrambled naked around the room, picking up her clothes.

'It's your own fault,' he accused. 'Cheating so soon before the big day.'

'I didn't cheat. I told you, I'm an addict.'

'A sex addict,' he said, laughing.

'Yeah, well, so are you!' She tugged on her top without her bra and hissed as she pulled up her jeans. 'Oooh! Ow! Oh!'

It was so pure Roma, Jake collapsed onto the floor in a fit of laughter. 'God, you crack me up.'

'Laugh all you want, lover boy. If I end up having to cut this out of my hair, you'll be laughing out of your belly button.' She started for the door, but stopped suddenly. She pivoted around. 'I'm out of shampoo.'

He pointed across the room. 'In my gym bag.'

'Thanks,' she said, unzipping it and grabbing what she needed.

'No problem,' he said as she darted out of the door.

Lying back, he folded his hands across his chest and stared at the ceiling. Oh yeah, life with Roma Hanson was never boring. He could hardly wait to see what would happen next.

Chapter Eleven

Friday after work, Roma was getting in one of her final workouts. She didn't want to let up now, not when her reunion was only a week away. She couldn't believe how well things were coming together for the big event. Her new figure was rockin', her dress was slinky, her hair was peanut free, and her escort was drop-dead gorgeous. Underscore that last one. Jake couldn't have been more perfect if she'd special ordered him out of a hunk-of-the-month catalogue. All they lacked was an appropriately hot car to match.

Maybe they should rent something snazzy. If they were going to make an impression, they might as well go all out. A limo would certainly draw attention. No ... too ostentatious and obviously a rental. Maybe a Caddy. Or a Hummer!

A snappy old tune from Katrina and the Waves came on the radio, and she cranked up the volume. The song fitted her mood perfectly. She increased the speed on the treadmill and began bee-bopping along.

Heh, heh, heh! This silly piece of equipment hadn't gotten the better of her. She could listen to the radio, handle the controls, and even look around the room without holding onto the support bar any more.

'I'm walkin' on sunshine. Whoa oh!' Katrina belted out the happy lyrics, and Roma nodded her head. Yep, sunshine – that's what she felt like. A big ball of light and warmth. Well, scratch that. She didn't feel like a big ball any more. She was just happy and content. Everyone should feel this way.

'And don't it feel good? Yeah! All right now.'

You go, Katrina. Yes, sir, she felt good. She was ready to take on Ellie Huffington and her cronies. Even they couldn't make a dent in her confidence any more. She had a good life. A great life. They had no power over her. If they even tried to get under her skin at this reunion, she was more than prepared to kick a little ass.

Jake had lived up to his promise on that.

'I'm walkin' on sunshine. Whoa *oh*!' The happy song disappeared, and she lost her rhythm. Stumbling, she grabbed for the support bar. Somebody had just plucked her headphones right off her head. Looking around, she found Hawk. 'What do you think you're doing?' she snapped.

'You're singing!'

'I'm what?'

'You're caterwauling like a stuck pig. Nobody can concentrate.'

Eyes wide, Roma glanced around the room. Sure enough, people were staring. Nothing new there. She looked at the guy on the treadmill next to her. 'Was I really singing?'

'If you want to call it that.'

She grimaced. 'Oops.'

'You didn't realise?' Hawk said in disbelief. 'You were at about an eight on the volume scale.'

'Oh, goodness.' She snatched her headphones back from his greedy paw and looped them about her neck. With a quick slap on the controls, she turned off the treadmill. She waved at her unwitting audience. 'Sorry to intrude everyone. Go back to whatever you were doing. I'll just be going to the locker room now to hide my face. As usual.'

Before she could escape, Hawk passed her the cleaning solution and a rag. Gym rules. She sprayed down the machine and wiped off the droplets of sweat she'd left behind.

206

'Does it really feel that good?' he teased as she polished the display.

'Yes. It does,' she said, chin raised. She and Jake were solid – a true couple.

'Good,' he replied. She took a step backwards and, almost nonchalantly, he looped an arm about her waist just as she tripped over her towel. She'd draped it across the machine as she'd been working out, but it must have fallen off. Righting her on her feet, he gave her a quick slap on the rear. 'I need to go through things one more time.'

Roma lurched and spun around, holding her bottom. *Had Jake told him about what they'd done in his office?* No, she realised as she watched him closely. As always, Hawk was just being a pain in the butt. She looked at him tiredly. 'Again?'

'Just once more.'

Grumpily, she put the cleaning supplies back on the shelf where they were kept and picked up her towel. 'Hawk, we've gone through everything a million times already. You've got it.'

He ran a hand over his glistening head. 'There are still a few loose ends. Like ... I made the reservation at that fancy Italian restaurant you recommended, but we never talked about what I should order.'

'Oh, for heaven's sake! Order anything you want – except maybe spaghetti. That's tough on a first date. Too messy.'

'Right. Good point. Should I order for Missy, too?'

'God, no. Women hate that.'

He grabbed the end of her towel and patted his brow. She had a sneaking suspicion his workout wasn't what was making him sweat.

'I'm worried about this conversation thing,' he confided. 'What if we run out of things to talk about?'

Aaaggh! She couldn't believe he was still hung up on that. He had a million things he wanted to know about the woman. The list took up two entire pages, and she knew that Missy had one just as long. 'You won't run out,' she promised. 'She's going to be asking you questions, too.'

Apparently, he hadn't thought about that.

'Questions like what?' he asked, in a near panic. 'We didn't practise that. What's she going to want to know?'

Roma sighed and threw a glance at the clock on the wall behind the reception desk. Saved by the bell! 'We haven't got time to cover all the possibilities now. You need to leave.'

When his eyes opened in alarm, she grabbed his chin and made him look. 'You've got an hour and a half to get cleaned up, dressed and over to her apartment. You told her you'd pick her up at seven o'clock.'

His face paled. 'Shit. How did it get that late?'

When he stood frozen, still looking at the clock, she did something really stupid. Reaching out, she returned his playful slap on the ass. It nearly bruised her hand. 'Get a move on, Hoss.'

His head turned. Slowly, his gaze dropped. 'That was probably a mistake.'

'Probably.' She clenched and unclenched her fingers, trying to regain some sense of feeling. 'But so would be making Missy wait.'

'Damn.' His gaze flew back to the clock, and she could almost see his worries flooding back in. He threw her one last forlorn look before hurrying out of the room.

Roma sighed. He might not think he was ready, but she was happy the big night was here. The man had her exhausted. She'd only been his dating coach for three days, but it seemed like three years. The questions just didn't stop. What should we do? Where should I take her? What should I wear? What's she going to wear? Can I touch her?

'Is he gone?'

She turned around to find Jake standing behind her. 'Where have you been?'

'Hiding in the massage room. I never volunteered to help him with this date thing. I couldn't take it any more.'

'You? I'm the one he's been hounding.'

'Yeah, but you weren't getting the sex questions.'

'Wanna bet?'

Jake's eyes narrowed, but then Hawk was flying by with his gym bag and all his gear. He hit the front door so hard, it nearly flew off its hinges.

'Well?' Jake asked. 'How do you think it's going to go?'

Roma let out a long breath. 'Hard to tell. If he opens up, everything will be all right.'

'And if he doesn't?'

'Then the only one who will be visiting the closet is the janitor.' She wiped the towel across the back of her neck. 'I wish the poor guy luck – for our sanity as well as his.'

Hawk's palms were sweaty on the steering wheel when he pulled into the parking lot for Missy's building. God, his nerves felt like they were trying to poke through his skin. His breaths were ragged, and he felt almost light-headed. If he didn't watch it, he was going to start hyperventilating.

All because of a stupid date.

He turned off the engine and stared at her front door.

What the hell were they doing?

This wasn't what they needed. Dressing up in fancy clothes? Going to a restaurant whose name he couldn't even pronounce? How was that supposed to fix anything? If she'd just let him touch her ...

But she wouldn't.

His hand fisted tightly around the steering wheel. Apparently touching was the problem. He still couldn't quite figure out whose genius idea that had been. Sex between the two of them had always been fantastic. The problems hadn't started until the fucking had stopped.

And those problems were quickly reaching crisis stage.

He shifted uncomfortably in his seat. The last few days had been hell. Pure hell. Every time he'd tried to get close to her, she'd turned away. He couldn't take much more of the cold shoulder she'd been giving him. Being without her was killing him. Inch by inch by inch. He missed her in his bed. He missed her in his arms. He missed her. Period.

Reaching for the door handle, he gave it a yank. He still didn't quite understand what this 'more' thing was that she wanted, but he'd try to give it to her.

For her, he'd try.

The suit he wore actually gave him a bit of confidence as he strode up the front sidewalk. Roma had helped him pick it out and, looking at himself in the mirror, he'd realised he looked damn near respectable in the thing.

Almost like a man who could be with an educated, classy lady.

Holding onto that thought, he knocked on her door. He was surprised when she opened it almost instantly.

'You're early,' she accused.

Words died on his lips as he took in the sight of her. She looked incredible. He'd never seen her dressed up before. Dressed down was more their style. Way down. Like naked. She looked great that way, but this was a close second.

Her hair looked soft and shiny as it swung about her shoulders. She was wearing a little black dress. He'd never quite understood the allure those things were supposed to have, but he got it now. The dress was sleeveless with a neckline that teased him with just a peek at her cleavage. The skirt was nearly as bad, curling close around her bottom and hips and stopping well above her knees.

The shoes, though. Damn. He couldn't stop staring at her shoes. The heels must have been at least four inches high and the straps ... They wound up around her ankles and tied in sexy little bows.

He couldn't help himself. All of Roma's warnings and instructions flew out of his head. Instinct took over, and he reached for her.

Missy flinched and pulled back sharply. 'What are you doing?' she hissed.

His empty hands curled into fists. 'Picking you up for our date.'

'I know that!' She caught him by the arm and pulled him inside. Quickly, she scanned the parking. 'What are you doing at my front door? You know I always meet you out in the parking lot.'

The irritation he'd been feeling about this whole charade came back with a vengeance. She was dumping her lazy-ass boyfriend anyway. What did she care if he found out about them now? He nearly said something before he remembered he wasn't supposed to know. 'I looked,' he said, gritting his teeth. 'His car isn't here.'

She rubbed her hands up and down her arms as if standing in the doorway was making her cold. 'That doesn't mean he couldn't show up.'

'Then get your coat,' Hawk said. He'd had just about enough of this 'jumping-through-hoops' crap. He wasn't the type of guy who snuck around. Why she was making everything so complicated was beyond him. 'Let's go. We've got reservations.'

The look she threw at him wasn't happy. In fact, he hadn't seen her smile for days. She was the one who'd caused this estrangement, but it looked as if it was wearing just as hard on her as it was on him.

'If you don't want to go, we don't have to,' she said a bit sadly.

It was the sadness that got to him. 'Missy,' he

said, taking a step towards her. 'It doesn't have to be this way.'

Her eyes were limpid as she looked up at him. He threaded his hand through her hair and pulled her close. Just the scent of her perfume made him hard. 'Come home with me. Let me take you to bed and make everything right again.'

Her gaze went shuttered. 'You don't even want to try, do you?'

Try? He was standing here in a freaking monkey suit, wasn't he?

'I'm the one who asked you out,' he reminded her. 'You said yes.'

She looked into his eyes for a long time. What she was looking for, he didn't know. Hell, if he knew, he'd have given it to her a long time ago.

'Fine,' she said tiredly. 'Let's get there before they give our table away.'

The way she said it made him want to put his fist through the wall. It was almost as if she was giving up hope. *On them.* His stubbornness reared its ugly head.

She could give up all she wanted.

He wasn't going to lose her.

She picked up her wrap from the back of the couch, and he moved to help her put it on. When she felt his touch at her shoulders, though, she looked at him strangely – almost as if she'd never expected graciousness out of him. It irked him even more. He wasn't the senseless clout she seemed to think he was. Was there ever a time he hadn't opened a door for her?

His gaze slid over her body. Had there ever been a time when he hadn't let her come first?

Her hand brushed across her dress nervously. 'Stop looking at me like that.'

'Sorry, little miss,' he said gruffly. 'That ain't gonna happen.'

He put his hand at the small of her back and

started leading her to his truck. She might want 'more', but sex was an integral part of their relationship. Integral and goddamned necessary if you asked him. She might not want to admit that, but he wasn't going to let her forget it. They could add 'more', but they weren't going to leave the sex behind.

Not if he had anything to say about it.

Dinner was tense.

Missy could tell that Hawk hated the restaurant on sight. The lighting was too dim, the writing on the menu was too fancy and they were seated at a table out in the middle of the room. So much for being able to relax. Her nerve endings were snapping.

She watched as he shifted uncomfortably. The chair looked to be too small for him. She was having a hard time sitting still, too. The atmosphere was one that begged for romance. Intimacy. It was impossible to achieve. She felt like everyone in the room was staring at them.

She was certainly staring at him.

God, she'd missed him – and he looked so good. She would never have put him in a suit, but it worked. The dark-blue colour gave him a conservative look. Crisp white shirt, muted red tie ... The fancy trappings couldn't hide the raw strength underneath. She wanted to crawl right across the tiny table and strip him bare.

She gripped the cloth napkin in her lap tightly. She was the one who'd made the no-touching rule; she had to keep it.

He blew out a breath. 'How did your day go?' he asked.

The simple question tongue-tied her. It was the first time he'd ever asked her anything like that. Her heart rate increased, and the napkin crumbled into a little ball. 'Fine,' she said quickly.

He stared at her, waiting.

She licked her dry lips and shivered when his observant gaze followed the motion. She could practically feel his tongue sliding across hers. 'And yours?'

'Fine.' He toyed with one of the forks in front of him. She could see him looking at the array in confusion. There were four of them. 'Classes going OK?'

She crossed her legs. 'Fine.'

He waited.

'It's been a tough semester,' she added when the silence got to be too much. 'I'm glad it's going to be over soon.'

'When is that?' he asked, hopping on the subject.

'Three weeks.'

He nodded, and the table went silent again.

The silence screamed at her. She'd had so many things she wanted to ask him. So many things she wanted to know. Looking at him across the table, she couldn't think of a one.

He didn't look happy to be here. They should have gone someplace with smoke in the air and peanut shells on the floor. Maybe if he was comfortable . . .

Then again, maybe not.

With Hawk as grumpy as he was, she got the distinct feeling he was just biding his time until he could get her back into the sack. The thought made her shoulders slump. She wanted like anything to be there, but she was just coming out of a dead-end relationship. She knew how unfulfilling they could be.

He leant back in his chair. With the way he'd spread his legs, it wasn't the most cultured pose. It was, however, masculine as hell. She saw more than a few female gazes dart in his direction, and her jealousy flared.

Just like his had when the waiter had put the

napkin in her lap. She'd thought he was going to deck the guy.

'How's your car running?' he asked.

Her car. Of all the things he could ask her, he wanted to know about her car. 'Fine,' she said with a sigh. 'The battery hasn't failed me once since you changed it.'

'Good,' he said. 'That's good.'

Fine. Good. If everything was so fine and good, why were they both sitting here miserable?

The conversation went downhill from there. With each question, Missy tightened up even more. It was as if he was checking off a list or something – and he avoided anything personal like the plague. It gave her no encouragement to ask what she wanted to know of him. Why should she? He wasn't going to answer.

He picked up his wine glass and drained it. She followed suit.

Their meal showed up, and he looked even more disgruntled. 'A bird could eat more than this,' he grumbled.

The bird could gladly have hers. She'd lost her appetite completely. For the last few days, she hadn't been able to eat. She hadn't been able to sleep. Without his warm body at her side, she couldn't relax. This wasn't any better. His plate was clean within minutes, but she poked at her food listlessly.

The tension at the table pressed heavily on both of them.

'Not hungry?' he asked.

She finally looked up at him. 'What are we doing here, Hawk? Really?'

He looked at her face with that piercing gaze that had first caught her attention at the gym.

'Good question,' he said. He threw his napkin onto the table. 'Let's get the hell out of here.'

She went still.

'We'll go to my place.' He reached for her hand. 'For dessert.'

Her heart fell – and splattered. The sex. It was the only thing they had in common. He didn't want to know her. He'd tried to act the part for her sake, and she did appreciate that. He wasn't a heartless man. In his own way, he cared about her.

But he didn't love her like she loved him.

Her napkin dropped onto the floor. 'OK,' she whispered.

One more night. She'd spend one more night in his arms, but then it was through. She wasn't a woman who accepted less than she deserved.

Not any more.

Hawk reached down to help Missy out of her chair. Finally. If he got her home, they would both be more comfortable. She'd always liked it there, and if he got this tie off from around his neck and oxygen to his brain, he might be able to think.

He wrapped his arm about her waist and led her to the door. He felt her leaning towards him, almost as if she couldn't help herself. He pulled her closer. With the added height of those sexy shoes, she could rest her head right on his shoulder.

He couldn't get his wallet out of his pants fast enough.

They got as far as the parking lot before he pulled her into his arms. 'God, I've missed you,' he murmured as his head dropped.

When their mouths met, the kiss was nearly combustible. He let one hand slide down to cup her bottom as the other dived into her hair. He'd never felt it so soft. She cupped her hand around the back of his neck and ran her thumb across a bump at the base of his skull. He shivered. He'd never known how sexy that could feel, but she'd found that spot early on.

During their first fuck in the closet if he remembered rightly.

Slowly, he pulled back from her. 'Let's go home,' he said, sucking in air.

At the words, though, she looked sadder than ever. The look cut right through him. She didn't appear upset as if she were going to cry. It went deeper, as if the weight of the world was on her shoulders. It nearly sent him into a panic.

Before he could figure out what to say, though, she turned to his truck. She got there before he could open the door for her, but he helped her up inside.

Yeah. Going home was the best idea for both of them. He wanted his girl on his turf. He could put things right there. He knew he could.

He had to.

By the time he got her to his house, Missy wasn't saying anything. He pulled into the garage and hit the automatic control to close the door. They were both quiet as they stepped into the kitchen.

'I'll meet you out on the deck,' he said as he whipped off his jacket and tie.

She was as quiet as a mouse as she walked over to the sliding glass doors. She turned on the outside light and let herself out. He watched through the window as she dropped her purse onto the deck table. She seemed to sink into the cushions of one of the outdoor chairs as if her legs wouldn't hold her any more.

Things still weren't right.

He felt his nerves tightening. Damn it, what was wrong? Why wasn't this working? Roma had promised.

He swore under his breath as he began opening cupboards. He wanted this woman badly. Just sitting across the table looking at her had made the palms of his hands ache. That dress had teased him with glimpses of her breasts and thighs. He wanted her in his bed and in his life.

What the hell did he have to do to make that happen?

He stomped out onto the deck. He put the supplies down on the table and turned to the gas grill. He opened the lid, turned the knob and hit the ignite switch. When he turned back to the table with the long-handled grilling fork in his hand, he found Missy looking at him like he'd just hopped off a little green spaceship from Mars.

'What?' he asked, stopping.

'What are you doing?' she asked.

'Making you dessert.'

He reached down and grabbed a marshmallow from the bag. 'You like s'mores, don't you? Chocolate and marshmallows...'

She looked astonished – and uncommonly pleased. 'You actually meant dessert.'

'Of course I did,' he said, pausing as he stuck the marshmallow onto the fork. 'What did you think?'

She glanced shyly towards his bedroom.

He felt his cock jerk. 'We could do that instead,' he said, quickly stepping towards the table.

Her smile faltered.

But he got it. *He finally got it.*

She'd come here thinking he was going to drag her off to bed – like he always did. She still came, though. She'd come because she wanted him. He could see it in her eyes. He'd felt it in her kiss.

More, though. She wanted 'more'. It suddenly occurred to him that she wasn't asking for rocket science. 'More' was simple things like making her graham cracker sandwiches with sweet filling. It was simple things like talking to her, laughing with her, *enjoying her.*

His head was pretty damn thick, but when something got through, it stuck.

'My name is Oscar.'

Her gaze flashed up, and she froze.

'You asked me once what my name was.' He shrugged. 'It's Oscar.'

Missy swallowed hard, not trusting her ears.

Hawk twirled the fork restlessly. 'I was quiet as a kid, but I got teased a lot. I started working out to get tougher.'

He glanced at her with half a smile on his lips. 'I got the tattoo at seventeen. Nobody's called me Oscar since.'

Missy's heart began pounding so hard, she could barely hear him. He was actually confiding in her, trusting her with something he hadn't told anyone for over a decade. She'd been waiting for this – something that would tell her she was more to him than a hot body and a pretty face.

He'd just given it to her. In spades.

Unable to sit still any longer, she burst out of her chair. She hurried around the table. He stepped back in surprise and quickly held the fork away when she jumped into his arms. She wrapped her arms around his brawny neck and hugged him tight.

'Oscar is a very sexy name,' she said. She tucked her face into the crook of his neck. 'I wish you'd told me sooner.'

His arms came around her, pulling her closer. 'If I'd known you'd react this way, I would have.'

She lifted her head to whisper in his ear. 'Want to know a secret? My name isn't Missy.'

He pulled back so sharply, they bumped into the chair behind him. 'What did you just say?'

She put her finger across his lips. 'Melissa is actually my middle name. I was named Esther after my grandmother. Don't tell anyone.'

He laughed. He looked at her and belly laughed. His eyes crinkled at the corners and a dimple dented his left cheek. He looked so handsome, she could hardly stand it.

'Oscar and Esther,' he said, threading his fingers into her hair. He leant down and planted a kiss on her smiling lips. 'Aren't we the pair?'

They were. Others might not see it, but they were a perfect match.

'Still want that dessert?' he asked, his lips moving against hers.

'Yes,' she said. 'And *yes!*'

He held the marshmallow out for her, and she took a nip. 'Mmm.'

'This isn't half bad,' he said as he took a bite, too.

'No, it's not,' she said. 'And I'm starving.'

She wriggled out of his arms and hopped up onto the table. 'Tell me more, Oscar.'

'What do you want to know, Esther?'

'Everything.'

He smiled and turned back to the grill. He began melting marshmallows as she opened the box of graham crackers and tore the wrappers off the Hershey bars.

From that point on, no subject was off limits. Missy couldn't have been happier. If she asked, he answered. He told her about himself, but he was just as curious about her. He asked her about her schoolwork. When she'd told him she wanted to work with cardiac rehab patients, he couldn't have been more supportive. Her love for pop music distressed him a bit, but he'd finally decided he could live with it.

Through it all, he fed her. She watched him hungrily, getting more and more turned on as they talked and nibbled on the unhealthy, but delicious dessert.

God, he looked good. He'd gotten rid of the jacket and red tie. His crisp white shirt was open at the neck and the sleeves were rolled up. The casual way he wore the dress clothes showed off his thick chest and muscular arms. His dress pants fitted even better. They showed off his rock-hard bottom so well, her fingers itched.

'Last one,' he said as he tucked the marshmallow inside a graham cracker sandwich. 'I'm out of marshmallows.'

He turned off the grill. Picking up the sweet, he walked right towards her. He stepped close, standing between her legs as she sat at the edge of the table. Watching her closely, he held the s'more to her lips.

Feeling sexy, Missy took a bite. She licked her lips seductively, and his pupils narrowed. Bold as he was, he took a bite of his own, treating her to the same show. When he finally leant down to kiss her, she had some ideas of her own.

She slipped off the table as their mouths ate at one another's. Planting her hands on his chest, she encouraged him to walk backwards. He took a glance over his shoulder. 'The swing?'

He had a wooden two-seater. She'd been enchanted with it since the first day he'd brought her here. She liked to sit on it in the early mornings, tucked in a woollen blanket as she drank her coffee.

She'd never sat on it with him.

'Did you make that, too?' she asked.

He murmured something that sounded like 'Mm hm' as he nuzzled the side of her neck.

Something inside Missy flared. 'Let's christen it,' she whispered.

She gave him a solid push to the chest, and he went down like a big old tree. The swing swung backwards under his weight, but he planted his feet on the deck before it swung back into her. 'God, you're sexy,' he said hoarsely.

'You make me that way,' she whispered. Grabbing the swing on both sides of his shoulders, she climbed on with him. The skirt of her dress was too tight. She tugged up the material until it was at her waist and then straddled him.

He made a choking sound. Looking at him quickly, she saw he was staring at the tiny slip of red between her legs. She shivered.

A look. It still took just a look from him to get her wet.

'Is that what I think it is?' he asked in a low voice.

Her hips swung towards him. 'Find out for yourself,' she whispered.

She took his free hand and guided it between her legs. When he cupped her, his hand tightened possessively. She shuddered and looked into his eyes. The heat there was so strong, it nearly burnt.

His fingers began exploring the open slit in the teddy, and she moaned. 'Like it?'

His fingers plunged deep. 'Get over here,' he growled.

Her hands went to his zipper as he pulled her higher on his lap. When his erection sprang out of his pants, it was thick and hearty. She licked her lips, tasting chocolate. She hadn't wanted to base their relationship on this, but oh how she'd missed touching him. At nights, her body had ached for his. She'd wanted him inside her so badly, she'd nearly given up fighting him. If he'd just wanted sex, she would have given it to him.

Now, she knew she could have more than just his huge cock.

She could have him.

Spreading her legs wide, she climbed on board. She felt his broad tip find the notch in her lacy red teddy. Then he found her notch.

Her head fell back as he determinedly ploughed into her. 'Ohhhh,' she groaned.

A muscle ticked at his temple. 'You feel tighter,' he grunted.

And he felt bigger. She squirmed on his lap as his hips twitched. Together, they swivelled and ground until he was seated inside her as far as he could go. Missy leant her forehead against his as he palmed her breast. He plucked at her nipple until it showed through the two layers of clothes she was wearing.

'A sweet for my sweet?' he crooned.

He still had the last s'more in his right hand. He pressed it against her lips. Missy had never felt so sensual in her life. She opened her mouth, and he fed her. She took a bite, and then he was kissing her.

She began to move on him, and the swing began to creek. The chocolate disappeared fast, and then his hands were on her. Neither of them had removed a stitch of clothing. Somehow, it made the experience all the hotter.

Hawk's hand slipped under her skirt to examine the thong back of her teddy. Her hand slid inside the open V at the top of his shirt. His chest felt like hot granite.

His cock was even harder.

He fucked her fiercely, making up for lost time. Each thrust went as deep as it could go. Outside in the silence of the night, their mating sounded animalistic. Primal.

Missy felt thoroughly taken. In every sense of the word.

'I . . . I love you,' she panted. 'I love you, Hawk.'

His grip on her tightened and he thrust so hard, he lifted her right off her knees. 'I love you, too.'

Another thrust, just as violent and intense, followed. 'My little miss.'

She came calling his name.

His real name.

'Oscar!'

Chapter Twelve

Roma loved to sleep in on Saturday mornings. It was part of her weekend routine. She'd curl under her comforter, savour her pillow and sleep until she just couldn't sleep any more. This Saturday morning, though, she was on her third cup of coffee when the phone rang bright and early. She snatched it up before its second ring.

'Missy?' she asked, not even bothering with a hello.

'Jake,' replied a low voice. 'I take it you haven't heard from them either.'

Her shoulders slumped. 'No, and it's killing me. I want to know how things went.'

'Call her,' he encouraged.

'I can't.' She'd already considered that idea and vetoed it. 'If Danny answers and she's not there, the cat will be out of the bag. I'm her cover story.'

'Damn. That won't work.' He paused for a moment. 'I'll call.'

'Who? Hawk?'

'Hell no. If things turned out the way he wanted, I don't want to interrupt anything.'

'And if they didn't?'

'Even I'm not that brave. He'll be as surly as a bear. I'll call Missy. If the kid answers, I'll just say I need her to sub for an aerobics class or something.'

'That won't work,' Roma said, thinking quickly. 'He'll start looking for her.'

'Shit. You're right.'

Roma started pacing with her cordless phone. She walked into her living room and looked out of the picture window. The birds were the only other ones awake and moving. 'This is driving me crazy. Did they fix things between them? Did they have a big blowout? Or did Hawk have a panic attack before they even made it to the restaurant?'

'The odds are pretty even on all three.'

'I want the first one.'

'Me, too.'

Frowning, Roma swirled her coffee around in her mug. 'I can't believe how tied up in knots this has got me. I've never been this nervous about someone else's date.'

'OK, that settles it,' Jake finally declared. 'We have to go jogging.'

'*Jogging?*' She turned away from the window and trudged back to the kitchen. That was his answer for everything. Stressed? Pump a little iron. Depressed? Hit the aerobics floor. Crazy? Go jogging.

'Saturday mornings are for resting,' she growled. 'We agreed on that.'

'Listen to me,' he said persuasively. 'I know you hate to jog, but there's a bike path on the opposite side of the creek behind Hawk's house.'

She stopped with her cup of coffee halfway to her lips. 'You want to *spy* on them?'

'Is it too much?'

She was already tossing the coffee into the sink and heading to her bedroom. 'Just let me get changed.'

'I'll be there in fifteen minutes.'

'Make it ten.'

The little creek running through the countryside was beautiful. Roma had never been to this part of town. It was on the outskirts, and really still more country than city. At such a low angle, sunlight darted between the trees that lined the creek. Spring was in full bloom, and flowers were poking up alongside the jogging path. Not that she saw them. She was in sprinting mode. Curiosity and a double shot of caffeine had given her more get-up-and-go than she was used to.

'Slow down,' Jake warned. 'You're going to run out of steam before we get there.'

He kept pace with her easily. The macho stud wasn't even huffing. Roma was huffing. She was puffing, too. There was a reason she hated running.

It was hard.

'How much further?' she panted.

'His house is at least another mile down the path.'

'Another mile?' she said, her head snapping to the side. 'You didn't tell me it was that far.'

He threw her a grin and sped up so she couldn't catch him. Turning around, he trotted backwards. 'No, but I did manage to get you out of bed for an early Saturday workout.'

'Trickster.'

'No, that's "trainer", Goldie.'

She swiped at him, but he was just too fast. Realising he was right, she settled down into a slower pace. She couldn't believe that now he was trying to get her *out* of bed. She must be losing her charm.

'Sometimes trainers have to be tricksters to get the results their clients want,' he said, falling in beside her again.

'Don't even say it.'

'Reunion.'

He liked to use that word for incentive. By now, she was pretty darn sick and tired of it. He ducked, but not quite fast enough. She managed a glancing blow to his shoulder.

'Reunion,' he repeated. 'Ree-ewe-nyun.'

'Aaaggg!' Putting her head down, Roma clicked off the steps.

It was the motivation she needed, though, and he

slowed down sooner than she expected. 'There it is,' he said. 'Let's cool down and walk the rest of the way.'

She put her hands on her hips, trying to catch her breath. Really, that hadn't been so bad. Having a clandestine mission at the other end of a run really made it go by fast. She squinted through the trees. 'Which house is it?'

He pointed a ways down the path. 'That one with the big deck on the back.'

Her eyebrows rose. 'Impressive.'

'Isn't it?' He veered off the cleared path and into the brush. 'Let's cut across here. The creek looks shallow.'

She followed. The tall grass tickled against her legs, and she giggled. They were such idiots. 'I can't believe we're doing this.'

He held his hand out to her when the terrain got a bit rockier. 'Want to go back?'

'Are you kidding? I feel like James Bond – but with boobs.' She held onto a tree and watched her step. Strategically, she picked her way to the edge of the water. 'Do you really think they're in there together?'

'If Hawk had his way, I could tell you exactly which room they're in right now.'

Jake stepped on a smooth rock in the middle of the stream. With a lunge, he hopped to the other side. He held his hand out to her. 'Be careful.'

Roma bit her lip. She put out her right foot. The rock was wet and slippery, but her tennis shoes had good traction. Leaning forwards, she grabbed Jake's hand. 'One. Two. Three.'

She skipped across like a gazelle.

He looked surprised. 'Huh,' he said, looking at the water.

This time when she punched him, she didn't miss. 'You thought I was going in the drink.'

He winced and rubbed his shoulder. 'Can you blame me?'

She rolled her eyes and strutted away. He caught up with her quickly and took her hand. Together, they climbed up the other bank. Soon, they were on Hawk's property. Weaving their way through the trees, they stopped at the edge of the backyard. The view of the home was breathtaking.

'Wow,' Roma said, planting her hands on her hips. 'That's –'

'*That's them!*' Jake caught her about the waist and pulled her behind a tree.

Hawk and Missy had just stepped out of the sliding glass door onto the back deck. Both were in natural, blissful, naked glory. Actually, Hawk had stepped out. Missy's arms and legs were wrapped around him like vines. And, technically, she wasn't naked.

'The red teddy!' Roma said, recognising the lingerie from the store.

'The red teddy,' Jake repeated appreciatively.

She looked at him sharply.

'We've got to get one of those for you.' When he looked down at her, there was a secret smile on his face. 'Think they've got one in pink?'

He wiggled his eyebrows so outrageously, she laughed. Aghast, she slapped a hand over her mouth. They couldn't let Missy and Hawk know they were here.

She snuck a peek around the tree and let out a snort. Like anything was going to distract those two! They were so immersed in each other, the deck could have been on fire and they wouldn't have noticed.

She melted a bit inside as she watched them. They looked good together. Hawk so masculine; Missy so feminine. The picture they made was so erotically beautiful, she couldn't look away.

Apparently, neither could Jake.

'Looks like they made up,' he said close to her ear.

From the way Hawk was groping Missy's bare butt, that seemed to be a good bet. The thong back of the teddy allowed him free access, and he took it. As they kissed, his hands squeezed and moulded her tight cheeks.

Jake and Roma watched avidly as their friends made love. All the same, Roma went right up onto her tiptoes when Jake's hands slid up under her shorts and started groping her the same way. 'What are you doing?' she gasped.

'Just keep watching,' he whispered into her ear.

'I don't think we should. Oh, damn!' Watching them while he touched her? Why, that was just scandalous.

And so hot, she just might faint.

Carrying Missy as if she didn't weigh a thing, Hawk walked over to the table. He carefully laid her upon it, and she lay back trustingly. The look that passed between the two was passionate and private. Jake's hands rubbed her bottom more aggressively, and Roma felt herself getting aroused.

With an intense look on his face, Hawk pulled Missy hips to the very edge of the table. She moaned and spread her legs wide. When he stepped up between them, Roma saw something she hadn't seen before.

'Oh, my God!'

Jake saw where she was looking and gave her a stinging nip on the ear.

She just couldn't look away. She'd been in the closet with that man. She'd felt the bulge in his pants as he'd rubbed it against her, but *holy cow*! That was the biggest cock she'd ever seen. It was thick and unbelievably long.

Jake's hands slid higher under her shorts. He pushed aside the panel of her panties and began touching her – just like Hawk was touching Missy. Roma shuddered hard.

As they watched, Hawk reached up to Missy's breasts. He plucked at the strategically placed ribbons and, suddenly, her nipples were pointing through. They were so hard, they stood up like two red points. Apparently, that wasn't good enough for him. Using his thumb and forefinger, he pinched a red nub. Firmly.

Missy's cry of delight echoed in the woods around them.

Jake's breath came a little harder in Roma's ear. His fingers were still investigating her wetness below – just like Hawk's were deep inside Missy. Reaching up, he pinched her breast through her jog bra.

Roma sagged back against him. Oh, dear Lord!

He was copying the couple's lovemaking move by move.

And from the impressive erection he rubbed against her bottom, they were both getting off on the voyeuristic game.

'Take your clothes off,' he ordered, his voice low and intense.

He didn't need to tell her twice. They were naked before they could miss a thing. Roma felt her exhilaration sharpen when Jake's hands found her pussy and her breast all over again.

Everyone waited to see what Hawk would do next.

Roma let out a soft sound when he bent down and took Missy's stiffened nipple into his mouth. She could almost feel him at her own breast. His cheeks hollowed out as he suckled and, from the way Missy was writhing on that table, he was tugging hard.

Insistently, Jake turned her. He bent her back over his arm, and then she felt his mouth at her breast. Her right one. Just like Hawk was on Missy.

The fantasy pulled Roma under.

Missy's hand came up to cup the back of Hawk's head.

She did the same to Jake.

'Legs up.'

The order drifted across the yard, and her legs buckled. She watched as Missy obediently lifted her legs and rested her ankles against Hawk's shoulders. Suddenly, Roma found herself on her back in the dirt. Jake's hands slid up the backs of her thighs, and she assumed the position.

Hawk stepped forwards, and her excitement peaked. Missy hadn't been exaggerating. He was hung like the state of Florida – only Florida had just gotten flipped upside down. She licked her lips.

Oh, God. They shouldn't be watching this. It was too private.

Hawk grabbed his big cock in his hand and lined himself up. Roma felt Jake bump against her.

'Are you with him?' he asked.

Her head turned away from the erotic scene playing out in front of them. When she looked at Jake, she didn't find anger or jealousy. She saw arousal. Scorching-hot arousal.

'Are you with her?'

Missy suddenly groaned from the deck, and his gaze flew towards the sound.

Hawk was penetrating his lover.

Roma felt the pressure inside her increase as Jake's hips swung forwards. He shuddered, and she realised that he was playing out a long-held fantasy, too.

This *was* private.

A private interlude for four.

She quickly turned her head to watch. Hawk was burrowing deep. With the way Jake mirrored the action, the link was inevitable. Inside her head, it suddenly became her that Hawk was screwing.

Her back arched. Oh, God. This was so hot she could hardly stand it. Reaching up, she grabbed Jake's shoulders. Her fingernails bit into his skin.

Hawk went deeper – and then ground his hips. Roma moaned low and long.

Missy let out a cry, and Jake bucked.

Both men began moving more fiercely, and Missy and Roma's bodies undulated wildly. Hawk was just as rough as Roma thought he'd be. He fucked like a barbarian, and she felt every thrust and jerk.

Jake bent over her, bracing his arms on either side of her head. The position gave him even more leverage. Roma raked her hands down his chest, copying Missy's animalistic response.

'Son of a bitch,' he swore. His body was quaking.

Roma felt herself quickly spiralling upwards. Her hips raised to meet Hawk's. Jake's . . . whoever's.

Bodies slapped together, and sighs filled the air. Missy came first. Her cry wafted through the morning mist, and Jake stiffened. Hawk let out a curse, and Roma's body bowed. She came, joining in the pleasure with her friends.

'Oh, damn,' she said with a sigh as she came back to earth.

Literally. She was lying in a bed of grass and dirt. Breathing hard, Jake relaxed on top of her.

'Holy shit.'

The couple on the deck was having just as much difficulty recovering. Limp and satiated, Roma watched as they touched each other languorously in the aftermath of lovemaking. Missy was running her fingers up and down the planes of Hawk's back as he whispered into her ear. The intimacy between them made her smile.

With a heavy sigh, Hawk pushed himself away from his lover. He disengaged their bodies and stretched like a lazy mountain lion. Scratching his chest, he walked to the spot on the deck where the steps led down into the backyard.

'So are you two going to keep pretending you're big horny rabbits?' he called, blatantly ignoring his own nudity. 'Or do you want to come in for breakfast?'

Roma felt her face grow hot, and she glanced with embarrassment at Jake. 'Peter Cottontail, I presume?'

His eyes narrowed. 'Thumper?'

Her jaw dropped. 'If anyone should be Thumper, it's you.'

'Why me?'

She looked pointedly at the spot where they were still connected. 'You should know the answer to that.'

He grunted and pulled back. 'I think we've been spotted.'

'Ya think?'

Tiredly, he pushed himself to his feet. He rubbed the back of his head as he walked out into the clearing. Nudity, schmoodity. Neither of the guys seemed to care.

'Was it as good for you two as it was for us?' he called.

Hawk started laughing as Missy rolled onto her side and gawked.

'It was fucking fantastic. Where's Blondie? It's only fair that I get a peek at her.'

Roma timidly stepped out from behind the tree. She wasn't as audacious as the men. Pressing her legs together tightly, she gave her friends a hesitant wave. 'Morning.'

Hawk's eyes narrowed, and his cock surged. 'Looking good, Blondie. Real good.'

'Hey,' Jake snapped.

Hawk pointedly looked at his friend's softening boner. 'Don't try to pretend my woman had nothing to do with that.'

Jake looked down, but finally had to shrug. What could he say?

'Oh, stop it you two,' Missy said as she climbed off the table. Embarrassed, she began tying the ribbons at her breasts. 'I'm hungry.'

Hawk rubbed the top of his head. 'Come on in. It sounds like I'm cooking.'

Hawk and Missy were nowhere to be found by the time Roma and Jake got dressed and stepped into the back door of the house. Roma looked around in awe. Vaulted ceilings, open-aired beams, and the kitchen! Envious, she walked in and examined the appliances. Everything was top of the line.

'Nice, huh?' Jake said.

'I had no idea.'

'He's good.'

She threw a mischievous look over her shoulder. 'That, I already knew.'

He gave her a stinging slap on the behind. 'Guest bathroom is down the hall to your left.'

She was grinning broadly as she hurried away.

She snooped a bit as she went and eventually found the bathroom. It was just as sumptuous as the rest of the house. The decorating was minimal, to say the least, but Missy would have that fixed in no time. Roma hopped into the shower.

By the time she got back to the kitchen, Hawk was clattering around in the cupboards. She was relieved to see he'd found a pair of sweatpants. His bare chest was extremely distracting, however. Missy was setting the table, wearing a rather slinky blue robe. Roma's tongue clicked against the back of her teeth. She wondered how many other things her friend kept here.

'Hungry, Blondie?' Hawk asked when he spotted her.

'Famished.'

'Worked off a few calories, did you?'

She blushed, but she wasn't going to let him rattle her. 'Jake made me run on that path to get here.'

Hawk chuckled. 'Then you're first in line. What do you want?'

She nibbled on her lip, and glanced at her friend for help. 'Can he actually cook?'

'To die for,' Missy assured. 'Try the egg-white omelette. That's what I'm having.'

'Sounds good,' Roma said. She pulled a chair away from the table in the breakfast nook and sat down. 'Fire it up, Mr Chef.'

Jake appeared in the hallway fresh from his shower and propped his arm against the archway.

'What about you, peeping Tom?' Hawk asked as he sprayed a pan with non-stick coating.

'Voyeurism is hard work,' Jake returned. 'Make it French toast for me.'

'Hey,' Roma said, complaining. 'That's not fair.'

'One week,' he promised as he crossed the room and sat down beside her. 'Then you can ease up on the diet.'

Still ... Roma was concerned that the world might be coming to an end if Jake Logan was eating French toast, and Hawk Miller had the supplies on hand to make it. The health freaks. Breakfast was supposed to be those icky protein drinks. She was reassured when Hawk pulled out a loaf of wholewheat bread and sugar-free syrup. That was more like it.

Missy finally sat down at the table with them. Roma lifted her eyebrows, silently questioning her. Her friend smiled shyly and gave her a thumbs up.

Roma leant in closer. 'Did he tell you his name?'

Missy threw Hawk an amused look. 'He did, but I can't tell. Ever.'

Hawk laughed and cracked an egg with one hand.

Roma's forehead crumpled in confusion. 'Can't you give me a hint?'

'He's a grouch,' Missy said flatly.

'Hey!' Hawk warned. He pointed the spatula at her.

'Fine,' Roma said, sitting back in her chair. 'Be that way.'

Breakfast turned out to be delicious. Jake had at least six pieces of French toast, and Roma helped him polish off the last one after finishing her omelette. She wished she knew how to make those things. Every time she tried, she got fried eggs instead.

Holding her stomach, she relaxed back in her chair. 'Hawk, that was awesome.'

He tilted his head in acknowledgment. 'Consider

it payment. You two can provide manpower. Today's moving day for Missy.'

Missy looked at him sharply. 'It is not.'

'Today,' he said firmly.

'I have to talk to Danny first. I can't just walk out.'

'Sure you can.'

'I want to handle this right.'

'Getting out of there today is right,' he said, not giving an inch.

Roma watched the back and forth volleys like a tennis fan. Hawk was imposing, but Missy was holding her own. It was nice to see.

'I'll talk to him this morning,' her friend promised, meeting him halfway.

'Then we'll hold off on moving your stuff over here until this afternoon.'

It wasn't much, but it was a concession. Missy nodded her head in agreement. It was decided. She was moving in with Hawk that afternoon.

'I can help,' Roma said, raising her hand.

'My truck's just down the road,' Jake volunteered. He pushed himself away from the table, but his cell phone rang. 'Whoa. That's me.'

He unclipped the phone from his waistband and looked at the caller ID. 'Excuse me. I need to take this.'

Roma started to help Missy gather up the dishes. She noticed Jake's brow furrowing, though.

'How bad is it?' he asked.

She stopped with one hand holding the syrup and the other gripping a sticky plate. Who was on the other end of that line? Tito? Had something happened at the gym?

'Does the doctor say you'll be healed in time for the competition?'

Competition? Roma sighed. He was talking to Liz. Rolling her eyes, she continued with what she was doing. Stacking her plate on top of his, she headed for the kitchen sink.

He glanced at her as she walked by and tilted his head apologetically.

'It doesn't sound that bad, Liz. If the doctor says you need to rest it, we'll rest it. Don't worry. We can work around it.'

Roma walked off in a huff. That woman. She called whenever she broke a fingernail.

'Now's not a good time, Liz,' Jake said patiently. 'I can't come over; I'm right in the middle of something.'

Roma stopped. Oh, he'd better not.

'Liz? Liz, stop crying.'

Oh, for heaven's sake. Jake looked up at her ruefully, and she wanted to kick him in the shin. The tears got to him every time. Didn't he know they were the oldest tools in women's belts of manipulation?

'Liz, don't say that. I'm not giving up on you. Liz?' Closing his eyes, he reached up and rubbed his temple. 'Ah, hell. Just stay put. I'll be right over.'

If Roma hadn't been in someone else's kitchen, she would have thrown the syrup right against the wall. Missy and Hawk saw the look on her face and took a step back. Way back.

Jake hung up from the call with an excuse already on his lips. 'It really sounds like something serious this time, Roma.'

'Sure it does.'

'She pulled a muscle. With two weeks until the show, that could be disastrous. She's got some strength moves that put a lot of stress on that leg.'

'Can't she wait?' They were here enjoying an intimate breakfast with their friends. A very intimate breakfast. They'd just engaged in a virtual orgy, for goodness sake. Was he just going to run off after that?

'She's pretty upset.'

He was just going to run off. She couldn't believe it.

He clipped the phone back at his waist. 'Do you want to come along?'

Her eyebrows lifted. 'What do you think?'

'Right,' he said, looking sheepish. 'Hawk?'

'I can give her a ride home.'

'Thanks.'

Roma tried to avoid Jake when he reached out and grabbed for her waist, but her reflexes weren't quick enough. He pulled her close and looked down into her eyes.

'I just have to keep her happy until the show is over,' he said quietly. 'I'm doing this for us.'

She counted to ten.

'Don't be mad,' he coaxed.

She rolled her eyes, but she did understand. In fact, she understood all too well. He couldn't help being a nice guy. If a woman in need called, he was going to run to the rescue. What she didn't appreciate was the woman who used this knowledge to her advantage.

He gave her a quick kiss and hugged her. 'I'll ditch her as soon as I can.'

'You'd better,' Roma said, pouting. She'd allow this for two more weeks.

Then, it was going to stop.

Jake left through the back door, and she watched out of the window as he trotted towards the creek. She sighed. All that hunkiness was supposed to be hers. 'Damn that Liz,' she said, tossing the plates into the sink.

Missy came forwards and rubbed her back. 'It's just work.'

'I know,' Roma said stubbornly. She couldn't help the way she felt. Even if there wasn't anything romantic, a closeness had developed between the two. 'I trust him. It's her that has me worried.'

Missy brushed her hair over her shoulder and glanced across the room at Hawk. 'Would you tell her there's nothing going on between Jake and Liz?'

Hawk climbed up on a barstool and rested his elbows on the breakfast bar.

'Liz Huffington?' He let out a grunt of disgust. 'Give me a break. Blondie, that bitch has nothing on you.'

Roma heard nothing past the name 'Huffington'. He might as well have screamed it at her with the way it ricocheted inside her head.

She pivoted sharply and stared at both of her friends. 'Huffington? Liz's last name is *Huffington*?'

Hawk threw a look at Missy. 'Well, yeah.'

Reaching out, Roma grabbed the counter. Her knees suddenly didn't feel all that steady.

Missy lurched forwards and wrapped an arm about her shoulders for support. 'Roma, what's wrong? You're as white as a sheet.'

That was because she suddenly couldn't breathe. 'Ellie's last name is Huffington.'

Her friend's eyes widened dramatically. 'No!'

'Who's Ellie?' Hawk asked.

Missy shushed him with a wave of her hand. 'It's a coincidence. It's got to be.'

Roma wasn't so sure. Liz. Elizabeth . . . Ellie?

'Yeah, a coincidence,' she said, clinging to the hope. 'People don't change their names after high school.'

Hawk and Missy exchanged a look. Roma felt a bit sick when they didn't back her up. 'But why would she do something like that?' she asked.

'Could be anything,' Hawk said.

Panic started to seep into Roma's system. Oh, this was terrible. A nightmare. A horror story told in broad daylight. But how could she find out for sure?

'What does she look like?' she demanded. She flapped her hands frantically, trying to get her brain to function. 'Height. Hair colour. Anything.'

Missy looked worriedly at Hawk. 'Blonde.'

'Dirty blonde,' he agreed.

Ellie had had brown hair, but it could always have been coloured or highlighted.

'She's relatively petite,' Missy added. 'Five foot four maybe.'

Wrong answer! The rock in Roma's gut cut deeper. Jake had said that Liz did backflips in her routine. Ellie had been a tumbler.

Reaching out, she grabbed Hawk's wrist. 'You said she was a bitch. How big?'

He didn't hesitate. 'The biggest one I've ever met.'

Oooh. Not good. Roma flung her hands up in the air and began to pace. 'Do you have any pictures of her?'

Both shook their heads.

'How old is she?'

'Thirty?' Missy guessed

'Thirty-five?' Hawk said.

Roma perked up. That was too old – but the gross feeling in her stomach didn't let up. She had to know for sure. But how? She snapped her fingers when the light bulb popped on inside her head. That was it!

She spun around towards Hawk. 'Take me to the gym. Please!'

By the time they got to the gym, the Saturday morning crowd was in full swing. Tito was behind the desk, but he was surprised to see them. 'Hey guys. What are you doing here?'

As a trio, they stomped right on by.

'Guys?' Tito called weakly.

Roma opened the door to Jake's office with her key. Marching straight over to the filing cabinet, she yanked on the 'H' drawer. It held tight.

'Damn!'

She began searching frantically for a way to open it. Her keys wouldn't fit. Neither she nor Missy had a hairpin – although that would have been a small miracle. Women hadn't worn their hair in pin spirals for half a century, and fewer still knew how to pick locks. Frustrated, Roma began yanking on the drawer. 'Open!' she demanded.

Missy pulled her back. 'Careful. It might fall on you if you do that.'

'I want it open.'

'Then get out of the way.'

She pulled back sharply when Hawk walked up with a ten-pound free weight. He'd heard the story of Ellie on the ride over. He wasn't that big a fan. Lifting the weight, he drove the flat end into the lock. There was a bang and an ear-piercing screech.

Reaching up, he hit the button for the top drawer and gave the handle a pull. The sound of more metal scraping against metal made Roma clap her hands over her ears. Hawk wasn't to be denied. He prised the drawer open until he could stick his hand inside. When he reached the lock, he twisted it manually.

'Open,' he said as he stepped back.

'Oh, thank you,' Roma said, rushing in.

She whipped open the drawer with the 'H's and began thumbing through the files until she found Huffington. Her hand shook as she pulled it out of the drawer.

'How will you know if that's her?' Missy asked, stepping in to peek over her shoulder. 'I've never seen Jake take pictures of clients.'

Roma was thumbing through the thick file, trying to find what she needed. Comments like 'hard worker' and 'shows potential' slowed her down. 'Ellie's birthday was on New Year's Eve,' she said. 'She always threw a big party. It was the social event of the winter season.'

She knew, because she'd never been invited.

Her breath caught when she found the page listing Liz's personal information. She scanned the page until she found the date of birth. Her friends had been wrong. Liz was twenty-eight.

Roma's arms went limp, and the file dropped to the floor. Turning, she pressed her face into Hawk's wide chest. His arms automatically came up around her.

'It's her,' she groaned.

Liz was Ellie. Ellie was Liz. Her long-time, evil nemesis was Jake's star pupil.

Chapter Thirteen

When Hawk and Missy finally dropped Roma off at home, she went straight to the kitchen. Convincing her friends that she was calm and rational had been no small feat. Hawk, in particular, had been like a mama bear – not that she'd say that to his face. He'd just been overly protective of her.

She didn't need protecting right now.

She needed chocolate.

Opening the cupboard, she pulled out her secret stash of Snickers. Jake might have confiscated those he'd found in her briefcase, but he'd yet to find her other hiding places. The lid went flying off the fake flour canister and rolling across the countertop. Reaching inside, she pulled out the first of the many candy bars she planned to eat.

Liz was Ellie. *Unbelievable!*

As if she hadn't developed a big enough dislike for this 'Liz' character already.

Because she felt like it, Roma grabbed the metal lid and banged it against the counter. The reverberating clatter gave her a sense of satisfaction. She felt like creating some mayhem. Making a scene. Throwing a good, old-fashioned hissy fit.

Jake was with Ellie right now. He'd been with her for the past three months – plus whatever additional time he'd trained her before she'd met him. The wrapper crinkled as Roma ripped into it, and she savagely bit off a mouthful of chocolate and peanuts. She knew how he'd trained her. How many times had he touched Ellie's shoulders to make sure her posture was straight? Or her stomach to make sure she was strengthening her abs? Or her butt to . . .

Well, he just liked to do that.

With her, at least. He'd better not be grabbing Ellie's butt.

More importantly, Ellie better not be grabbing his. She knew how that witch worked.

'Arrggg!' Roma snarled.

The trainer–trainee relationship was just so physically intimate. She knew Jake could keep things professional, but could Ellie? Did she even want to?

Ha! Of course not. What kind of a question was that? Just look at all the phone calls. The messages. The trips to the bikini store and Chicago.

'That Lizard!' Roma hissed.

This was just so totally unfair.

She'd worked her ass off for the past three months to get ready to face Ellie. Liz . . . Whatever her name was these days. She'd hoped to get a foot up on the bitch at the reunion, but noooooo. Her arch-enemy had one of the best bodies in the Midwest. She could search state after state and not find someone as fit.

'Oh, you got me good,' she said, waving her Snickers in the air. She could practically hear the Fates having a chuckle at her expense.

All that stretching. The sweating. The pain. The time. Roma groaned as she remembered all the workouts she'd pushed herself through.

Had it all been for nothing?

'Screw that.' She wasn't even going to go down that road. She had to have accomplished something – other than nab a sexy lover. Jake was wonderful, but this whole undertaking had been about her. Improving her self-confidence. Reaching a goal.

A goal.

Her head snapped up. That was it. She had set a goal, and it had nothing to do with Ellie Huffington. With purpose, she headed out of the kitchen. Thinking twice, she swung back around for her Snickers.

No sense leaving them behind. She clutched the canister to her chest and walked to her bedroom.

Setting it on top of the dresser, she wiped her suddenly damp palms on her shorts. Slowly, she approached the closet and slid open the door. Peering into the very back, she found what she wanted.

Her band uniform.

'Come here, you.' She pulled the garment bag off the hanging rod and unzipped it. A big green 'W' stared up at her from the sweater, challenging her. Her nerves began to twitter.

The big day had arrived.

All that running, lifting, stretching and straining had better damned well have been worth it!

She tossed the garment bag on the bed and began tearing off her clothes. Her shoes flipped end over end as she kicked them off, and she hopped from one foot to the other as she tugged at her thick exercise socks. Her shorts went next, and she decided to change into fresh underwear. The jog bra had to go, too. Only her best push-up would do.

Finally, she turned and faced her foe.

The sweater went on first. She pulled it over her head and tugged it down to her waist. Objectively, she evaluated herself in the mirror. It was a bit snug but, overall, very nice. She'd filled out a bit on top since her high-school days, but she had no problem with that.

It was the filling out below that had left her a bit peeved.

Feeling like she was dressing for battle, she pulled on the opaque white panties that went with the outfit. At last, she eyed the skirt. 'Ah, we meet again.'

She unclipped it from its hanger and gave it a little flip. The material snapped loudly. 'Feeling feisty, are you?'

Opening the waistband, she stepped inside. The moment of truth had arrived. Anxiously, she began pulling the skirt upwards. The fit over her hips was a bit tight, but she got it up to her waist without too much difficulty. The zipper, however, decided to be difficult. It stopped halfway up.

'Oh, no you don't,' Roma said. She hadn't come this close only to be denied.

Sucking it up, she tried again. The zipper closed another inch.

'Dang it. Don't do this to me. Didn't you hear that Liz is Ellie? Work with me.'

She tugged again, and the zipper closed all the way.

'Yes!' she exclaimed. 'Now just let me –'

She pulled in her stomach and managed to loop the hook at the top of the skirt through the eyelet on the other side.

'Yes,' she said hopping up and down. 'Yes, yes, yes.'

She whirled around to look at her reflection in the mirror.

It fit!

All that torment and suffering at the gym had been worth it. Jake had promised, and he'd delivered. She was back to fighting weight.

Bounding over to the dresser, she found a pair of bobby socks. Cute. Frilly. She teamed them with a pair of Keds. When she finally looked in the mirror, she could have sworn the last ten years had never happened.

'Take that, Ellie,' she said laughing sarcastically. 'You might be buff, but nobody would ever confuse me for thirty-five.'

Snatching up another Snickers bar, Roma voraciously bit off a chunk. She had the witch there. Feeling victorious, she let her hips swivel. The skirt swung saucily against her thighs.

'Ha! I'm buff, too, and I still look young.'

Petty and shallow be damned. It was something.

For a long time, Roma stood in front of the mirror, eating chocolate and admiring herself. She was twisting and gyrating her hips when the doorbell rang, cutting her triumphant celebration short. She threw an impatient glare towards the front door.

'Go away. I'm busy here.'

Whoever it was started knocking, too. The doorbell rang incessantly, and she rolled her eyes. Hawk. She should have known he'd come back. Pivoting in her spunky pair of Keds, she stomped to the living room. Knowing him, he was coming in one way or the other and she rather liked her front door.

Not bothering to glance out the peephole, she swung it open.

Jake stopped, frozen with his fist raised. He blinked. What the hell? From the sound of Missy's voice on the phone, he'd known something was wrong – but she hadn't prepared him for this. His gaze slowly travelled down Roma's form. Good God! Talk about ten different fantasies all wrapped up in one.

'Oh, it's you,' she said flatly.

He let his hand drop. That hadn't sounded encouraging.

'What's wrong?' he asked. 'Missy called and told me I should get over here. Are you OK?'

Roma shrugged. 'I'm having a minor meltdown. I figure it's about halfway over now.'

His eyes narrowed when she obstinately lifted a Snickers bar to her mouth and gave it a chomp. She seemed rather unaffected at having him catch her in that get-up. In fact, she seemed rather proud of it. Not that she shouldn't ... It was her chilly attitude that had him worried.

'What happened?' he asked. She'd been fine when he'd left her, although she hadn't been too happy about him going to take care of Liz. Ah, hell. Liz. Was that what this was about? 'I thought you were OK with things.'

One of her eyebrows arched. 'I reconsidered.'

'Come on, Goldie,' he said patiently. 'We talked

about this. There are only two weeks left until the show. Don't get mad at me now.'

'I'm not mad at you.'

The hell she wasn't. He took a step towards her. 'Then what's with the attitude?'

'*Attitude?*' Her other eyebrow lifted to match the first.

'The attitude. The strange sense of style. The chocolate.' He reached for the Snickers bar as if it were a weapon. 'Don't do this to yourself. Just tell me what I did wrong.'

She jerked the candy bar away and turned to block him from getting it. 'Nothing. I'm not mad at you.'

He sighed. 'If you won't tell me, I can't fix it.'

'Are you deaf? *I'm not mad at you!* Or at least I wasn't.'

He raked a hand through his hair. Women. He didn't understand them on the best of days, but she had to be the most confounding female on the planet.

He took a deep breath and tried a different tactic. 'If it makes you feel any better, Liz really is hurt. It's just a minor muscle pull, but we're icing it down and –'

'Ellie!' Roma hissed.

He stared at her. 'What?'

Her eyes lit with fire. 'Her name is Ellie.'

He still didn't understand. Did he have it all wrong? Had her high school enemy crawled out of the woodwork while he'd been gone?

With a growl of frustration, Roma spun on her heel. Her hair flounced behind her with nearly as much enthusiasm as that short skirt as she marched to her bedroom. Cautiously, he followed. He found her bent over, searching through a box on the floor. The way her skirt hiked up, he didn't pay much attention to the box until she pulled something out of it.

The book looked heavy. When she slammed it on

the dresser, he flinched. She flipped it open, thumbed through the pages, and pointed. 'Ellie.'

He moved closer. All he saw was a haughty teenage girl.

Roma let out a sound that was almost savage.

He looked again.

'Change the hair to dirty blonde,' she growled. 'And apparently add some wrinkles.'

'I don't understand –' It suddenly hit him like a two-ton brick. He stared at the picture hard and felt his blood pressure escalate. 'Liz!'

'Give the man a prize.' Roma slapped her hand on the dresser and stepped back. She popped the last piece of chocolate into her mouth as she watched him.

Jake could hear his blood thumping in his ears. Liz was Ellie – the same little snot who'd terrorised Roma throughout her high school years. He remembered some of the things she'd done. The nasty, cruel things.

'That bitch,' he said through gritted teeth.

Nonchalantly, Roma pulled another candy bar out of what he'd thought was a flour canister. She offered it to him. 'Snickers?'

He dumped the chocolate back inside. 'I can't believe it. This can't be right.'

'Believe it. Ellie is Liz. Liz is Ellie. Isn't life just a hoot sometimes?'

No wonder Missy had called and demanded he get his butt over here. He needed to have it kicked. Reaching up, he clenched his hands together at the back of his neck. He couldn't believe how much time he'd spent with that woman – time he could have spent with Roma. He felt guilty, somehow, as if he'd betrayed her. 'Goldie, you've got to believe me. I had no idea.'

'None of us did.'

'She hasn't said a word about a reunion. If she had, I might have made the connection.'

'Oh, please.' Roma waved her hand at him. 'She knows she has the reunion in the bag. All her concentration is on the Midwest Fitness Show. She might actually have some competition there.'

He felt the words like a punch in the gut. That was his doing, too. He felt so unbelievably gullible. He'd known Liz was a problem. Hell, she'd been through three trainers before she'd landed with him. He was the only one in town who could put up with her.

And look at where his patience had gotten him.

Well, no more. Rigidly, he turned and headed back out into the hallway.

'Where are you going?' Roma called.

'To see Liz. The Show's over for her.'

'What?' she snapped.

'She's got to pay for the things she did to you. It's about time somebody set her straight. Believe me, it will be my pleasure.'

He hadn't made it two steps when he felt a yank at the back of his shirt. Turning around, he found Roma in his face. If he'd thought she'd been fiery before, he'd been wrong. Sparks shot from her lavender eyes, and electricity crackled all around her.

'You're going to do no such thing,' she growled.

'The hell I'm not.'

Her cheeks turned red. 'This is my fight,' she said, her voice rising.

'Yeah? Well, your fights are my fights,' he shot right back.

'Why?' she yelled, stepping up toe to toe with him. 'Because you think she can take me?'

'Because I love you, damn it,' he yelled right back.

The confession made Roma's entire body jerk. Her eyes went wide, and her mouth dropped open. When she tried to say something, though, nothing came out.

Jake was left speechless, too. Oh, shit. Panic started to creep into his system. That wasn't nearly

252

as romantic as he'd planned. His fingers curled around the door jamb as the tension in the room skyrocketed.

He waited for her to respond. To laugh in his face. To say *something*.

When she finally moved, though, he wasn't ready.

'Well, I'm stuck on you, too,' she said, bounding up on her tiptoes to glare into his eyes. Her voice was at an all out bellow. 'That's why you're not going anywhere.'

The bottom of his stomach fell out entirely, but she wasn't through.

She poked him in the chest. 'You're not going to risk your gym over her. We stick with the plan and squeeze her for every penny she's worth.'

A slow smile spread across Jake's face. Now that was the blonde dynamo he knew – full of vim and vigour, up for any challenge and loyal to the core. It warmed him that she wanted to protect him as much as he wanted to protect her.

'OK,' he said.

She seemed surprised by his easy agreement.

'Well ... OK then,' she said, relaxing back down onto her heels. Her arms folded over her chest. At last, she started to look a bit uncertain. Her gaze flicked up to meet his, but then skittered away. 'So you love me?' she asked hesitantly.

He caught her by the waist and kissed her soundly. 'I'm wild about you, you crazy woman. Didn't you know?'

Slowly, she wrapped her arms around his neck. 'I thought maybe.'

He chuckled. 'I was pretty sure about you. You're not very good at hiding your emotions.'

He ran his hand down her back and encountered her tiny skirt again. Pulling away, he let his gaze trail down her sexy little uniform. 'Speaking of which ... Do you want to tell me what this is about?'

She finally blushed, but she gave him a flirty twirl

of the skirt. 'This was my goal. I wanted to fit back into my uniform by reunion time.'

The wattage of her smile nearly blinded him.

'I did it,' she said proudly.

'Yes, you did.' He tugged on the bottom of her sweater. 'I especially like how the "W" seems to swell in the middle.'

She laughed and slapped at his hand.

He smiled and backed her up against the door jamb. 'Cheerleader?' he asked.

The thousand-watt smile turned upside down. 'Ellie was a cheerleader.'

'Dance squad?' he said quickly.

'Sign holder,' she said, grabbing him by the shirt.

Roma wasn't in the mood to explain as she pulled Jake down to her. He loved her. She'd hoped he did, but now she knew for sure. How could she not? He'd practically screamed it to the world. This big, brawny, blond hottie was all hers. He kissed her, and her thrill just about put her through the roof.

She kissed him back hungrily, and her hands went everywhere at once. She pulled at his T-shirt, nearly ripping it, and he understood her urgency. Catching her by the waist, he started hurrying them backwards towards the bed.

'You look like a teenage boy's wet dream,' he growled against her lips. His heel caught on the box on the floor, and they went tumbling down on the mattress. Rolling, he pinned her underneath him. 'Most grown men's, too.'

'You say the sweetest things.' She finally worked the T-shirt over his head and flung it aside.

'Sassy,' he said, nipping at her lower lip.

His hand fisted in her tight sweater and, together, they pulled it off her. The 'W' landed face up when it hit the floor. Roma breathed deeply as Jake stared down at her.

She knew he liked her breasts, but things always heated up between them so fast.

Looking into his eyes, she saw that this time he intended to linger.

Arousal began seeping through her system, hot and strong. They'd been together before – many times – but this somehow seemed so much more intimate. When he softly fingered the front clasp of her bra, she shivered. The way the design plumped her up, she felt as if she were offering herself to him.

And she was. In so many ways.

Jake seemed entranced as he traced the edge of the lace cup across her breast. 'You are so pretty,' he said, his voice tight.

Watching her closely, he reached for the front clasp. Her heart began to pound when it popped open. Straddling her, he slowly flipped one cup aside and then the other. Roma could feel her nipples straining towards him. He cupped her greedily, and she arched into his hands. He rewarded her with flicks of his thumbs.

'Feel good?' he asked.

'So good,' she said with a sigh.

Scooting down, he settled his weight over her. When he dropped his head, she braced herself.

He was going to service her.

She let out a shuddering breath when he began to kiss her. He started with her left breast and worked his way to her right. Not a centimetre of skin went without a touch. Or a lick. Or a nip. By the time he made it to her nipples, she was groaning and squirming underneath him.

Knowing how he felt about her made everything more stimulating.

He carefully raked his teeth across a pouting tip. She let out a cry, and her body bowed. It was only then that he gave her what she needed. Opening his mouth wide, he took her nipple into his mouth. He began suckling fiercely, and she raked her fingernails down his back.

He'd only gotten started.

He moved to her other breast and gave it the same treatment. He took his time, experimenting to find what she liked most. With him, she liked everything. Cupping the back of his head, she held him to her tightly.

'Jake,' she said, her voice strained. She couldn't take much more of this. 'I need you.'

'Easy, Goldie.' Reaching up under her skirt, he caught her underwear. He gave them a tug. Her hips rose, but the panties stayed put.

He lifted his head, and she returned his confused look.

They usually came off when he did that.

He sat back on his knees. Impatient as she was, she lifted her skirt for him.

'There are two pairs,' she said, thinking that might be the problem.

'Two?' Curious, he slid his finger under the leg opening of the white ones. He found the mint green panties that were underneath. 'What the hell is that for?'

'They're called cheaters,' she said, squirming. She reached down and tried to tug them off herself. 'They hide a girl's panties if her skirt flies up.'

'Well, they're doing a bang-up job of that.' He got a good grip on everything and pulled.

Roma felt the uncomfortable tug at the small of her back. 'Wait. They're caught in the zipper.'

Jake started to laugh. 'Only with you.'

He flipped her over so she lay on her stomach. She propped herself up onto her elbows and craned her neck to look over her shoulder. Talk about the worst possible time for something like this to happen!

'Lie still,' he ordered. Catching the tab of the zipper, he tried to work it down.

Roma knew she wasn't helping, but she couldn't stop her hips from pumping. She was ready for him. Trying to find some relief, she ground her aching nipples against the mattress. 'Hurry,' she begged.

'I'm trying.' He saw what she was doing and attacked the zipper with a bit more gusto.

But it was stubborn.

He tugged and pulled and wiggled, but the thing refused to move. 'Damn,' he cursed. 'You never make it easy for me to get inside your pants, but this is ridiculous.'

Desperate, Roma reached back and began yanking at the zipper herself. 'Get this thing off me!'

He wiped the back of his hand across his brow. 'I can't.'

'Yes, you can.' Pushing herself upright, she twisted around. 'Jiggle the zipper.'

'I did.'

'Pull harder.'

'It just makes it worse.'

She looked at him mournfully. 'It's got to come off.'

His gaze burnt her naked breasts.

'You aren't kidding me.' He raked his hand through his hair and looked around the room. The bathroom caught his eye. 'Soap. Let's try soap.'

She sprang off the bed before he could move. Her breasts bounced as she ran to the bathroom. She was holding a bar of soap out to him by the time he got there.

Rubbing soap on the tracks didn't work. Neither did trying to pluck out the material with tweezers. Roma spun around like a whirligig, trying to get at the thing. Poor Jake was having to fight her as well as the zipper.

Finally, he sagged back against the wall. 'I give up.'

'No!' she shrieked.

She hurried about the room looking for something they could use. Her head suddenly snapped up. 'I know. Stay here. I'll be right back.'

Jake closed his eyes and banged his head back against the wall. God, whatever tricks she had in mind, they'd better work – or they were going to have to get very creative.

And very soon.

He waited. And waited some more. Just when he was about to go after her, she appeared in the bathroom doorway. A devilish look was on her face. Reaching out, she carefully set a pair of scissors on the edge of the sink. His gaze flashed to the scissors and back to her.

Lifting her hand slowly, she let two pieces of rectangular material flutter to the floor. One was white. The other was mint green.

'Think you can work with this?' she asked.

With a growl, he caught her around the waist. She laughed as he hoisted her over his shoulder. Marching to the bed, he dropped her on it. She bounced with a shriek, but then he was on her.

Straddling her once again, he flipped up her skirt. Tatters of her two pairs of underwear still remained. He flipped them up, too, and bared her curls to his gaze. Her laughter stopped abruptly when he petted her. She was soft and enticing. He pushed his fingers into her. Groaning, she pulled her legs up to her chest.

It was the only sign he needed. He yanked down his pants and grabbed his aching cock. He was inside her before she could even catch her breath.

The fuck was fast and furious. He latched onto her nipples again and tugged with his mouth as he banged her down below. She came with a shudder. He pulled out, tore off the rest of his clothes, turned her over and penetrated her from behind.

The flirty little skirt had given him a hard-on like he'd never had in his life.

Her fingers were raking against the sheets as he fucked her deeply. 'Jake,' she groaned.

He slid an arm under her hips and lifted her onto her knees. She pressed her face into the pillow as his thrusts became more jagged. With each push into her, he slapped against her white cheeks. The carnal sounds made him grit his teeth.

He heard her cry out, and then he was coming, too.

He came so hard, his entire body went rigid. When the end finally came, he crumpled down on the bed beside her. He doubted he'd ever be able to move again.

'Wow,' she panted. 'You weren't kidding when you said you could make that work.'

'You just told me you loved me.' He sighed tiredly. 'I had to make it memorable.'

She smiled. 'Mission accomplished.'

'Good, because that's about all I've got left in me.' He kissed her again, but then rolled onto his back. 'Damn woman. You're more exhausting than a triathlon.'

She snuggled closer, and he stroked her back as he waited for his energy to return. It was a lost cause. He was wasted.

'You know there was never anything between Liz and me,' he said, wanting to make sure they were clear on that issue.

'I know,' she said, drawing slow circles on his chest. 'You have much better taste in women than that.'

Damn straight he did. He hugged her closer.

'I still can't believe it.' He stared at the ceiling. 'Liz is Ellie.'

'The one and only.'

'That bitch. I'd love to tell you she's changed since

259

high school, but I can't.' He rolled his head on the pillow and looked Roma straight in the eye. 'Just say the word, and she's gone.'

'I'd rather she found out about us at the reunion.' She propped her chin on his chest. 'About that ... when I asked you to go with me before, I acted like you were eye candy or something. Will you go with me as my boyfriend?'

He fisted his hand in her hair. 'Goldie, you've got me any way you want me.'

Chapter Fourteen

'Stop fidgeting,' Jake said.

'I'm not fidgeting,' Roma replied. She was just overflowing with energy. She gripped his arm a bit tighter as they rode the elevator up to the third floor. Her class reunion was being held in the ballroom of the ritzy Stratton Hotel. The moment those doors opened, it would be show time.

'Did you see Mitzy Reeger and Dante Smith gawk at our car in the parking garage?'

'It's not our car,' Jake reminded her. 'It goes back to the rental company tomorrow morning.'

'Nobody needs to know that,' she hissed. She gave him a sideways glance. 'Besides, you looked awfully happy driving it.'

'It's a red Corvette, Goldie. I'm only human.'

The elevator dinged as they arrived at their destination, and Roma's pulse took off like a shot. Her fingers bit into Jake's biceps as the doors slowly pulled open. A sign pointing to the Washington High School Class Reunion greeted them, along with the driving beat of ten-year-old music.

He patted her hand. 'Ready?'

Unbelievably, after all the time she'd spent preparing for this, she found herself frozen. 'I don't know,' she said uncertainly. 'Am I?'

With a swift curse, he hit the close button for the elevator doors. Turning, he backed her up against the wall. 'You've got nothing to be nervous about, Roma. You're exactly what you wanted to be – a drop-dead, stop-'em-in-their-tracks, bombshell blonde. On top of that, you're an amazing woman. I thought I made that clear earlier.'

Oooh. She liked it when he got this way. He leant into her suggestively, and she rubbed against him. 'Yes, and you almost made us late.'

'It's that dress.' He made a tight sound and shook his head. 'I can't be held accountable for my actions when you look this way.'

She straightened his collar. 'Neither can I.'

He smiled and chucked her under the chin. 'Then let's go show ourselves off.'

Why not? She was having a good hair day. Her shoes were sexy, her dress was slinky and Missy had even found a purse to match. Even without all that, she had the best accessory possible – a gorgeous, supportive hunk on her arm. She nodded, feeling her excitement return. 'Let's go knock their socks off.'

'That's more like it,' he said. He opened the doors again before she could change her mind.

Confidently, they strode out of the elevator and down the hallway. A table had been set up outside the ballroom doors. A grin broke out on Roma's face when she saw Mr Carlton, her old science teacher, handing out nametags. 'Mr Carlton,' she said. 'I didn't know you were going to be here.'

His hair was greyer, and his glasses looked a bit thicker. The smile on his face, though, was the same. Time had treated him kindly.

'Roma Hanson,' he said in delight. Reaching out, he took both of her hands in his. 'Why, you don't look a day older than when you graduated.'

The compliment made Roma so happy, she felt like she could burst. She'd known she looked young. 'Thank you. You look as if you're doing well.'

'I'm retiring next year,' he said with content. 'My wife thinks it's time we travelled a bit. See the world – not to mention the grandkids.'

'That sounds wonderful.' Eagerly, she caught Jake's hand and pulled him forwards. 'I'd like you to meet my boyfriend, Jake Logan. Jake, this is Mr Carlton, the best high school science teacher around.'

Jake gave the older man a firm handshake. 'I'm honoured to meet you, sir. Roma's told me a lot about you. I appreciate the things you did for her back when she was a student, especially when the situation got difficult.'

The two men exchanged a look and Carlton gave a meaningful nod towards the ballroom. 'Well, I'm glad she's found an even better protector in you. It's nice to meet you, son.'

Roma didn't miss the look.

Ellie was already here.

Her spine straightened as she glanced towards the ballroom. Scores of people were wandering around, and amongst them was a mean one. She wasn't intimidated. Out of everyone in that room, Ellie was the one for which she was best prepared.

'Are we supposed to wear these?' she asked, pointing at the nametags on the table.

'Oh, look at me. You're so beautiful, you've got me forgetting to do my job.' Mr Carlton passed her a marker. 'Just write down your names. Here's a little booklet with the information everyone sent in. It will help you get updated on what your classmates are doing these days.'

'That should be interesting,' Roma said. She took the booklet as Jake filled out his nametag.

'Oh, and don't forget this,' Carlton said. He passed her a piece of paper. 'They're handing out awards after dinner. Don't forget to vote for your favourite nominees.'

'OK,' Roma said, adding the list to her growing collection. She caught Jake's hand when he held it out to her. 'It's been nice talking with you, Mr Carlton. Maybe we'll get a chance to speak more later. I'd love to hear about those grandkids.'

Her old teacher smiled and patted her on the head as she walked by. He'd saved another knowing look for Jake. 'You've got a good one here, Mr Logan. Treat her right.'

'I know that,' Jake said. 'And I'm trying.'

Roma smiled when his fingers squeezed hers intimately.

They looked at each other. He gave her a wink, and she took a deep breath. Then, together, they made their grand entrance.

As they crossed the threshold into the ballroom, though, Roma felt as if she were stepping back in time. The decoration committee had outdone themselves – although the end result gave the strong impression a high school prom. Streamers swung to and fro, and balloons bounced against the ceiling. Countless dinner tables had been set up in front of a large stage, and each had a centrepiece that looked like the school mascot. The music, though, was what brought everything together. She watched as a DJ bobbed his head to a song she hadn't heard for years.

The effect was a bit overwhelming.

She looked around in amazement. The only thing that seemed to have changed was the people. Jake had been right. Some had gained weight. Other had lost their hair. Most frightening, though, were the ones who'd obviously had some 'work' done. 'How am I supposed to recognise anyone?' she whispered.

'That's what the nametags are for,' he said, rubbing the small of her back. 'Although it looks like people are recognising you without it.'

Roma could feel the attention on them gathering – only it wasn't all reserved for her. She happened to catch Cindy McLaughlin, Ellie's best friend, just as she turned her head. The woman's appreciation of Jake was so obvious, it was a wonder her eyes didn't pop right out of her head. When she saw who he was with, though, she almost swallowed the olive in her martini whole.

The response made Roma want to do cartwheels across the dance floor.

Cindy was envious. Seethingly so. The woman scowled as she tried to find something wrong with the picture the two of them made. Roma could feel the glare intensifying as it scraped over her hair, her shape, her dress and even her shoes. Obligingly, she took on the pose of a fashion model.

Yes, she was hot.

Yes, she had a fabulous-looking beau with an even better personality.

But, no. So sorry. She hadn't put on fifty pounds.

Cindy McLaughlin, on the other hand, had gotten fat.

Roma knew she should be ashamed of herself. Taking pleasure in another person's plight was terrible. And from the degree of the pleasure she was feeling, she realised she had to be the smallest-minded person on the face of the earth.

Oh, well, her devilish side chuckled.

You can work on that after the reunion, her angelic side conceded.

Turning to Jake, she began to laugh.

His fingers curled into her hair. 'Was that the reaction you wanted?'

'Even better,' she said, trying to catch her breath.

'What did I tell you?' he whispered into her ear. 'One look at you, and the women are green with envy.'

'And the men?' she asked, looking up into his eyes.

'Sweating in their beer. Do you forgive me now for making you do all those lunges?'

'Oh, please,' she said, giving him a playful push to the chest. 'Nobody thanks somebody for making them do lunges.'

'Ma'am?' Somebody tapped her on the shoulder. 'Would you and your escort like to have your picture taken?'

Roma absolutely beamed. She couldn't think of anything better. She wanted this moment caught forever. Practically dancing, she hurried over to where the photographer had set up a green-and-white backdrop in honour of the school colours.

Jake stood at her side and wrapped a possessive arm about her waist. There was a smile on his face, too. 'Having fun, Goldie?'

'A blast,' she said with a grin. She put her hand on his chest and smiled brightly for the camera. The flash popped, and she saw stars in front of her eyes.

'Roma!' somebody called excitedly.

She waved a hand in front of her face, trying to make the blots of colour disappear. When she was finally able to focus, she saw a pretty woman standing in front of her. At first, she didn't recognise her. Slowly, though, her brain changed the deep auburn colour of the woman's hair back to mousy brown. The contacts were replaced with glasses, and the straight white teeth were bound in braces.

'Myrtha!' she exclaimed.

Reaching out, they caught each other in a hug. Unable to contain their excitement, they jumped up and down.

Finally, Myrtha pulled back. 'I almost didn't recognise you. You look beautiful. I absolutely love this dress.'

Myrtha was wearing a rather sharp suit herself. Roma was impressed. It was tailored, showing off her friend's sleek figure. 'You look incredible!'

Giddy, they hopped up and down again.

Finally, Roma reached out and grabbed Jake. She pulled him over excitedly, wanting to introduce him to someone who had been a true friend. 'Jake, this is Myrtha Snodgrass. She held the other end of the Washington High school sign.'

His eyebrows lifted. 'Another sign holder?' he

asked with interest. 'With the sweater and the skirt and the cheaters?'

Roma felt her face flare.

He laughed and shook her friend's hand. 'It's nice to meet you. I have the greatest appreciation for sign holders.'

Myrtha glanced at Roma. 'OK, I'm missing something – but he's cute enough for me to ignore it. Where did you find this one, Roma?'

'At the gym,' she said, hugging him tightly. 'He's my trainer.'

Myrtha snapped her fingers. 'I knew you got that body somewhere.'

'Believe me,' Jake said. 'She had it before she got to me.'

'And he's charming, too. My, my, what a combination.' Myrtha pointed across the room. 'That's my charmer over there – the one in the cast. My last name's Kramer now.'

'That doesn't look good,' Jake said, expertly eyeing what appeared to be an ankle injury. 'What happened?'

'A bike.' Myrtha rolled her eyes. 'Don't ask. Artie's not an athlete, but, boy, you should see him with a microscope. There's nobody better.'

'He's waving at you,' Roma said.

'He needs another drink. I should go and help him.' Myrtha gave her one last hug. 'Sit with us for dinner? I've got most of the rest of the mathlete team joining us.'

'The mathletes?' Roma said with surprise. 'I haven't seen anyone from that group in years.'

'*Mathletes?*' Jake said with more than a bit of scepticism.

'We competed at math bees.' Roma twirled around so enthusiastically, her asymmetrical skirt slapped against his legs. 'We were awesome. We were city champs my junior year.'

He chuckled. 'You really were a geek, weren't you?'

'Well, you were a jock,' she said, spitting out the word as if it left a bad taste in her mouth.

'You're a sexy geek, though,' he said, catching her by the waist and pulling her close.

'And you're a jock with an actual brain in his head,' she said, returning the backhanded compliment.

They shared an intimate smile. Then there, right in front of Cindy McLaughlin and the rest of her high school class, he kissed her. By their standards, it was a conservative kiss, but whoops of approval still went up in the air. Jake only took it as encouragement. He kissed her long and hard. By the time he pulled back, Roma was blushing.

Even conservative kisses could be hot.

He let out a long breath. 'Is all this showing off making you as thirsty as it's making me?'

Her mouth had just gone bone dry. Carefully, she wiped away any lipstick he might have smudged. 'White wine, please.'

'Stay here,' he said. 'I'll be right back.'

He started to weave his way through the crowd, and Roma noticed more than one woman craning her neck to take a peek at him. The reactions were actually kind of fun to watch. Poor Jake. He couldn't help that he was a good-looking man. And tonight, he was especially handsome.

He was wearing a dark-grey suit and a crisp white shirt. They'd decided he didn't have to wear the tie. He hadn't wanted to spend the night being strangled, and she was all for him showing some skin. There was something to be said for reverse sexual exploitation.

He was a hottie. Why try to hide it?

'*Aroma?*'

The sneering voice cut right through Roma's

happy reverie. Instinctively, the muscles at the back of her neck went rigid. She'd know that voice anywhere. It was as familiar as fingernails on a chalkboard. Turning slowly on her high heels, she faced her old nemesis.

'*Smellie?*' she returned, cocking her head.

A thrill shot through her. Where had that comeback been ten years ago?

Ellie's eyes narrowed dangerously, and the tension crept up a notch. Holding her purse under one arm, the woman rubbed lotion onto her hands as she scathingly evaluated Roma's outfit. Apparently, she'd just come out of the ladies' room. 'I'm surprised you decided to show your face.'

'Why wouldn't I?' Roma asked. 'I have a rather nice face.'

Unlike her old schoolmate. Oh, Ellie was coiffed to high heaven. She looked stunning in a curve-hugging, white sheath dress. The sleeveless style showed off her amazingly sculpted arms and back. The sedate heels lifted her slightly, making her calves look like they'd been carved from rock.

Her face, though ... The nickname of 'The Lizard' fit better than Roma could possibly have imagined. Her old classmate had done so much tanning, her skin looked rough and dry. Not even her perfectly applied make-up could hide the damage the UV rays had done.

'Why you mouthy ...' Ellie's chin came up. She plucked her purse out from under her arm and strutted forwards with purpose.

Roma held her ground. She planted one hand on her hip, and they faced off like two old-time gunslingers.

Ellie slowly sized her up, looking her over from head to toe. 'Nice dress, Aroma. A bit trashy for my taste.'

Was that the best she could do? Roma felt her

already high self-esteem bump up another notch. She was in shape, and there was nothing Ellie could do to change that. 'Thanks. I like yours, too.'

Dots of red colour showed through the heavy layer of foundation on the woman's cheeks. She'd been expecting her to flinch, to falter. 'Still a bitch, I see.'

Roma let her eyebrows lift. 'I think you've got that backwards.'

A crowd had started to gather around them. Ellie's minions, Cindy McLaughlin and Kelly Tanner, stood behind their friend. Roma didn't take her eyes off Ellie. She was ready for this. She'd trained for three months for this.

Bring it on.

Only Ellie couldn't seem to think of a thing to say. Her gaze raked over her, looking for a flaw to attack. She couldn't find one. Flustered, she looked at her girlfriends for support. She laughed sarcastically, and the twits joined in.

Roma let out a short laugh, too – one of disappointment. Talk about a letdown. She'd let herself get all worked up for this?

Jake finally returned with their drinks. With effort, he squeezed his way through what had become a tightly packed crowd. He looked from her to Ellie, quickly evaluating the situation. 'Is there a problem here?'

'No,' Roma said calmly, taking her drink. Her hand was rock steady as she lifted the glass to take a sip.

Ellie, on the other hand, did a double take and went as white as her dress. 'Jake? What are you doing here?'

'I'm with Roma.'

It was like watching a volcano erupt. First there were tremors. Ellie began to shake in her designer shoes. Redness rose up from her chest and into her face. Roma could almost see the steam pouring out of her ears. When she finally blew, she blew to high heaven.

'You bitch!' she hissed, taking a threatening step forwards. 'I can't believe it. You did it again.'

Roma's eyes narrowed. 'Did what again?'

'Stole my man!'

'*Your man?*' Jake said, coughing when his beer went down the wrong pipe.

He might have been surprised, but Roma wasn't. She'd expected as much. Calm and possessed, she also took a step forwards. She stood so close, her toes nearly brushed against her rival's. 'Don't go down this road again, Ellie. You'll only embarrass yourself.'

'Shut up, you slut!'

'Careful, Liz,' Jake warned in a dangerous, low voice.

Ellie's gaze darted to his. To Roma's amazement, she pressed her lips together tightly, stopping herself from saying anything more. Her eyes narrowed in cunning, though.

'I didn't mean it that way, Jake. You just don't understand what she did to me in high school,' Ellie said, playing the part of the helpless victim. 'She acted all sweet and innocent, but deep down she was terrible. She stole my boyfriend. All it took was a toss of that blonde hair and a shake of those big boobs.'

Roma rolled her eyes. 'I was Brian's math tutor. Nothing more.'

'You tutored him in something, all right.'

Jake stepped forwards, but Roma stopped him with a hand to his chest. 'I'm not going to play this game with you again, Ellie. It was pathetic then, and it's even more pathetic now.'

'You're the one that's pathetic.'

'No,' Roma said tiredly. 'You are. Everyone else has moved on since high school, but you're still trying to hold onto your glory days. But you know what? These are my glory days, and I'm not going to let you spoil them.'

With that, Roma did the unthinkable. Turning her back on Ellie, she summarily dismissed her. Reaching out, she took Jake's arm. 'Let's go find our seats. It looks as if they're ready to serve dinner.'

Ellie didn't know what to do. She looked around in vain but the crowd, seeing that nothing juicy was going to happen, began to disperse. Unwilling to concede defeat, she stepped forwards, following them. 'You're nothing, Roma Hanson.'

Roma smiled blandly over her shoulder. 'I wish you luck at the Midwest Fitness Show, Ellie. Honestly. Maybe you'll get the attention there that you so desperately need.'

With her head held high, she walked with Jake to their seats next to Myrtha and Artie.

'I'm impressed,' Jake said, low enough for only her to hear. 'You took the high road.'

She shrugged. 'That woman just isn't worth it. I want to have a good time tonight. I want to remember this reunion as something that was fun.'

'Still ...' He rolled his shoulders restlessly. 'Where's that loser boyfriend of hers? The one that fed you to the wolves?'

'Brian?' She looked around. 'I haven't seen him. I don't think he came.'

'That figures.'

'Why?' she asked in confusion.

He pulled her chair out from the table for her, looking uncharacteristically grumpy. 'You weren't the only one who came here with intentions of kicking some ass.'

She smiled. She liked this protective streak of his. 'I guess we'll just have to settle for going "zero for two" tonight.'

'Lovers instead of fighters?' he asked, his lips brushing against her temple.

A thrill went down her spine. 'That sounds good to me.'

Feeling proud of herself for acting like an adult, Roma sat down. Her angelic side was abnormally pleased with her.

'Are you OK?' Myrtha asked.

'I'm fine.' Perfect, in fact. She had Jake, and Ellie couldn't touch her any more.

Roma couldn't remember the last time she'd enjoyed herself so much. Dinner was good, but the company was excellent. Seeing her old friends was such fun, she could hardly contain herself. She took so many pictures and posed for so many more, her face hurt from smiling. And the stories! They had even Jake laughing.

Time passed quickly and, all too soon, the lights dimmed. Everyone watched as Kelly Tanner moved to the stage. As class president, she'd been in charge of organising the reunion. She might be one of Ellie's cronies, but even Roma had to admit she'd done a good job.

Turning her chair so she had a better view, Roma watched the prepared programme. She felt Jake scoot up beside her and then his arm was around her shoulders. 'Your mathletes are nice people,' he said quietly.

She smiled back at him. He'd been the perfect date this evening, boyfriend or not.

Kelly had prepared a slide show of pictures from their school days. Roma leant her head on Jake's shoulder as she took a trip down memory lane. When a picture of her and Myrtha holding the school sign appeared, a cheer went up from the entire table.

'That was during a parade,' Myrtha said.

Roma gave her a high five, and their attention turned back to the show. It was much too short. A few of their other classmates stood up and reminisced about old times, but the end of the night was approaching.

'And, now,' Kelly said excitedly. 'It's time for what everyone has been waiting for – the awards!'

Roma had nearly forgotten. Mr Carlton had walked around collecting the votes during dinner.

He seemed to be enjoying himself as much as everyone else. How he could remember students after teaching so many classes for so many years was beyond her.

'Our first award goes to the person who travelled the farthest to get here,' Kelly said, overplaying the enthusiasm just a bit. 'Would Jenny Olson come forwards? She came all the way from Vancouver.'

People clapped as Jenny walked up the steps to the stage and got her cheap little plaque. Roger Stine took the next award for having the most children. Five – including a set of triplets. Roma noted that he looked rather tired. So was she, she realised. The night had been like a roller-coaster ride. Going through so many emotions had left her exhausted. She reached for her purse as Mary Wolf took the award for having the strangest job. Nobody could quite understand how a strait-laced neat freak had ended up as a sanitation engineer.

'And finally to the last award of the night,' Kelly said.

Roma glanced at Jake as she slid her camera into her purse. He looked ready to go, too. 'Want to leave early and beat the crowd?' she asked.

He let one eyebrow rise. 'If we leave early, nobody will see your Corvette.'

She smiled and shrugged. 'It doesn't matter.'

He was kissing her on the forehead when applause broke out around them.

'Hey,' Myrtha said, reaching over to tap her on the shoulder. 'You won! Go up there and get your award.'

'I won?' Roma looked around in confusion. Everybody seemed to be staring at her. 'What did I win?'

'The comeback award!'

Roma gasped. It was the biggest award of the night.

'You!' Myrtha said, nudging her towards the stage. 'You made the biggest impression on everybody tonight. Get up there.'

'Yeah, Goldie,' Jake said. 'Get up there.'

Hesitantly, Roma stood. The applause intensified, and her heart began to thud. Impulsively, she leant down and gave Jake a kiss. Wolf whistles broke the air, and she blushed. She could hardly believe this was happening. From what she'd heard from previous classes, the comeback award was usually a popularity contest. She hadn't been popular in high school. She'd hardly been a blip on anyone's radar screen.

Apparently, she'd bleeped tonight.

Her legs were a bit shaky as she moved to the stage. She saw a dejected Ellie as she passed the table up front.

Don't trip on the stairs! her inner voices screamed in unison as she caught the handrail. *Whatever you do, don't trip.*

Her purple high heels performed flawlessly. Mr Carlton met her at the head of the short staircase and handed her the plaque. She accepted it and impulsively gave him a hug. When she turned to Kelly, she found the woman's smile a bit forced. Still, her old classmate graciously stepped back from the podium. Roma took her place in front of the microphone but, for the first time in her life, found herself speechless.

'I don't know what to say,' she admitted. She held the plaque in front of her and read the engraved words. She'd worked long and hard for tonight, wanting to be at her best. Winning an award, though, hadn't been her goal. 'I'm so honoured.'

She swallowed hard and looked out across the crowd. She didn't know why she'd been so afraid of coming here tonight. Most of these people were her friends. They didn't care if she was skinny, fat, ugly or poor. Image was such an illusive thing. In high school, it had meant everything. Now, as she stood here in front of everyone in her glamorous outfit and perfect body, it didn't mean quite so much.

Other things did.

'Thank you for thinking of me,' she said, smiling, 'But I haven't done anything impressive enough to deserve an award like this. Yes, I dressed up for tonight, and I'm proud of the person I am. I have a good job, wonderful friends and an amazing boyfriend.'

She threw a little wave at Jake. 'Really girls,' she said, her voice dropping to a confidential whisper. 'An amazing, funny, be-careful-not-to-drool boyfriend.'

Laughs rose up throughout the room.

'But seriously,' she said. 'I'd like to pass this award on to someone else – someone who in just one week will be doing something more notable than putting on a pair of killer high heels.'

At the front table, Ellie's head snapped up. She looked stunned.

'I can't imagine the work this person has put in over the years since we were last together as a group. She's made sacrifices that not many of us would be willing to make, so I'd like to ask her to come up here to the stage.'

Setting down her napkin, Ellie rose from the table and started towards the stairs. With the lights pointed towards the stage, Roma didn't see her until the last minute. When she did, she was so surprised all she could do was watch in mute stupefaction.

Ellie's gaze locked with hers. To Roma's amazement, the dimwit nodded her head. *In thanks.* Then the cockiness was back. Lifting her chin until her nose was planted firmly in the air, she skipped up the steps.

Until she got to the top one.

The whole thing seemed to happen in slow motion. One moment, Ellie was strutting her stuff. The next, her toe caught on the lip of the stage. Shock, dismay and alarm crossed her face in rapid-fire succession.

Her hand lifted to the railing, but it was too late to catch herself. Mr Carlton stepped forwards to help, and she instinctively lunged at him as she went down hard on her knees.

'Mmmph.'

Ellie came to a skidding stop with her arms wrapped around Mr Carlton's waist and her face pressed firmly against the zipper of his khaki pants.

A roar went up from the crowd.

Roma felt laughter bubble up in her throat. She'd taken the high road, but this was just too much.

She knew she was a shallow, petty, pathetic person. But she was also a shallow, petty, pathetic person with a digital camera! Whipping it out of her purse, she took aim.

And got the shot she'd been waiting a lifetime for.

She nearly doubled over with laughter as she looked at the picture that had been stored forever in her camera's memory. It was even worse than the one Ellie had posted of her.

'Oh, man,' she said, stepping up to the podium again. She wiped tears of laughter from her cheeks. 'Thanks, Ellie. I didn't actually mean you, but this photograph is the only award I'll ever need.'

The crowd was going crazy. There wasn't one of them who hadn't seen the nasty pictures Ellie had posted of her on every wall in the school building.

'What do you think, people?' she asked the crowd. 'We have classmates who weren't able to make it tonight. Should I post this on our class reunion web site?'

The suggestion met with great approval.

Roma laughed. Her stomach hurt so badly, she had to hold it. 'Don't worry, Ellie,' she said as the woman tried to slink off the stage. 'I won't lower myself to your level.'

But she would keep the picture in case she ever did need it.

Wiping the last tears from her eyes, she slipped her camera back into her purse. She picked up the plaque and polished a smudge off from its corner.

'Myrtha Snodgrass Kramer,' she said clearly into the microphone, 'would you please come to the stage?'

She shielded her eyes from the glare of the lights and saw her friend's head snap up in surprise. The response couldn't have made Roma happier. This was absolutely the right thing to do.

'For those of you who haven't had a chance to read your booklet tonight, you should know that Myrtha's become a microbiologist. She's a top researcher in her field, but in one week she and her husband, Artie, are taking a sabbatical. They're heading over to Africa where they'll be donating their time training people on how to keep their food and water systems clean and safe. In essence, she's saving lives.'

Heads in the audience turned as Myrtha shyly made her way to the stage. Roma walked over to offer a helping hand to her friend when she came to the steps. Keeping hold of that hand, she pulled her to the podium. 'I give the comeback award to you, Myrtha, for doing more in the past ten years than most of us will do in a lifetime.'

Amid the applause, Roma quietly left the stage. Jake was waiting for her when she got back to their table. Not even trying to hide it, he pulled her into his arms. He kissed her soundly, and she felt her heart turn over.

'That was classic,' he whispered into her ear. 'And classy, all at once.'

She wrapped her arms around him and hugged him tightly.

He kissed the top of her head. 'Has your reunion turned out to be all you wanted it to be?'

'And more.' She tilted her head back to look at him.

'Want to get out of here?'

With him? She smiled. What more could a gal ask for? She had the job, the body and the guy. Only one thing remained.

'I'll race you to the car.'

A red Corvette and Jake Logan. Mmmm. She couldn't wait for a private reunion of their very own.

Epilogue

Roma was nervous. The crowd at the Midwest Fitness Show was packed, and anticipation was running high. Energy flowed through the air, catching up everyone in its wake. Only three women remained on stage. The rest had been sorted through and rejected, leaving only the best of the best. Anxiously, she reached over and caught Missy's hand.

'Ladies and gentlemen, this has been a tough competition,' the announcer said. 'Let's give these ladies the round of applause that they deserve.'

The crowd cheered. Hands clapped and feet stomped, but the noise quickly fell back to a low roar.

'Would he just get on with it?' Roma hissed.

Missy looked down at her hand. Her fingers were turning white under Roma's grip. 'I thought we hated her. Why are we cheering for her again?'

'We don't hate her. We just dislike her immensely. Besides, we're cheering for Jake.' Roma scooted around on the hard auditorium seat. The wait was driving her crazy.

'Come on!' she yelled. The handsome announcer looked down at his score sheet. That little slip of paper held the secret everyone wanted to know. She was ready to hop up on stage and rip it out of the guy's hands. 'Just tell us already.'

'Our second runner-up is –' the announcer flashed a smile, drawing out the suspense '– Mary Henderson.'

Mary's face fell, but the crowd cheered. Pasting

her plastic smile back in place, she waved to her fans. Hastily, she took a bow and left the stage.

Hawk scowled at the two remaining competitors. Both had bodies that had been honed to perfection. Stretching, he settled his arm over the back of Missy's chair. 'You could be up there, little miss. They haven't got anything you haven't got.'

With as much room as Hawk took up, the man sitting on the other side of him looked a bit cramped. The poor guy had sat that way through the entire show, though, without saying a word. Roma couldn't blame him.

Missy smiled and gave her boyfriend a peck on the cheek. 'You're so sweet.'

Hawk's face reddened, and he glanced around to see if anyone had heard. Mr Cramped slipped a little lower in his chair. He'd heard nothing. Absolutely nothing.

Roma craned her neck, trying to see around the heads of the people sitting in front of her. 'I can't take this.'

'And we're down to two,' the announcer said, finally giving in to the pressure of the fans. The final contestants caught each other's hands and bounced nervously on the balls of their feet. 'The first runner-up in the Midwest Fitness Show is . . .'

'Yes?' Roma said breathlessly. 'Yes?'

'Liz Huffington.'

'Yes!' She exploded out of her seat. She jumped right up into the air, scattering the people around her, and let out a victorious howl.

Missy and Hawk stood and clapped more politely.

'I thought we were cheering for her,' Missy yelled over the din of the crowd.

'We were.'

'But she didn't win.'

'I know. Isn't it great?' Roma stuck two fingers in her mouth and gave an ear-piercing whistle.

'But . . .'

She caught her friend by the shoulders. 'Jake just wanted her to end up in the top five. She got second place. Second! This is fantastic.'

Quickly, she grabbed her things as the announcer congratulated the winner. She needed to find her boyfriend. They had some celebrating to do. 'Excuse me,' she said as she worked her way to the aisle. 'Excuse me.'

Ellie had done well enough to put Jake's plan into action, but not well enough to make her a pain in the ass. In Roma's opinion, things couldn't have ended better. Her worst enemy had just potentially made her boyfriend a very wealthy man.

She broke into a run when she saw Jake standing on the ground floor near the back of the stage. Leaping into his arms, she gave him a resounding smack on the lips. 'Congratulations!'

'You're happy,' he said, rocking back a step under the impact. He looked a bit surprised.

'Of course, I am.'

'But that was Ellie,' he said.

'Liz,' Roma corrected. She caught his face with both hands and gave him another kiss. 'Onwards and upwards, Mr All-Star Trainer. Forget the past. It's time we looked ahead.'

'Oh, yeah?' His arms tightened around her as he held her with her feet dangling a foot off the ground. Devilishly, he rocked his hips forwards. 'Got anything specific in mind?'

She did. All she wanted to concentrate on now was their future together.

Because it looked great.